ViVi's Rose Garden

Gordon Jacobson

Contents

Chapter 1

*Vi*vi had always been different. Born beneath the shade of twilight skies and raised on lullabies sung by the wind, she found beauty in the darkness where others saw fear. Dressed in her usual lace gown, skin pale as moonlight, and raven hair cascading down her back, she walked like a shadow through the town. But Vivi wasn't interested in the living. She had long since abandoned that world.

The cemetery, cold and overgrown, was her sanctuary. Its ancient stone mausoleums and ivy-choked statues stood like sentinels, protecting her from the outside world. At the edge of the cemetery, she had nurtured her rose garden—black and crimson petals blooming with a life that seemed unnatural in such a place of death. No one knew how she did it. The roses were too dark, too beautiful to belong in a place like this. And yet, there they grew, flourishing under her care. She tended to them daily, her thin, pale hands brushing the velvety petals, her voice whispering to the flowers as though they could hear her secrets.

But the roses had a secret of their own.

Every night, when the town fell silent and the last flickers of light vanished from the horizon, Vivi could hear voices rising from the earth beneath her feet. They were soft at first, whispers carried by the wind, but soon they became clearer—fragments of long-forgotten conversations, desperate pleas, and bitter cries for revenge. At first, she had dismissed them as figments of her imagination. The mind plays tricks when you're alone in the dark. But night after night, the voices persisted.

One evening, as she trimmed the thorns from a particularly stubborn black rose, a voice rose louder than the rest. "Come to me," it whispered, faint but filled with urgency. Startled, Vivi dropped her shears, her heart racing. The cemetery was colder than usual, the air thick with an eerie stillness. She looked around but saw no one, only rows of headstones bathed in the silver light of the moon.

"Come to me," the voice repeated, its tone commanding now.

It seemed to be coming from beneath an old oak tree, near the grave of a man named Elijah Blackthorn—a name she had often noticed but never lingered on. Drawn by some invisible force, Vivi found herself walking towards it, her footsteps light on the soft earth. The ground beneath the tree was uneven, disturbed as though something had recently been unearthed. She knelt beside the grave, her fingers brushing the rough stone, and suddenly, a chill ran up her spine. The ground beneath her shifted, and a single black rose bloomed from the soil, its petals shimmering unnaturally in the moonlight.

She plucked the rose, feeling its energy pulse through her veins, and in that moment, she understood. The roses in her garden were not ordinary—they were connected to the dead, feeding off the souls buried beneath the earth. Each rose represented a life, a soul trapped between worlds, waiting for release. And Elijah Blackthorn, whoever he was, was desperate to escape.

Over the next few days, Vivi couldn't shake the feeling that something was watching her, lurking just beyond the edge of her vision. The roses began to wilt, their once vibrant petals curling inward, blackening at the edges. The voices grew louder, more insistent, and the air around the cemetery grew thick with the stench of decay.

One night, as she stood in the garden, staring at the withering flowers, the ground beneath her feet trembled. The earth cracked open, and from the shadows, Elijah Blackthorn emerged. He was not a man, not anymore. His form was skeletal, his eyes glowing with an unnatural light, his voice a rasping whisper.

"You've been feeding me," he said, his voice cold as the grave. "Every rose you planted, every petal you nurtured, brought me closer to the surface."

Vivi backed away, her heart pounding in her chest, but it was too late. The roses, once beautiful and alive, now twisted into something dark and malicious, their thorns extending like claws. They wrapped around her legs, holding her in place, drawing her closer to Elijah.

"You gave me life," he whispered, his bony fingers reaching out to touch her face. "And now, I will take yours."

In a final, desperate act, Vivi reached for the shears at her side and slashed at the roses, severing their connection to the earth. The roses shrieked, a sound like the wailing of a thousand souls, and Elijah's form flickered, fading into the night. But as he disappeared, his voice lingered in the air.

"You cannot escape the garden. The dead are always hungry."

Vivi collapsed to the ground, gasping for breath, her body trembling with fear. The roses lay in ruins around her, their petals scattered like ashes. But even as she lay there, shaken and broken, she knew the truth.

The garden would grow again. It always did. And one day, it would claim her, just as it had claimed so many before.

Vivi was the keeper of the roses, bound to the cemetery by a force darker than death itself. And as long as the dead whispered, she would never be free.

Chapter 2

ViVi didn't return to the garden the next day. Or the next. For the first time in years, she felt something she hadn't in a long time—fear. She stayed inside her small, candle-lit home near the edge of the cemetery, watching the wind stir the branches outside, hearing the soft tapping of rain on her window. But even in the quiet, the voices were there, creeping in the silence, whispering through the walls. She knew she couldn't ignore them forever.

Three days passed before she finally returned to the cemetery. The gate creaked as she pushed it open, a sound that echoed in the stillness of the night. The roses were exactly where she had left them—broken and wilted, their black petals lying in the soil like forgotten dreams. But beneath the surface, she could feel it. The pulsing energy, the hunger. The dead weren't done with her.

"Why do you keep calling me?" she whispered to the garden as she stood before it, her voice barely more than a breath.

The air around her shifted, cold and thick. The wind picked up, and with it, the scent of decay. A soft voice answered, one she recognized but wished she could forget.

"Because you are one of us, Vivi."

It was Elijah again. She hadn't seen him since that night, but his presence lingered, just beyond the edge of the living world. She could feel his eyes on her, watching, waiting.

"I'm not like you," she whispered, her hands trembling as she reached for the dead roses. "I don't belong to the dead."

But even as she said it, she knew it wasn't true. Vivi had always been drawn to the dark, to the forgotten places where the dead lingered. She had felt more at home in the cemetery than anywhere else. And the roses—those unnatural blooms—had been a part of her life for as long as she could remember.

"You do belong here," Elijah's voice rasped, growing louder. "You've always belonged here. The garden is your legacy, just as it was mine."

She shook her head, trying to block out his words, but it was no use. She could feel the truth of them sinking into her bones, seeping into her soul. The garden wasn't just a part of the cemetery; it was a part of her. And as long as it existed, so would the connection to the dead.

"You can't make me stay," she said, more to herself than to him. "I won't be trapped here."

Elijah's voice softened, but it was no less threatening. "You're already trapped. You've been tending to us for years, feeding us, growing us. And now, we're part of you."

Suddenly, the ground beneath her feet trembled, and from the earth, new roses began to sprout. Their black petals unfolded in the moonlight, vibrant and full of life, as though they had never withered at all. But these roses weren't like the others. Their thorns were sharper, their stems twisted, and their scent was sickly sweet—like rot and perfume mingled together.

Vivi stepped back, heart racing. She could feel them growing, pulling her toward them. Each rose was a life, a soul, trapped in the twilight between the living and the dead. And she knew, deep down, that each one was connected to her.

"Why me?" she whispered, her voice breaking. "Why am I the one who has to keep this garden?"

Elijah's voice was closer now, as if he stood right behind her. "Because you were chosen. The moment you touched the first rose, the garden became yours. And so did we."

Tears pricked at the corners of her eyes. She had never asked for this. She had never wanted to be the keeper of the dead, to be bound to this cursed place. But it didn't matter what she wanted anymore. The garden had chosen her, just as it had chosen Elijah before her. And there was no escape.

Unless…

Her mind raced, searching for a way out. She had severed the roses once before, breaking their hold on Elijah. If she destroyed them all, maybe—just maybe—she could free herself.

With a burst of determination, she reached for the shears strapped to her waist. Her hands were steady this time, her resolve strong. She wouldn't let the dead claim her. Not yet.

She began cutting, one rose at a time, slicing through the thick, thorny stems. The roses shrieked, their cries piercing the night, but she didn't stop. Each cut brought her closer to freedom, closer to the life she had almost forgotten.

But as she worked, the ground beneath her shifted again, harder this time, and a cold wind swept through the cemetery. Elijah's voice echoed around her, louder, angrier.

"You can't kill the garden, Vivi. It *is* you."

She ignored him, slashing at the roses, her breath coming in ragged gasps. But the more she cut, the faster they grew, their roots twisting beneath the earth, crawling toward her like living things. They wrapped around her ankles, pulling her down, their thorns digging into her skin.

Panic set in as she struggled, the shears falling from her grasp. The roses tightened their hold, dragging her closer to the ground, their black petals brushing against her skin, soft as death.

Elijah's voice was calm now, a dark whisper in her ear. "You can't run from this, Vivi. You were born for it."

With one final pull, the roses enveloped her, their dark blooms closing in, suffocating her in their embrace.

And then, everything went still.

The garden stood silent once more, its roses swaying gently in the night breeze. They were as beautiful and terrible as ever, their petals glistening in the moonlight like drops of blood.

But at the center of the garden, where Vivi had once stood, there was nothing left—nothing but a single black rose, blooming quietly among the others.

A new flower for the garden.

And the dead were always hungry.

Chapter 3

ViVi didn't feel pain. Not at first. As the roses closed in around her, there was a strange warmth, like being submerged in the embrace of shadows. Her body no longer obeyed her mind; the thorns, though sharp, felt distant, as if her consciousness had floated away from the prison of flesh and bone. It was as if she was dissolving into the garden itself, becoming one with the earth, the darkness, and the souls that lingered there.

Her vision blurred, and for a moment, all she saw were the roses—endless rows of black and crimson, stretching out into eternity. A beautiful, deadly maze of flowers. She felt her thoughts slipping away, becoming quiet, heavy with sleep.

But then she heard it. A sound, faint at first, but growing stronger by the second—a heartbeat.

Her heartbeat.

It pounded in her ears, louder than the whispering voices, louder than Elijah's taunts. It was the sound of life—her life, fighting back.

This isn't over.

With a sudden jolt, Vivi's mind snapped back into her body. She gasped, her lungs burning as if she'd been underwater for hours. She was still trapped, the roses tightening around her like a vice, but she was *awake*. And with that awareness came a surge of defiance. She wasn't going to be consumed. Not yet.

Her eyes flickered open, and through the tangle of vines and thorns, she saw something she hadn't noticed before—a small flicker of light glowing at the center of the garden. It wasn't natural, not like the moon or the stars. This light was softer, pulsing gently, like a beacon.

Vivi knew it was important. She could feel it calling to her, just as the roses had, but this was different. This light felt warm, safe, even in the midst of all the darkness.

She struggled against the roses, but they held her tight, their thorns biting deeper into her skin. Blood dripped down her arms, her legs, staining the black petals red. But she didn't stop. She couldn't. The light was the key—she knew it, somehow. It was her way out.

With a burst of strength she didn't know she had, Vivi grabbed one of the thorns and snapped it in half. The roses recoiled, as if they had felt pain. Encouraged, she tore at the vines, ripping them away from her body one by one. The thorns cut deep, but the more she fought, the looser their grip became.

Elijah's voice returned, echoing in her mind. *"You're wasting your time. You belong to the garden now. You belong to me."*

"Not anymore," Vivi whispered through gritted teeth, her hands raw and bloody as she tore the last of the roses away.

She fell to the ground, gasping for breath, the taste of iron in her mouth. Her body ached, but she didn't have time to stop. The light was fading, growing dimmer by the second.

With shaky legs, Vivi pushed herself up and stumbled toward the glowing heart of the garden. The roses swayed angrily around her, their thorns lashing out, trying to pull her back. But she was faster now, stronger. She had tasted freedom, and she wasn't going to let them take it from her again.

The light pulsed brighter as she neared it, and as she reached the center of the garden, she saw it—an old, weathered gravestone, half-buried beneath the earth. The name carved into it was almost unreadable, but she could just make out the letters: *Vianna Blackthorn.*

Her heart skipped a beat. The grave was hers.

For a moment, everything clicked into place—the pull she had always felt toward the cemetery, the strange connection to the roses, the whispers of the dead. She was a part of this place, bound to it by something older and darker than she had ever imagined.

But the light… the light was still there, glowing from beneath the gravestone. And as she knelt beside it, she realized what it was.

It was a seed. Small, fragile, but pulsing with life. The last remnant of something pure that had survived the garden's corruption.

Elijah's voice was a hiss in her ear now, desperate and furious. *"Leave it! You can't escape what you are! The garden will always be your prison!"*

But Vivi ignored him. She reached down, her fingers brushing against the seed, and the moment she touched it, a warmth spread through her. It was like sunlight, filling her with strength and hope she hadn't felt in years. The roses around her shrieked, their petals curling as if scorched by fire, retreating from the light.

Elijah screamed, his form flickering into view, a twisted shadow at the edge of her vision. *"No! You don't understand! You'll doom us all!"*

But Vivi didn't stop. She wrapped her fingers around the seed and pulled it free from the earth. As she did, the light exploded outward, blinding and pure, sweeping through the garden like a tidal wave.

The roses withered in its wake, their once-beautiful petals turning to ash. The ground trembled beneath her feet, and the air filled with the wails of the dead as they were released from their prison, their souls finally free.

Elijah's form disintegrated, his screams fading into nothingness as the light consumed him. The last of the thorns fell away, and for the first time in years, the garden was silent.

Vivi stood there, the seed cradled in her hands, the only thing left alive in the barren wasteland of the garden. The cemetery was still, the air clear, the sky above painted with the first hints of dawn.

She looked down at the seed, the small, glowing fragment of life she had saved. It was delicate, fragile, but she knew it held something powerful. Something new.

For the first time in years, Vivi smiled. She wasn't bound to the dead anymore. The garden was gone, and with it, the darkness that had claimed her.

But she wasn't done.

With the seed in her hands, she turned and walked toward the edge of the cemetery, leaving the ruins of the garden behind.

There was a new garden to plant—one filled with light, not shadows.

And this time, it would be hers.

Chapter 4

ViVi wandered through the cemetery's ruined paths, clutching the seed tightly in her hand, its warmth a quiet reminder that there was still life, still hope, even after all the darkness. The morning sun was rising now, casting long shadows over the gravestones, the soft orange glow melting away the cold that had gripped the land for so long. The cemetery felt… different. Lighter. Freed from the oppressive weight of the garden's curse.

For the first time in her life, Vivi didn't feel alone.

But she couldn't ignore the lingering emptiness inside her. She had lived for so long under the shadow of the cemetery and the garden, that its absence left a hollow space in her heart. The voices were gone, but the silence that followed felt unnervingly loud. She had escaped the prison of the dead, yes—but what now? What was she without the garden? Without the roses? Who was she, truly, outside this graveyard of lost souls?

Vivi left the cemetery that day, walking down the path that led into town. It had been months, perhaps even years, since she had ventured beyond the iron gates. The town had always seemed distant, like another world entirely, filled with lives that had nothing to do with her. People didn't look at her the way they looked at each other. They saw her as a ghost even when she was alive, a strange girl who wandered among the graves, tending to a world no one else wanted to see.

But today, she wasn't that ghost. Today, she was just Vivi
—a girl with a seed in her hand and an uncertain future.

She found herself standing at the edge of a small park, its
flowerbeds overgrown, the grass damp with dew. The town
seemed to move slowly in the early morning, people trickling out
of their homes, starting their day. But she didn't belong among
them. Not yet. Vivi knelt in the park's soil, feeling the earth
beneath her fingertips. It was soft, untouched by the corruption
that had once twisted her roses into something sinister. Here, the
ground was alive with possibility.

Vivi dug a small hole, her hands moving carefully, and
placed the glowing seed into the soil. As she covered it, she felt
the pulse of warmth spread through her fingers, as if the seed
recognized her touch, as if it knew that it had been waiting for this
moment.

She sat back, her legs tucked beneath her, and waited.

Nothing happened at first. The world was still, the town
waking up around her, its noises and voices beginning to rise with
the sun. But then, slowly, the ground began to shift. From the soil,
a tiny sprout emerged, fragile and green, stretching upward
toward the light. It grew quickly, faster than any normal plant, its
leaves unfurling with delicate grace. The sprout blossomed into a
small flower, its petals a deep crimson with streaks of silver,
unlike anything Vivi had ever seen.

It wasn't like the roses from the cemetery—this was
something new, something untouched by the death and decay that
had surrounded her for so long. It was a flower born of light, not
darkness.

She smiled, her heart lifting for the first time in what felt like forever.

As the flower bloomed, she noticed something peculiar. Around her, the park seemed to brighten. The air felt clearer, fresher. And then, one by one, other flowers began to emerge from the ground—wildflowers, daisies, violets, and marigolds—until the once-overgrown patch of earth was a vibrant, living garden.

The transformation wasn't just in the garden. Vivi felt something change inside her too. The dark weight that had pressed on her heart, the connection to the dead that had always felt like chains wrapped around her soul—it was gone. Completely.

She wasn't their keeper anymore.

She had set herself free.

As she sat there, watching the flowers sway gently in the breeze, she heard footsteps approaching from behind.

A voice, soft but familiar, broke through the morning quiet. "I thought I'd find you here."

Vivi turned to see an older woman standing at the edge of the park. Her long, silver hair was pulled back, and her face, though lined with age, held a warmth that matched the morning sun. Vivi knew her instantly. She was Mrs. Adelaide, the town's historian and keeper of old stories—the woman who had always looked at Vivi with knowing eyes, as if she could see the shadows that followed her.

"You've done something incredible," Mrs. Adelaide said, her gaze sweeping over the newly bloomed flowers. "I've been waiting for this day for a long time."

Vivi frowned, confused. "You… knew?"

The old woman nodded, stepping closer. "Oh, I knew. I knew what the cemetery was hiding, and I knew you would be the one to break the curse. You've always been connected to it, even before you understood why."

Vivi felt a chill run down her spine. "What was it? Why was the garden… mine?"

Mrs. Adelaide smiled sadly. "The Blackthorn family was cursed long ago, tied to the souls buried in that cemetery. Your family's bloodline was bound to the dead, to keep them from rising, to keep them quiet. The garden was a prison—a beautiful one, perhaps, but still a prison."

"But I'm free now," Vivi said softly, more to herself than to the old woman. "The garden's gone."

Mrs. Adelaide knelt beside her, her eyes filled with wisdom and a kind of pride. "Yes, you are free. But you're also something more. You've turned death into life, darkness into light. Not many can do that."

Vivi looked down at the flowers blooming around her, their bright colors painting the ground in a way she had never thought possible.

"You've given this town something it's never had before," Mrs. Adelaide continued, standing slowly. "Hope."

Vivi stood too, the weight of her past falling away like an old coat she no longer needed. She wasn't just the girl who belonged to the cemetery anymore. She was something else, something new.

As Mrs. Adelaide turned to leave, she paused and looked over her shoulder. "The world is full of gardens waiting to be planted, Vivi. Some of them will need your light."

Vivi smiled as the old woman walked away, disappearing into the morning crowd. She looked back at the new garden she had created, its flowers dancing in the breeze, alive and vibrant. For the first time in her life, Vivi felt like she truly had a future.

And she knew, deep down, that there would be more gardens. There would be more seeds to plant, more darkness to turn into light.

Because the dead may have been hungry, but the living had an even greater hunger—for life, for hope, for beauty.

And now, Vivi had the power to give it to them.

Chapter 5

$\mathcal{ViVi}$ stood there, watching the flowers sway in the gentle breeze, feeling the shift inside her. The weight of the cemetery had been lifted, but now a new kind of responsibility settled in its place. This was a different kind of power, not the dark pull of the dead, but a quiet strength—a power to bring life where there had been only death.

For the first time, she wasn't afraid of it.

The park around her buzzed with the hum of life—birds chirping, bees flitting between the newly bloomed flowers. It was a sharp contrast to the eerie silence of the cemetery, the place she had once called home. Vivi hadn't realized how much she had missed this kind of noise, the small, living sounds that reminded her of the world beyond the graves.

But as she stood there, something flickered at the edge of her vision. A shadow, subtle and faint, moved between the trees on the other side of the park. It was barely noticeable, but it sent a shiver down her spine, a ghost of the feeling she had experienced in the cemetery.

Vivi's heart skipped a beat. She wasn't alone.

She turned slowly, her eyes scanning the park. The morning sun bathed everything in warm light, but there was something lurking just beneath it, something that felt wrong.

Out of the shadows stepped a figure—a tall man, dressed in black, his face half-obscured by the brim of a wide hat. His clothes were old-fashioned, like something from another century, and his eyes, when they locked onto Vivi's, were cold, empty.

"You thought you could leave us," the man said, his voice as hollow as the graves she had left behind. "But the dead never truly let go."

Vivi's breath caught in her throat. She didn't recognize him, but the energy radiating from him was unmistakable. He was connected to the cemetery, to the dark power she thought she had left behind.

"I don't belong to you anymore," she said, trying to keep her voice steady. "The garden is gone. I'm free."

The man's lips curled into a thin smile, one that didn't reach his eyes. "The garden may be gone, but you are still part of this. You can't plant new life without consequences."

"What do you want?" Vivi asked, taking a step back, her hand instinctively reaching for the small pouch at her side, where the shears from the cemetery still rested.

"I want balance," the man replied, his voice low and dangerous. "For every life you create, something must be given in return. That is the way of things. You cannot escape the darkness without paying a price."

Vivi's pulse quickened. She had felt the truth in his words even before he spoke them. She had taken something from the cemetery, freed herself from the curse—but nothing in this world was without cost. The roses, the souls, the power she had left behind—they weren't simply gone. They had merely shifted, finding a new way to return.

"What price?" she whispered, though she already feared the answer.

The man's gaze flicked toward the flower blooming beside her, the one she had planted with the glowing seed. It stood tall, its crimson petals shining in the sunlight, so full of life. But as she watched, a single petal blackened at the edges, curling inward like burnt paper.

"You gave life to this garden," he said, his voice soft but sharp as a blade. "Now, the darkness wants something back."

Vivi's hand tightened around the shears. "I won't let you destroy it."

The man took a step closer, his presence darkening the space around him, casting long, unnatural shadows over the flowers. "You can't stop what's coming, girl. The garden of the dead is never truly gone. It's inside you now. Every flower you plant, every life you nurture—it draws the darkness closer. Soon, you won't be able to tell where one ends and the other begins."

Vivi felt a cold wave of fear wash over her. The garden *was* still inside her—she had known it, deep down, ever since she had pulled the seed from the earth. It hadn't been a simple escape. It had been a trade, a new beginning, but one that came with its own risks.

"I won't let the darkness take this," she said, more to herself than to the man. "I'll find a way to keep it at bay."

The man's smile widened, but there was no warmth in it. "You can try. But the dead are patient. They will wait."

He turned and began to walk back into the shadows, his form fading into the darkness. "Remember, Vivi," he called over his shoulder, his voice echoing in the air, "life and death are two sides of the same coin. You can't have one without the other."

And then he was gone, the park returning to its peaceful stillness as if he had never been there at all.

Vivi stood frozen, her mind racing. She stared down at the flowers, at the single petal now fully blackened, and felt a sinking dread settle in her chest.

There was still time. The darkness hadn't fully claimed her new garden. But the man's words echoed in her mind, a warning she couldn't ignore.

For every life she brought into the world, the shadows would come for her. The garden of the dead wasn't finished with her yet.

But Vivi wasn't the girl she had been before. She had already faced the darkness and survived. Now, she had the light.

She knelt beside the flower with the blackened petal, gently touching its stem. Closing her eyes, she focused on the warmth inside her, the part of her that had been reborn in the light of the seed. She felt it pulse through her fingers, a soft glow of energy spreading into the soil.

When she opened her eyes, the blackened petal had returned to crimson, as if the darkness had been pushed away, at least for now.

"I won't let you win," Vivi whispered to the shadows, her resolve hardening. "Not this time."

She stood and looked out over the garden, knowing that this was only the beginning of a new struggle. The dead may have been patient, but so was she. She had learned their ways, understood their hunger, and now she had something they couldn't take from her.

She had hope.

And she would fight to protect it.

With one last glance at the flowers, Vivi turned and walked out of the park, her head held high. The dead may have followed her, but she wasn't running anymore. She was moving forward, into the light, and whatever darkness lay ahead, she would be ready for it.

Because now, Vivi wasn't just the keeper of the dead.

She was the keeper of life.

Chapter 6

Vivi walked away from the park, her footsteps echoed through the quiet streets of the waking town. The encounter with the dark man lingered in her mind, a heavy shadow at the edge of her thoughts. She had always known, deep down, that freeing herself from the cursed garden wouldn't be as simple as pulling a seed from the earth. There were ancient forces at play—forces that didn't care about hope or new beginnings.

But she wasn't powerless anymore. She had survived the darkness, and now she carried something inside her, something that felt like light, though fragile and untested.

She wandered through town, letting her feet guide her until she found herself at the entrance to an old, forgotten greenhouse on the outskirts. It had been abandoned for years, its windows clouded with dust and vines creeping through the cracks. It had once belonged to an eccentric botanist who had disappeared under mysterious circumstances—another story lost to the town's strange history.

But Vivi saw potential here.

The greenhouse had the feeling of a place waiting to be reclaimed. Where others saw rot and decay, she saw the perfect place to cultivate life. And maybe, just maybe, it would help her keep the darkness at bay.

Pushing open the creaking door, she stepped inside. The air was thick with the scent of damp earth, and the light filtered in through broken glass, casting a patchwork of shadows on the floor. Inside, the remains of old plants stood brittle and forgotten, their once-vibrant leaves crumbled to dust.

Vivi felt the tug of something ancient in the air, but it wasn't malevolent. It was like the ghost of life that had once thrived here, waiting for someone to breathe new energy into it.

"This will do," she whispered to herself.

She moved to the center of the greenhouse, pulling the pouch from her side. Inside, along with the shears that had helped her fight through the cursed roses, were a handful of seeds—small, glowing faintly, remnants of the life she had awakened in the cemetery. These seeds were different from the one she had planted in the park. They were connected to the garden, but not entirely twisted by its darkness. They represented a fragile balance—one she could nurture.

Kneeling in the dirt, she planted the first seed carefully, covering it with rich soil. As she pressed her hands into the earth, she felt the pulse of life once again, that soft warmth spreading from her palms, through the soil, and into the seed.

It would grow here. She knew it would.

But even as she felt the stirrings of new life beneath the earth, the presence of the dark man lingered at the edges of her thoughts, his warning still fresh in her mind. Balance, he had said. Life for life. The dead were patient, waiting for their due.

Vivi stood up and surveyed the greenhouse. There was something she had to accept—she couldn't simply run from the darkness. It would follow her, creep into the cracks, no matter how much light she planted. The garden, the dead, the strange forces connected to her family's bloodline—they were a part of her now.

But perhaps, she thought, there was another way.

If the darkness demanded balance, then she would give it balance. But on her own terms.

The seeds she had planted in the park, and now in the greenhouse, held light and life—but they had also come from the garden of the dead. The forces that shaped them were tied to both worlds: the living and the dead. If she could harness that connection, maybe she could create something new—something that bridged the gap between light and dark.

Vivi felt a surge of determination as she glanced around the greenhouse. It was a place of forgotten things, just like the cemetery had been, but this time, she was in control. This time, she would be the one to decide what grew here. She would tend to both the light and the darkness, ensuring neither would consume her.

Over the next few weeks, Vivi dedicated herself to the greenhouse. By day, she tended to the seeds she had planted, carefully nurturing the strange, glowing plants that began to sprout. They were unlike any plants she had seen before—some had dark, glossy leaves that shimmered in the low light, while others bloomed with pale, almost ethereal flowers that seemed to glow faintly in the dark.

At night, however, she felt the presence of the cemetery growing stronger. The whispers of the dead crept into her dreams, sometimes gentle, other times insistent, as if they were watching her, waiting for her next move. And sometimes, in the quietest moments, she felt the cold breath of the dark man, lingering just outside the greenhouse, watching, waiting.

But Vivi didn't waver. She had chosen her path.

One evening, as she finished tending to her plants, she felt a shift in the air. The temperature dropped suddenly, and the shadows in the greenhouse seemed to grow longer, darker. She turned, and there, standing at the edge of the light, was the dark man.

"You've been busy," he said, his voice a low, ominous rumble. "But you haven't learned."

Vivi stepped forward, unafraid this time. "I've learned plenty," she said, her voice steady. "I know the dead want balance. I know you want something in return for the life I've created."

The dark man tilted his head slightly, curious. "And what do you plan to give them?"

Vivi looked around at the plants she had nurtured, their strange, otherworldly beauty filling the greenhouse with an energy that felt both vibrant and dangerous. "I'm not giving them anything. I'm creating a new balance. One that doesn't involve death."

The man's smile was thin, almost mocking. "You think you can rewrite the rules of life and death? You're playing with forces you don't understand, girl."

Vivi met his gaze, unwavering. "Maybe. But I know this —I'm not afraid of the darkness anymore. And I'm not afraid of you."

The dark man's eyes flashed with something—anger, perhaps, or amusement. "You'll regret this," he said, his voice dripping with menace. "The dead are patient, but they are also relentless. You cannot deny them forever."

Vivi's heart pounded, but she didn't back down. "I'm not denying them. I'm giving them something different."

The man stared at her for a long moment, the air between them thick with tension. Then, without another word, he turned and disappeared into the shadows, leaving Vivi alone with her plants.

But she wasn't truly alone. The seeds she had planted were growing, their light mixing with the darkness in a strange, delicate harmony. And as she looked at them, she knew she had made her choice.

She would walk the line between life and death, light and darkness. Not as a prisoner, but as a keeper of both.

And whatever the dead demanded, whatever the darkness tried to take from her, Vivi was ready.

Because now, she understood the rules.

And she was going to rewrite them.

Chapter 7

$Weeks$ passed, and the greenhouse thrived under Vivi's care. The plants she had nurtured grew into a mesmerizing mix of life and darkness, a strange harmony of light and shadow. Some of the flowers were luminous, their pale petals glowing softly in the twilight, while others had an almost haunting beauty, with black vines curling through the soil, their leaves shimmering with an unnatural iridescence. They were otherworldly, reflecting the balance Vivi was trying to create between life and death.

But the more Vivi nurtured her strange garden, the more she felt the presence of the dark forces lingering just outside her reach. The dead were watching, waiting, and she knew that the dark man was not the only one keeping an eye on her.

One evening, after a long day of tending to the greenhouse, Vivi sat in the center of her creation, watching as the glowing plants swayed in the soft breeze. The air was thick with the scent of earth and blossoms, but it also carried something else —something cold and ancient, like the cemetery's breath had followed her here.

Suddenly, the air shifted, growing colder, and the greenhouse dimmed as if a shadow had passed over the moon. Vivi's skin prickled as she felt the familiar presence of the dark man. She stood, turning toward the entrance, where he appeared once again, his tall figure cloaked in darkness, his eyes glinting with a malevolent curiosity.

"You think you've created something new," he said, stepping closer, his voice as cold as the night air. "But the dead are still owed a debt. The balance hasn't been paid."

Vivi clenched her fists, standing firm. "I'm not playing by your rules anymore. I'm creating my own balance—one that doesn't involve sacrificing life for the dead."

The dark man tilted his head, his expression unreadable. "You don't understand, girl. The forces you're tampering with are older than time itself. You can't change the natural order."

"I can," Vivi said, her voice resolute. "I'm not afraid of the darkness. I've faced it before, and I know how it works. Life and death are connected, but that doesn't mean they have to be enemies. There's a way to make them coexist."

The dark man let out a soft, menacing chuckle. "You're naïve. You think you can bargain with the dead and walk away unscathed?"

"I'm not bargaining with anyone," she said, taking a step forward. "I'm creating something new—a bridge between life and death. These plants, this garden, it's proof that the dead don't have to claim everything."

His eyes narrowed, his smile fading. "You think these flowers are enough to keep the dead at bay? They are nothing more than an illusion, a temporary distraction from what's coming."

Vivi's heart pounded, but she refused to show fear. "They're more than that. They're a symbol of balance. And if the dead want something from me, they'll have to come and take it themselves."

The man's expression darkened. "They will. And when they do, you'll regret challenging forces far beyond your understanding."

He turned to leave, but then paused, looking over his shoulder with a cryptic smile. "You've made your choice, Vivi. But the dead are patient. And they always collect their due."

Before she could respond, he vanished into the shadows, leaving Vivi standing alone in the cold, dim light of the greenhouse. The plants around her rustled gently, as if in response to the tension in the air, their delicate petals trembling.

For the first time, doubt crept into her mind. Was she truly strong enough to hold back the darkness? Could she really keep the dead at bay, or had she merely delayed the inevitable?

But as she looked around at the strange, beautiful garden she had created, her resolve returned. She couldn't let fear control her. She had already seen what the dead could do—she had lived with their whispers, their cold, suffocating presence. And she had survived.

She wouldn't let them take that from her.

With renewed determination, Vivi turned back to her plants, feeling the pulse of life beneath her hands as she touched the soil. The greenhouse had become a sanctuary, a place where the rules of the outside world didn't apply. Here, she could continue her work—continue to nurture the balance she was trying to create.

But the dark man's words lingered in her mind, like a shadow that wouldn't fade.

That night, her dreams were restless. She saw the cemetery again, but it wasn't like the one she had left behind. It was alive—twisted vines of black roses growing wild over the tombstones, spreading like veins across the earth. And standing at the center, surrounded by the dead, was the dark man, his eyes glowing with an eerie light.

He wasn't alone. Other figures stood with him, shadowy and indistinct, their faces hidden in the darkness. But Vivi knew who they were—the dead. The souls who had once been bound to the garden she had destroyed.

They were waiting for her.

When she woke, the morning light was just beginning to filter through the greenhouse windows. Vivi sat up, her heart still pounding from the dream, the dark images lingering in her mind.

The dead were growing restless. And they wouldn't wait forever.

But Vivi wasn't going to let them win. She had come too far to turn back now.

Over the next few days, she worked tirelessly, experimenting with the strange plants that had begun to thrive under her care. Some grew in ways she didn't expect—twisting in on themselves, their vines curling around the others like they were seeking something deeper, something hidden. Others bloomed with radiant beauty, their light pushing back the creeping shadows that seemed to haunt the edges of the greenhouse.

Vivi began to notice that the plants weren't just reacting to her care—they were reacting to her emotions. When she felt fear or doubt, the darker, shadowy plants grew stronger, their vines spreading faster, their leaves darkening. But when she focused on hope, on life, the luminous plants thrived, their glow becoming brighter, pushing back the darkness.

It was then that she realized the true nature of the balance she was creating.

The plants weren't just a bridge between life and death—they were a reflection of her own inner struggle. The darkness that haunted her wasn't something external; it was a part of her, just as the light was. She couldn't destroy it. She couldn't run from it.

But she could control it.

And as she stood in the heart of the greenhouse, surrounded by the strange, beautiful life she had nurtured, Vivi made a vow to herself.

She would find a way to make the darkness and the light coexist. She would master the balance.

No matter what it took.

Chapter 8

ViVi's days in the greenhouse became a ritual, a careful dance between light and shadow. As the luminous plants flourished, their soft glow filling the glass walls with a radiant energy, the darker ones grew too, with their twisting vines and black petals pushing up from the earth like the dead reaching toward the living. She spent hours tending to them, trimming and shaping, watching how they responded to her every movement, her every thought.

But each night, the dream returned—the cemetery, the dark man, the gathering of the dead. Their presence grew stronger, more insistent, and Vivi knew that time was running out. She could feel the pull of the cemetery, the weight of unfinished business pressing against her. The balance she sought to create wasn't stable yet, and the dead wouldn't wait much longer.

One morning, as she worked in the greenhouse, she noticed something strange. A single dark vine had begun to creep up the wall, its tendrils snaking between the cracks in the glass. She hadn't seen it the day before, but now it stood out starkly against the glowing plants, a reminder of the dark forces that still hovered just outside her control.

She reached out to touch it, and the vine responded immediately, twisting around her fingers like a serpent. Its touch was cold, and for a moment, she felt the chill of the cemetery wash over her, the scent of earth and decay filling her senses.

But she didn't pull away. Instead, she closed her eyes and focused on the warmth inside her, the light she had nurtured in the greenhouse. Slowly, the cold faded, and the vine loosened its grip. When she opened her eyes, it had stopped growing, its dark leaves quivering as if uncertain of its next move.

Vivi let out a breath she hadn't realized she was holding. She was getting better at this—better at controlling the balance. But the dark man's warning still echoed in her mind: *You cannot deny them forever.*

Later that evening, as she sat by the window of her small apartment, staring out at the moonlit town, she heard a soft knock at the door. Her heart skipped a beat, and for a moment, she wondered if it was him—the dark man, come to collect his due.

But when she opened the door, it wasn't the dark man. It was something—or someone—entirely unexpected.

A girl stood on the doorstep, her pale skin almost glowing in the moonlight, her dark hair falling in waves around her shoulders. She wore a long black dress, reminiscent of the style Vivi herself had once favored, but there was something ethereal about her, something that made her seem almost unreal.

"Are you Vivi?" the girl asked, her voice soft, but with an edge of urgency.

Vivi nodded, suspicion gnawing at her gut. "Who are you?"

The girl stepped closer, her eyes shining with an eerie light. "My name is Dahlia. I've been sent to find you."

Vivi frowned, her hand instinctively reaching for the shears she kept hidden by the door. "Sent by who?"

Dahlia hesitated for a moment, then spoke in a low voice. "The dead. They're restless, and they're looking for you."

The words sent a chill down Vivi's spine. She had known the dead were growing impatient, but she hadn't expected them to send someone like this.

"What do they want?" Vivi asked, her voice steady despite the unease creeping through her.

Dahlia's gaze flickered to the side, as if she was wary of being overheard. "They want the garden back. The one you destroyed. But they know you've created something new, something different. They want to see it—to understand it. And if they can't control it... they'll destroy it."

Vivi's heart pounded in her chest. The dead weren't just waiting anymore—they were coming for her. "And what do you want?" she asked, her eyes narrowing as she studied Dahlia's strange, glowing form.

Dahlia looked down, her expression suddenly sad. "I want to help you. I wasn't always like this. I used to be alive. But now... I'm part of them. They sent me because I can walk between worlds. But I don't want to be their servant anymore."

Vivi's suspicion softened slightly. There was something in Dahlia's voice, something fragile and desperate, that reminded her of herself. "Why me?" Vivi asked. "Why do the dead care so much about what I've done?"

Dahlia stepped closer, her voice dropping to a whisper. "Because you broke the rules. You took life from death without giving something in return. The balance is fragile, and they think you've upset it. But I think you're onto something—something bigger than just balance. You've created a bridge between life and death. And they fear it."

Vivi felt a flicker of understanding, like a puzzle piece falling into place. The dark man hadn't just been warning her about balance. He had been warning her about power. The garden she had created wasn't just a way to keep the dead at bay—it was a new kind of power, one that neither the living nor the dead fully understood.

"What do I need to do?" Vivi asked, her voice firm.

Dahlia looked up at her, hope flickering in her eyes. "You need to show them. Show the dead that the garden isn't a threat— that it can be part of the balance. But they won't listen to me. They'll listen to you."

Vivi hesitated for a moment, the weight of Dahlia's words sinking in. If she failed, if the dead rejected her garden, everything she had worked for would be lost. The darkness would consume her, and the dead would take their due.

But if she succeeded, she could change everything.

"Take me to them," Vivi said, her resolve hardening.

Dahlia nodded, relief washing over her face. "They'll meet you in the cemetery. But be careful. They don't trust you. Not yet."

Vivi grabbed her shears and followed Dahlia into the night, the moonlight casting long shadows over the quiet streets. As they walked toward the cemetery, Vivi felt the pull of the dead growing stronger, the weight of their gaze pressing down on her.

This was it. The final confrontation.

And she wasn't going to back down.

As they reached the gates of the cemetery, Vivi felt a familiar chill creep over her skin. The tombstones stood silent and foreboding, the earth beneath them heavy with the presence of the dead. But there, in the center of the cemetery, she saw them—dozens of shadowy figures, their faces hidden in darkness, their eyes glowing faintly in the moonlight.

And standing at the front, watching her with a cold, unblinking gaze, was the dark man.

"You've come," he said, his voice echoing through the still night. "Are you ready to pay your debt?"

Vivi stepped forward, holding her shears tightly. "I'm not here to pay any debt. I'm here to show you something."

The dark man's smile was thin and dangerous. "You think you can bargain with the dead?"

Vivi met his gaze, unafraid. "I'm not bargaining. I'm showing you a new way—a way where life and death don't have to fight each other."

She raised her hand, and from her palm, a small seed appeared, glowing faintly with the same light that had filled her greenhouse. She knelt down and pressed it into the earth, her fingers trembling slightly as she felt the pulse of life beneath her touch.

The ground shifted, and from the spot where she had planted the seed, a vine began to grow, twisting upward into the air. It was a strange, beautiful thing—half glowing with life, half dark and twisted with the energy of the dead. But it was balanced, a perfect harmony of both worlds.

The dead watched in silence as the vine grew, their glowing eyes fixed on the new creation. Even the dark man seemed momentarily caught off guard, his cold expression faltering as he watched the vine bloom.

"This is what I've created," Vivi said, standing tall. "A bridge between life and death. A balance. You don't have to take anything from me. I'm giving you something new."

For a long moment, the cemetery was silent. The dead stood still, their shadowy forms flickering in the moonlight. And then, slowly, they began to move forward, drawn to the vine that now grew in their midst. They reached out to touch it, their cold fingers brushing against the glowing leaves.

The dark man's eyes narrowed, his expression hardening. "You think this is enough? You think a single plant can undo the laws of life and death?"

Vivi turned to him, her eyes blazing with defiance. "It's not just a plant. It's a beginning."

The dark man stared at her for a long, tense moment, the shadows around him growing darker, deeper. But then, slowly, he smiled.

"We'll see, girl. We'll see."

And with that, he turned and melted into the darkness, leaving Vivi standing in the cemetery, the dead gathered around her creation, their cold presence no longer threatening, but curious.

Vivi let out a breath of relief. The confrontation wasn't over, but for now, she had shown them the possibility of something different. Something new.

And as the first light of dawn began to break over the horizon, Vivi knew that she had taken the first step toward rewriting the rules.

The garden of the dead had become something more. Something alive.

As dawn cast a soft light over the cemetery, the dead slowly withdrew, retreating into the shadows of their graves, leaving only the dark vine twining through the tombstones as evidence of what had transpired. Vivi stood in the silence, her heart still pounding from the confrontation. The dark man's parting words lingered in her mind—*We'll see, girl. We'll see.*

Dahlia stood by her side, her ethereal glow dimming as the sun rose higher. "You did it," she said quietly. "But this is only the beginning. The dead—they're curious now. But they haven't decided what to do yet."

Vivi nodded, her eyes still on the vine. The strange plant seemed to pulse with life and death in equal measure, its blackened leaves shimmering faintly in the early light. She had shown the dead something new, something that bridged the gap between their world and hers. But she knew the dark man was right—this wasn't over. The dead might still come for her if they felt the balance wasn't in their favor.

"I need to make this stronger," Vivi said, more to herself than to Dahlia. "This vine, this bridge between life and death—it's not enough yet. I need to grow it, expand it, make it something they can't ignore or destroy."

Dahlia nodded, though there was uncertainty in her eyes. "But how? The dead won't wait forever. They're watching you, and if they don't like what they see, they'll act."

"I'll need your help," Vivi said, turning to Dahlia. "You said you can walk between worlds. If I'm going to make this garden strong enough to hold the balance, I need to understand both sides. I need to know what the dead want—what they fear."

Dahlia hesitated, her gaze dropping to the ground. "I'll help you, but... there's something you need to know. The dead— they don't just want balance. They want control. Some of them are older than anything you can imagine, and they've been waiting for someone like you—a living soul who can create something like this. But not all of them agree with what you're doing. Some think you're playing with forces you can't control."

Vivi clenched her jaw. "I'm not afraid of them."

"You should be," Dahlia whispered. "They're not like the living. They don't think the way we do. They don't feel the way we do. And if they decide you're a threat, they'll take everything from you."

Vivi met Dahlia's gaze, her determination unwavering. "Then I'll make sure they don't see me as a threat. I'll prove to them that this garden can be part of their world, not against it."

Dahlia nodded slowly, though her worry remained clear. "There's a place where you can learn more—about the dead, about their desires. But it's dangerous. If you go there, you might not come back."

"Where?" Vivi asked, her voice steady.

"The Cradle," Dahlia whispered, her voice barely audible over the breeze. "It's where the oldest of the dead reside, where their power is strongest. If you want to understand them, to truly know what they want, you'll have to face them there."

Vivi had heard of the Cradle before, though only in whispers—an ancient burial ground, hidden deep within the forest beyond the cemetery. It was said to be a place where the veil between life and death was thinnest, where the dead could manifest in ways they couldn't in the mortal world.

"If that's where I need to go, then I'll go," Vivi said, her resolve firm.

Dahlia looked at her with a mixture of admiration and fear. "I'll guide you, but once we're there, I can't protect you. No one can."

Vivi gave a small nod, her thoughts already focused on the journey ahead. The Cradle was dangerous, but it was also the key to understanding the dead's true intentions. And if she wanted to keep the balance she had created, if she wanted to protect her garden and her life, she had to face them on their terms.

The following night, Vivi stood at the edge of the cemetery, staring into the dark forest that loomed beyond the graves. The path to the Cradle was barely visible, a winding trail swallowed by the trees and the thick mist that clung to the ground like a shroud. Dahlia stood beside her, her form even more translucent than usual, as if the proximity to the Cradle was weakening her connection to the living world.

"This is it," Dahlia said, her voice quiet. "Once we cross into the forest, we'll be in their territory."

Vivi took a deep breath, feeling the weight of what lay ahead. She wasn't just walking into the unknown—she was walking into the heart of death itself. But she had come too far to turn back now. The garden she had created was too important. It wasn't just a bridge between life and death; it was her defiance, her refusal to accept the rules the dead had imposed on the living.

"I'm ready," Vivi said, stepping forward.

As they entered the forest, the air grew colder, and the mist thickened, swirling around them like ghostly tendrils. The trees towered overhead, their branches twisted and gnarled, blocking out the moonlight. It felt as though the forest itself was alive, watching them, waiting for them to make a wrong move.

The deeper they went, the heavier the air became, and Vivi began to feel the presence of the dead more acutely. It was as if they were all around her, unseen but palpable, their whispers brushing against her skin, their eyes following her every step.

"Stay close," Dahlia warned, her voice barely a whisper. "They're watching."

After what felt like hours, they reached a clearing. In the center stood a massive stone altar, covered in moss and vines, with ancient symbols carved into its surface. This was the Cradle.

The air here was thick with the energy of the dead, and Vivi could feel the weight of their presence pressing down on her. The shadows around the altar shifted and flickered, and one by one, figures began to emerge from the darkness—tall, imposing beings with eyes that glowed faintly in the dim light. These were the ancient dead, the ones who had ruled over the balance for centuries.

And at their center, standing taller than the rest, was the dark man.

"You've come," he said, his voice carrying the weight of ages. "But why? Do you think you can bargain with us, girl?"

Vivi stepped forward, her heart pounding but her resolve unshaken. "I'm not here to bargain. I'm here to show you something. Something new."

The dark man's eyes glinted with cold amusement. "You think you can create something the dead will accept? Something that will change the order of things?"

Vivi held up her hand, revealing another seed, glowing faintly with the same strange light as the vine she had planted in the cemetery. "I've already started," she said. "This garden I've created—it's not just for the living. It's for you too."

The ancient dead watched her in silence, their expressions unreadable. But Vivi could feel their power swirling around her, testing her, weighing her worth.

"The balance between life and death doesn't have to be about taking and giving," Vivi continued. "It can be about sharing, about coexistence. This garden—it's a place where the living and the dead can both thrive. I'm offering you something more than just balance. I'm offering you a new way."

The dark man stepped closer, his eyes narrowing as he studied her. "And why should we trust you? Why should we believe that you, a living soul, can create something that will benefit us?"

Vivi met his gaze without flinching. "Because I'm not just a living soul anymore. I've touched death. I've walked with it, and I understand it. I'm not asking you to trust me. I'm asking you to see what I've created."

She knelt down and pressed the seed into the ground at the base of the altar. Immediately, the earth shifted, and a vine began to grow, twisting upward with unnatural speed. It was like the vine in the cemetery, but stronger, more vibrant, its dark and glowing leaves intertwining in perfect harmony.

The dead watched in silence, their cold eyes fixed on the vine as it grew. The dark man's expression remained unreadable, but Vivi could sense the tension in the air, the uncertainty that rippled through the ancient dead.

Finally, after what felt like an eternity, the dark man spoke. "You've created something new. Something we do not fully understand."

He looked down at Vivi, his eyes glinting with a strange light. "But we will watch. We will wait. And if this creation of yours proves to be a threat to the balance, we will take what is owed."

Vivi stood, her heart still racing. "It won't be a threat. It will be a new beginning."

The dark man smiled, but it was not a kind smile. "We'll see, girl. We'll see."

With that, the dead began to fade back into the shadows, their forms dissolving into the mist until only the dark man remained, watching Vivi with a gaze that held both curiosity and danger.

As he too disappeared into the darkness, Vivi felt a weight lift from her shoulders. She had done it—she had faced the dead and shown them her creation. But she knew this wasn't the end. The dead were watching, and if her garden faltered, they would come for her.

But for now, she had bought herself time.

And with that time, she would make sure her garden grew stronger than ever before.

Chapter 9

The walk back from the Cradle was silent, save for the soft rustle of leaves in the wind. Vivi's mind was racing. She had managed to present her creation to the dead without being torn apart, but she knew she was living on borrowed time. The dark man's words echoed in her mind—*We'll see, girl. We'll see.* It wasn't approval, just a temporary reprieve. The dead were waiting, watching, and if her garden didn't live up to their expectations, she would face their wrath.

Dahlia walked beside her, her glow flickering faintly as if the strain of being in the Cradle had sapped her strength. "You did it," Dahlia said softly. "But they'll test you. The dead don't just watch—they push. They'll find the weak spots in your garden, in you. If you can't hold it together…"

"I know," Vivi replied, her voice grim. "I'll be ready."

As they stepped back into the cemetery, Vivi felt the familiar chill of the tombstones around her. The dead here were quieter, less focused on her than before. The vine she had planted earlier was still there, twisting up between the graves like a dark sentinel. It was growing, stronger now, its leaves glowing faintly in the twilight. But she could sense its fragility—how easily it could be destroyed if the balance shifted.

"I need more than just vines," Vivi said, her mind working furiously. "The garden has to be bigger, more stable. I can't just rely on a few plants to hold the balance."

Dahlia nodded. "The dead won't be satisfied with just one small patch of life. They need to see something… grander. Something that proves you can balance both worlds."

Vivi's gaze shifted toward the horizon, where the edges of the town met the sprawling woods. "The cemetery isn't enough. If I want to create a true balance, I'll need to expand beyond these boundaries. I'll need to grow the garden into something that stretches between life and death, not just here, but everywhere."

Dahlia hesitated. "That's dangerous, Vivi. The more you expand, the more you draw attention. Not just from the dead, but from things older and darker. There are forces in this world that don't care about balance. They'll want to twist what you've created into something else."

"I know the risks," Vivi said firmly. "But I can't stay small. If I'm going to change anything, I have to go all the way."

Dahlia looked at her for a long moment, then sighed. "Then I'll help you. But you'll need more than just me."

Over the next few days, Vivi threw herself into her work. The greenhouse became a hub of life and death, its walls alive with glowing plants and dark, twisted vines. She experimented with new species—flowers that could thrive on the edge of decay, plants that glowed in the dark and withered in the light. Each one was a piece of the balance she was trying to create, a fragile harmony between two worlds that constantly sought to pull apart.

But it wasn't enough.

Every night, the dreams returned—the dark man, the gathering of the dead, their cold eyes watching her as they waited for her to falter. And she knew that time was running out.

One evening, as she was working late in the greenhouse, a soft knock echoed through the glass walls. Vivi looked up, expecting to see Dahlia, but it wasn't her.

A figure stood in the doorway, half-hidden in the shadows. It was a man, tall and thin, dressed in dark clothes that seemed to blend with the night. His face was pale, almost ghostly, but his eyes were sharp and alive.

"Vivi," he said in a low voice. "I've been watching you."

Vivi's hand instinctively reached for the shears on her workbench. "Who are you?"

The man stepped forward, into the faint glow of the greenhouse. "My name is Lucien. I'm… like you. Someone who walks the line between life and death."

Vivi narrowed her eyes, her grip on the shears tightening. "You're not dead."

"No," Lucien said with a small smile. "But I'm not fully alive either."

Vivi didn't relax. "What do you want?"

Lucien's smile faded, and he looked around the greenhouse, his gaze settling on the strange, glowing plants that filled the space. "I've heard about what you're trying to do. The balance you're trying to create. It's dangerous, you know."

"I'm aware," Vivi said coldly. "If you're here to stop me—"

"I'm not," Lucien interrupted, raising a hand. "I'm here to help."

Vivi's eyes flickered with suspicion. "Why?"

Lucien stepped closer, his expression serious. "Because the dead aren't the only ones watching you. There are others—ancient forces, things older than the dead. And they're interested in what you're doing. They think you're creating something new, something powerful. But they don't care about balance. They want to twist it to their own ends."

Vivi felt a chill run down her spine. "What are you talking about?"

Lucien leaned in, his voice low. "There's a darkness coming, something far worse than the dead. It's been waiting for an opportunity like this, and you—your garden—might be the key to unleashing it."

Vivi's heart pounded in her chest. "What do you mean? What kind of darkness?"

Lucien's gaze was intense, his voice almost a whisper. "The kind that doesn't care about life or death. It feeds on both. And if you're not careful, you'll open the door for it."

Vivi's mind raced. The dead were one thing—she had been preparing for them, trying to find a way to balance their world with hers. But this… this was something else. Something deeper, more primal.

"What do I need to do?" Vivi asked, her voice steady despite the fear creeping into her heart.

Lucien's eyes darkened. "You need to strengthen your garden. Not just with plants, but with something more. You'll need to bind it to the land, to the earth itself. And you'll need allies—people who understand what you're doing, who can help you fight back when the time comes."

Vivi swallowed hard. "And what about you? Why are you helping me?"

Lucien's smile returned, though it didn't reach his eyes. "Let's just say I have my own reasons for wanting to keep the darkness at bay."

Vivi studied him for a moment, her instincts warring with her need for allies. She didn't trust him, not fully. But she also knew that she couldn't do this alone. The dead were already a threat, and now, if Lucien was right, there was something even worse waiting in the shadows.

"Alright," Vivi said finally. "I'll take your help. But I'm not making any deals. If you're hiding something from me…"

"I'm not," Lucien said, his voice smooth. "I'm on your side. For now."

Vivi nodded, though the unease in her gut didn't fade. "Let's get to work, then."

As Lucien began explaining his plan, Vivi couldn't shake the feeling that she was walking a fine line, one that could easily collapse beneath her if she wasn't careful. But for now, she had no choice but to move forward.

The dead were watching.

The darkness was coming.

And she had to be ready.

Chapter 10

The days following Lucien's arrival passed in a blur.

His knowledge was unsettling, vast in ways Vivi couldn't quite place, yet undeniably useful. Under his guidance, she began weaving stronger connections between the garden and the cemetery itself, binding her plants not just to the soil but to the very essence of the land. The vines spread farther, creeping up ancient gravestones and wrapping around crypts, their dark, glowing leaves pulsing with the eerie energy she had learned to harness.

But it wasn't enough.

Despite the progress, the presence of the dead grew more palpable. At night, the cemetery felt more crowded, as though the spirits were gathering in greater numbers, drawn to the power of her garden. And Vivi could feel them testing her, probing at the edges of her creation, searching for any weakness.

Lucien remained a shadow at her side, always offering advice but never revealing too much about himself. Vivi still didn't trust him, but he seemed committed to the same goal—strengthening the garden, solidifying the balance. Dahlia, on the other hand, had grown quieter, her once-constant companionship becoming sporadic. She seemed uneasy, avoiding Lucien and often watching from a distance.

One evening, as the last rays of sunlight faded and the cemetery slipped into its usual shroud of mist, Dahlia appeared again. Her form was faint, flickering as though she was struggling to maintain her connection to the living world.

"Vivi," she whispered, her voice barely audible over the wind. "Something's wrong. You need to stop this."

Vivi looked up from the vine she was tending, her brow furrowed. "What are you talking about?"

"The garden," Dahlia said, her eyes wide with fear. "It's growing too fast. The dead—they're not the only ones noticing. Lucien—he's not who he says he is."

Vivi felt a cold chill run through her. "What do you mean?"

Dahlia floated closer, her glow dimming even further. "Lucien isn't just some wanderer between life and death. He's tied to the darkness he warned you about. He's been manipulating you, using your garden to open something—something terrible."

Vivi stood, her heart pounding. "No, that can't be true. He's helped me. He's given me the knowledge I needed to—"

"To what?" Dahlia interrupted, her voice rising with urgency. "To create something that could destroy the balance entirely? Vivi, you've been pushing too far, too fast. The dead, the darkness—they're converging on your garden, and if you don't stop it soon, you'll lose control."

Vivi's mind reeled. She looked around the cemetery, at the creeping vines, the glowing plants, the unnatural energy that seemed to pulse from the very earth. It had felt right—like she was building something strong, something that could protect both the living and the dead. But now, doubts gnawed at her. Had she gone too far?

Before she could respond, a figure emerged from the mist. Lucien, his dark eyes gleaming in the dim light, walked toward them. His presence seemed to suck the warmth from the air, leaving the night colder, heavier.

"Vivi," he said, his voice smooth and calm. "Is something the matter?"

Dahlia floated backward, her form flickering even more. "Don't listen to him, Vivi. He's not on your side."

Vivi's eyes darted between Dahlia and Lucien, her pulse racing. She could feel the weight of the decision pressing down on her. She had come so far, built something she thought could change the world, but now everything felt fragile, like it could shatter with the wrong move.

"I think we need to slow down," Vivi said cautiously, her gaze fixed on Lucien. "This garden… it's growing too fast. I don't want to lose control."

Lucien's expression remained unreadable, but there was a flicker of something in his eyes—something dark, calculating. "Control?" he said softly. "Vivi, you've never truly had control. That's the thing about walking between life and death—neither side can be tamed. You're not building a garden. You're opening a gate."

Vivi's breath caught in her throat. "A gate… to what?"

Lucien's smile was cold. "To the true power of the dead. To the darkness that binds them. The balance you think you're creating—it's not balance at all. It's a doorway, and soon, it will swing open."

"No," Vivi whispered, stepping back. "That's not what I wanted."

"Isn't it?" Lucien asked, his voice low and persuasive. "You've felt the power, haven't you? You've seen what you can do. Why stop now? Why not let the garden grow, let it consume everything? You could be more than just a caretaker of the dead, Vivi. You could rule both worlds."

Vivi shook her head, her heart pounding in her chest. This wasn't what she had planned. She had wanted to create something beautiful, something that bridged the gap between life and death. But now, she saw the truth—the garden wasn't a bridge. It was a trap.

"You lied to me," she said, her voice trembling with anger. "You used me to create this… this gateway."

Lucien's smile widened, his eyes gleaming with malice. "You were so eager to defy the dead, to prove yourself. I just gave you the tools to do it."

Vivi clenched her fists, fury building inside her. She had been a fool. All her efforts, all her work—it had been for him, to feed the darkness that lurked just beneath the surface of her creation.

But it wasn't too late.

With a deep breath, Vivi reached into her pocket and pulled out one of the seeds she had been saving—a seed from the very first vine she had planted. It glowed faintly in her palm, pulsing with life and death in equal measure.

"I'm ending this," she said, her voice steady.

Lucien's smile faltered. "What are you doing?"

Without hesitation, Vivi knelt down and pressed the seed into the ground. As soon as it touched the soil, the earth trembled, and the vines that had spread throughout the cemetery began to writhe and twist. The dark energy that had been building in the garden surged, but instead of growing, it began to collapse inward, drawn back into the earth by the seed's power.

"No!" Lucien shouted, his calm demeanor shattering. He lunged toward Vivi, but Dahlia intervened, her glowing form solidifying as she placed herself between them.

"You can't have her," Dahlia hissed, her voice fierce.

Lucien snarled, but the power of the collapsing garden forced him back. The vines twisted and coiled, pulling themselves from the tombstones and crypts, sinking back into the soil. The glowing plants withered, their energy dissipating into the night air.

Vivi felt the weight lifting, the oppressive darkness receding as the garden she had created unraveled. She had done it—she had stopped the gateway from opening.

But the price was high.

As the last of the vines disappeared into the ground, the cemetery fell silent. The garden was gone, and with it, the fragile balance she had tried to create. The dead still lingered, watching from the shadows, but their presence felt muted, distant.

Lucien stood at the edge of the cemetery, his eyes burning with fury. "You think this is over?" he growled. "You can't stop what's coming, Vivi. The darkness is already here."

And with that, he vanished into the mist, leaving Vivi standing alone in the empty cemetery.

Dahlia floated beside her, her form flickering weakly. "You did it," she said softly. "You stopped him."

Vivi nodded, though her heart felt heavy. She had stopped Lucien, but at what cost? The garden was gone, her connection to both life and death severed. And the darkness that Lucien had spoken of… it was still out there, waiting.

"I'm not done yet," Vivi said, her voice quiet but resolute. "I'll find another way. I'll rebuild. And this time, I'll make sure no one can twist it."

Dahlia smiled faintly. "I'll be here. Whenever you need me."

Vivi looked out over the cemetery, the graves bathed in the pale light of the moon. The dead were still watching, but now, they were waiting—for her next move, for her to prove that she could still be the bridge between their world and hers.

The balance wasn't broken.

Not yet.

Chapter 11

The nights grew longer after Lucien's departure, the cemetery steeped in a cold that felt deeper than before. Though the oppressive energy had dissipated, something darker still lingered, a shadow just beyond the edges of perception. Vivi could feel it in her bones. Lucien had been a catalyst, but he wasn't the source of the darkness. He had merely shown her what was coming, what had always been there, waiting for a moment to break through.

But now, she was alone. Her garden was destroyed, its vines and plants consumed by the very power she had unleashed. The dead, once drawn to her, kept their distance, murmurs of judgment trailing in their wake as she walked among the graves. She had disappointed them. She had failed.

And yet, Vivi refused to give up.

Each day, she returned to the cemetery, rebuilding from the ground up. It wasn't the same as before—this time, she worked carefully, weaving smaller patches of life and death into the soil, experimenting with new mixtures of energy that would not spiral out of control. Her work was slower, more deliberate, and though the progress was less dramatic, it was stable. But even as she toiled in the shadows, her mind wandered back to Lucien's words. The darkness is already here.

The question haunted her: what had she truly unleashed?

Dahlia, too, was a shadow of her former self. Though she lingered near, her energy had grown faint, and Vivi could sense her spirit struggling to maintain its connection to the world of the living. They didn't speak much. There was little to say. The bond between them had changed, strained by the weight of the unknown forces pressing in on both sides.

One evening, as Vivi knelt by a patch of freshly planted vines, the air around her grew colder than usual. A deep, penetrating chill that made her breath come out in clouds of frost. She stood slowly, her instincts telling her that something was coming.

The cemetery had gone silent, the usual sounds of the night—rustling leaves, distant whispers of the dead—vanished. And then, from the mist that curled around the gravestones, a figure emerged.

Not Lucien. Not Dahlia.

This figure was taller, more imposing, draped in robes that seemed to shift and flow like smoke. Their face was hidden beneath a hood, but Vivi could feel their gaze upon her, heavy and cold.

"Vivi," the figure spoke, their voice deep and resonant, echoing as though it came from the depths of the earth itself.

Vivi's hand instinctively went to the shears she kept at her side. "Who are you?" she demanded, her voice steady, though her heart pounded in her chest.

The figure stepped closer, their presence suffocating, as though the very air around them was thick with power. "You've stirred something ancient, something that was never meant to wake," they said. "I've come to ensure it does not consume you."

Vivi's grip tightened on the shears. "And what would that be?"

The figure tilted their head, and for the first time, Vivi caught a glimpse of their face beneath the hood. Pale skin, eyes dark as voids, and a mouth set in a grim line. "The darkness," they said simply. "It has always been here, hidden beneath the surface, waiting. Your garden—it was a doorway, yes, but not to the dead. You were drawing from something far older, far more dangerous."

Vivi felt a knot form in her stomach. "Lucien… he said the same thing. That I was opening a gate."

"He was right," the figure replied. "But he sought to use you for his own ends. I, on the other hand, seek to prevent the worst from happening."

"And why should I trust you?" Vivi asked, her eyes narrowing.

The figure's mouth twisted into something like a smile, though there was no warmth in it. "Because unlike Lucien, I am not bound to the darkness. I am its guardian, its warden. I am here to ensure that it remains sealed."

Vivi's mind raced. She had spent so long believing that her garden was a bridge, a way to balance the worlds of life and death. But now, it seemed that the very power she had sought to control was tied to something far beyond her understanding.

"What do you want from me?" she asked, her voice barely above a whisper.

The figure raised a hand, and the ground beneath Vivi trembled, the earth shifting as though something beneath it was stirring. "You must finish what you started," they said. "You have the power to seal the darkness, but you must be willing to sacrifice for it."

Vivi's pulse quickened. "Sacrifice?"

The figure nodded. "The darkness feeds on the space between life and death. Your garden was drawing from that space, creating a conduit. To close it, you must sever that connection. You must give up the garden."

Vivi's heart sank. She had already lost so much—her plants, her connection to the dead. The garden was all she had left, the only piece of her that still felt like it belonged in both worlds.

But the figure's presence loomed over her, a reminder that the darkness was far greater than her personal desires.

"And if I don't?" Vivi asked, though she already knew the answer.

"Then the darkness will grow," the figure replied, their voice cold and final. "It will consume everything, starting here, in this cemetery. The dead will not be safe. Neither will the living."

Vivi clenched her fists, her mind racing with the weight of the decision. She had fought so hard to create something meaningful, something that could change the way life and death intertwined. But now, she was being asked to let it all go, to undo everything she had worked for.

"I'll do it," Vivi said finally, her voice hollow. "I'll seal the garden."

The figure stepped back, their form becoming less solid, more ethereal, as though they were fading into the mist. "Good," they said. "I will return when the time comes."

And with that, they disappeared, leaving Vivi standing alone in the cold, empty cemetery.

The next few days passed in a blur of preparation. Vivi knew what she had to do, but the thought of destroying the garden—the last remnant of her connection to the worlds she had tried to unite—was almost unbearable. Dahlia stayed close, offering quiet support, though her own energy was fading, her spirit growing weaker with each passing day.

When the time finally came, the cemetery was shrouded in thick fog, the air heavy with the weight of impending finality. Vivi stood at the center of what remained of her garden, the last of the vines curling weakly around her feet. She held the seed—the same one she had used to collapse the garden before—its faint glow the only light in the encroaching darkness.

The figure appeared again, just as they had promised. This time, they did not speak, simply watching as Vivi knelt before the garden, her hands trembling.

"I'm ready," she whispered, though her heart ached with the knowledge of what she was about to do.

With a deep breath, Vivi pressed the seed into the soil, just as she had before. But this time, instead of drawing the garden's energy inward, she pushed it out—letting the power flow from her into the ground, into the air, into the very fabric of the cemetery itself.

The earth trembled, and the vines began to unravel, their dark tendrils withering as the energy of the garden dissipated. The connection between life and death—between the living world and the dead—began to fade, severed by the power of the seed.

Vivi could feel it slipping away, her hard-earned balance unraveling as the last of the vines disappeared into the earth. The cemetery was silent, still, as though the very air had been emptied of all life.

And then, it was over.

The garden was gone.

The darkness had been sealed.

Vivi stood, the weight of the moment pressing down on her, heavier than she had imagined. She had done what was necessary, but the loss was profound, an emptiness that echoed deep within her soul.

Dahlia appeared beside her, her form flickering faintly. "You did it," she said softly, though there was a sadness in her voice. "It's over."

Vivi nodded, though the victory felt hollow. "But at what cost?"

Dahlia looked at her, her eyes filled with sympathy. "You saved them all, Vivi. The living and the dead. That's what matters."

Vivi took a deep breath, staring out at the empty cemetery. The dead were still there, but their presence was distant, muted. The garden—the bridge she had tried to create—was gone, and with it, her connection to the worlds she had once sought to unite.

But even in the silence, she knew that her fight wasn't truly over.

The darkness was sealed, for now.

But it would always be there, lurking beneath the surface, waiting for another chance to break through.

And when that time came, Vivi would be ready.

Chapter 12

Though the darkness had been sealed and her garden was gone, Vivi felt the weight of unfinished business clinging to her like a second skin. The silence of the cemetery, once a comfort, now felt ominous. The dead were still watching, but their presence was faint, withdrawn. Whatever balance she had once sought, it was fractured now, leaving her with an unshakable sense of isolation.

For days, she wandered the cemetery, feeling the empty space where her vines had once thrived. The patches of earth that had been so full of life now lay barren, and the dead, who had once come to her in whispers and gentle touches, stayed away. Only Dahlia remained, her form growing more transparent with each passing day.

"How much longer do you think you have?" Vivi asked one evening, her voice barely more than a whisper as she stood at the edge of a broken gravestone, the moonlight casting long shadows over the ground.

Dahlia hovered beside her, her glow dim. "Not long," she admitted. "The connection we had through the garden—it was what kept me here. Now that it's gone..."

Vivi nodded, the familiar ache in her chest growing stronger. She had lost so much already, and now she was losing her only friend in this strange, in-between world. "I thought there would be peace after I sealed the darkness. But it doesn't feel like peace. It feels like a wound that never heals."

Dahlia gave her a sad smile. "Maybe that's the nature of what we deal with, Vivi. Life and death… they don't come with easy answers. You tried to build a bridge between them, but maybe some things aren't meant to be connected like that."

Vivi sighed, staring out over the gravestones. She had believed so fiercely in her vision, had fought so hard to create something that could change everything. But now, standing in the aftermath, she wondered if she had been wrong all along.

Before she could speak again, a strange noise echoed through the cemetery—a low, rumbling sound, almost like a distant growl. Vivi froze, her eyes scanning the dark, mist-shrouded landscape.

"Did you hear that?" she asked, her pulse quickening.

Dahlia's form flickered, her expression growing tense. "Yes. I did."

The rumbling grew louder, and the ground beneath them began to tremble. Vivi's heart raced as she realized that the very earth was shifting, the graves around her quaking as though something deep within the cemetery was trying to break free.

"No," Vivi whispered, fear seizing her chest. "It can't be."

Dahlia floated closer to her, her voice urgent. "The seal. Something's wrong with the seal, Vivi."

Panic surged through her. She had used everything she had to close the gate, to seal the darkness, but now, it seemed as though her efforts hadn't been enough. She looked down at the ground, where cracks were beginning to form, the soil splitting open as a foul, dark energy began to seep through.

Vivi dropped to her knees, pressing her hands against the earth. "I closed it! I did everything I was supposed to do!"

But the darkness wasn't stopping. It was rising, crawling up through the cracks, black tendrils of shadow coiling around the gravestones, twisting toward the sky like fingers reaching for the surface.

"It's breaking free," Dahlia whispered, her voice barely audible.

Vivi's mind raced, trying to think of what she could do. The seed she had used to collapse the garden had been her last line of defense—her only way to stop the darkness. But now, with that power spent, she had nothing left.

Except… herself.

A realization hit her with the force of a cold wind. She was the one who had created the garden, who had drawn the power of the dead and the living into a delicate balance. If she was the source, then maybe—just maybe—she could be the final piece needed to close the darkness for good.

"I have to go," Vivi said, her voice steady but filled with a grim understanding.

Dahlia's eyes widened in alarm. "What are you talking about?"

Vivi looked up at her, her heart heavy with the weight of what she was about to say. "I'm the key, Dahlia. It was my connection to the garden, to the dead, that opened the gate. I think… I think I'm the only one who can close it."

Dahlia shook her head, her form flickering with desperation. "No, Vivi. You can't. You've given so much already. You don't have to do this."

But Vivi knew, deep down, that this was always where her path had been leading. The garden, the darkness, the balance—it was all connected to her. She had been drawn to the cemetery for a reason, and now she understood why.

"I do have to do this," Vivi said softly, standing up. "If I don't, the darkness will consume everything. I can feel it."

Dahlia reached out, her ghostly hand passing through Vivi's shoulder, her voice trembling. "You'll be lost. If you do this… you won't come back."

Vivi swallowed the lump in her throat, her mind already made up. She looked at Dahlia, her only friend, and gave her a sad smile. "Maybe I wasn't meant to come back."

Tears shimmered in Dahlia's ghostly eyes. "I don't want to lose you."

"You won't," Vivi whispered, her voice filled with a quiet resolve. "I'll be here. In the cemetery. In the garden. I'll be part of it, part of the balance, just… not the way we thought."

With one last look at Dahlia, Vivi turned toward the center of the cemetery, where the cracks in the earth had grown larger, the tendrils of darkness writhing like living shadows. She took a deep breath and walked toward it, her footsteps steady despite the fear that clawed at her heart.

As she approached the center, she could feel the pull of the darkness, the cold, insidious energy that had been trying to break free for so long. It whispered to her, tempting her to let it consume everything, to let the worlds of the living and the dead collide.

But Vivi was stronger than that. She had fought too hard, given too much, to let the darkness win.

She knelt down at the edge of the largest crack, placing her hands on the cold earth. The energy surged through her, filling her veins with a chilling power, but she didn't resist. Instead, she embraced it, letting the darkness flow into her, letting it fill her completely.

And then, with one final act of will, Vivi gave herself to the earth.

The ground trembled violently, the cemetery shaking as the darkness surged toward her. But instead of consuming everything, it stopped—drawn into her like a magnet, coiling around her, pulling her down into the soil.

The last thing Vivi felt was the cool embrace of the earth as the darkness sealed itself within her, the cracks in the ground closing, the tendrils of shadow disappearing into the void.

And then, there was silence.

The cemetery was still once more. The gravestones stood untouched, the air calm and peaceful. Dahlia floated above the place where Vivi had knelt, her heart aching with loss.

But she knew that Vivi's sacrifice had saved them all. The darkness was sealed, and it would never rise again.

Vivi was gone.

But her spirit, her essence, was now part of the cemetery, part of the balance she had fought so hard to protect.

Dahlia closed her eyes, her form flickering as she whispered, "Thank you."

And then, with a faint glow, she, too, faded into the night.

The cemetery stood silent, a testament to the girl who had once tended its garden, who had bridged the worlds of the living and the dead—and who had given everything to save them both.

Chapter 13

Years passed, and the cemetery remained largely forgotten by the living, tucked away at the edge of a town that moved on without noticing its quiet presence. The graveyard stood still, as it always had, but there was an undeniable change, a feeling that those who dared to walk its grounds could sense immediately: an odd calm, heavy but peaceful, like the air just before a storm.

Vivi's sacrifice had not only sealed the darkness but had woven her presence into the very soil of the cemetery. The ground, once cold and lifeless, now hummed with a subtle energy. Those sensitive to such things could feel it—a quiet hum, as if something was watching over the resting dead.

Among the whispers of local legends, there was one story that persisted: the tale of a goth girl named Vivi, the guardian of the graveyard. People spoke of seeing her late at night, a shadowy figure tending to flowers that no longer grew, her silhouette flickering at the edge of sight before vanishing like mist.

They said that if you were brave enough to venture deep into the cemetery at midnight, you might catch a glimpse of her standing beneath the oldest tree, her pale hands hovering just above the soil, as though still tending to her lost garden. And if you were respectful—quiet, calm, without fear—you might feel her presence, a cool breeze, a touch of comfort from beyond the veil.

The cemetery had become a place of both fear and reverence. Some came to pay their respects to the dead, leaving flowers by the headstones, not for the lost souls, but for Vivi, the unseen protector who watched over them. Others stayed away, fearing the stories of the strange power that lurked beneath the ground, of the girl who had given her life to save them all.

One evening, a young girl named Emmeline, dressed in dark clothes and feeling more out of place than ever, wandered into the cemetery. She had always been fascinated by the stories, drawn to the quiet mystery of death and what lay beyond, but the tale of Vivi—the goth girl who had protected the world from an ancient darkness—was the one that had captured her imagination most.

Emmeline felt a kinship with Vivi, though she didn't fully understand why. Maybe it was the way people looked at her—the same way they must have looked at Vivi, with suspicion and misunderstanding. Maybe it was the loneliness, the feeling of not belonging anywhere but in the shadows, surrounded by things people didn't want to think about.

As the sun set, casting long shadows over the gravestones, Emmeline found herself standing in the center of the cemetery, where the cracks in the earth had long since healed. She knelt down, brushing her fingers over the soil where, according to legend, Vivi had made her final stand.

"I don't know if you're still here," Emmeline whispered, her voice barely audible in the stillness of the evening. "But I hope you are. I hope you found some kind of peace."

The wind stirred gently, rustling the leaves of the ancient tree nearby, and for a moment, Emmeline felt something—an odd, comforting presence, as though the cemetery itself was acknowledging her words.

She stayed there for a long time, the twilight deepening around her, lost in thought.

It wasn't until she stood up to leave that she noticed something strange at the edge of the clearing. A single flower, pale and delicate, had bloomed from the soil. A rose—its petals a deep, almost black crimson—stood alone, a solitary sign of life in the graveyard.

Emmeline knelt down, staring at the rose in awe. There had been no flowers here for years. The soil was barren, or at least it had been.

The stories had said that the garden was gone, but maybe… maybe it wasn't.

She reached out to touch the rose, but stopped herself at the last moment, unsure if it was right to disturb it. Instead, she smiled faintly, a small flicker of hope lighting in her chest.

"Thank you," she whispered, though she wasn't sure who she was thanking—Vivi, the cemetery itself, or something else entirely.

As she turned to leave, she couldn't shake the feeling that someone was watching her. Not in a threatening way, but in a protective, watchful silence. And for the first time in a long while, she didn't feel quite so alone.

The next morning, when the sun rose over the cemetery, the single rose remained, standing tall and proud in the spot where Vivi had made her sacrifice.

And as time went on, others noticed small changes too—vines curling around gravestones, faint whispers in the wind, as though the cemetery itself was alive once more.

Vivi's garden was gone. But maybe, just maybe, it was beginning to grow again. Not in the way it had before—wild and uncontrolled—but slowly, carefully, nurtured by the lingering presence of a girl who had become the protector of the dead.

The darkness was sealed, and the balance restored.

But the story of Vivi, the guardian of the cemetery, would never truly end. It lived on, whispered among those who visited the graves, in the flowers that began to bloom once more, and in the quiet peace that settled over the cemetery like a gentle, protective veil.

And though Vivi herself was no longer of the living, her presence would always be there, watching over the cemetery and the souls who rested within it, forever a part of the world she had saved.

Chapter 14

Years passed, and the legend of Vivi the Cemetery Guardian deepened, growing in whispers carried by the wind. The cemetery, once a forgotten place, became a destination for those who felt lost, outsiders like Emmeline, and others who sought something they couldn't name—a sense of belonging, a connection to the invisible.

The cemetery now had an unspoken rule: respect the dead, and the garden would flourish. Some visitors brought offerings, leaving flowers or mementos by the ancient gravestones, while others came simply to sit among the quiet, feeling the weight of something profound in the air. The dark crimson roses, once a solitary bloom, began to appear more frequently, slowly reclaiming the space.

One cold autumn night, Emmeline returned. She had become a regular visitor over the years, always careful to honor the space that Vivi had guarded. Tonight, however, something felt different. As she walked among the gravestones, the air felt charged, as if the cemetery was holding its breath.

The old stories said that the dead, though silent, were never far away—that Vivi's sacrifice had bound her spirit to the land, protecting the balance between life and death. Emmeline often thought about this, wondering what it meant for Vivi. Did she still watch over the cemetery, or was she lost somewhere between the worlds, her sacrifice never truly understood?

She found herself again in the clearing where the first rose had bloomed, and to her astonishment, it wasn't alone. The entire patch was now alive with dark crimson roses, their petals velvety and luminous in the moonlight. They seemed to pulse faintly, as though imbued with a life force far older than the soil they grew from.

Emmeline knelt down, running her fingers gently through the petals. As she did, the wind stirred, and the night around her grew eerily quiet, the usual sounds of distant traffic and rustling leaves fading into nothingness. Her heart began to race.

And then, she felt it.

A presence—stronger, more tangible than ever before.

"Vivi?" Emmeline whispered, her voice trembling.

For a long moment, there was no response, just the heavy silence of the cemetery. But then, from behind her, a shadow moved. Emmeline turned slowly, her breath catching in her throat.

A figure stood at the edge of the clearing, barely more than a silhouette in the pale moonlight. Pale skin, dark clothes, and long black hair that swayed slightly in the wind—Vivi. Her eyes, shadowed and ancient, locked onto Emmeline's, and though her face was expressionless, there was something in her gaze—an understanding, a kinship.

"You…" Emmeline breathed, barely able to form the words. "You're still here."

Vivi didn't respond, but her form seemed to flicker, wavering between solid and translucent. She stepped forward, her movements slow and deliberate, and Emmeline noticed the ground around her feet—wherever Vivi stepped, the soil darkened, rich with life, as if she was still tied to the land, still nurturing it.

"Is it you?" Emmeline asked again, her voice steady this time. "Are you… protecting this place?"

Vivi stopped in front of her, her form now almost fully visible in the moonlight. Her face was serene, but there was a depth in her eyes—a sadness, perhaps, but also acceptance. She looked down at the roses and then back at Emmeline.

"You saved them," Emmeline said softly. "You're still saving them."

Vivi tilted her head slightly, as though acknowledging the truth of Emmeline's words, but there was no smile, no relief. It was as though she had come to terms with her fate long ago, knowing that her role was not to be celebrated, but simply to exist —to guard the fragile boundary between life and death, forever.

The wind picked up again, and with it came a faint whisper, like the rustling of leaves but with words just out of reach. Emmeline could almost make out what was being said, but the meaning remained elusive. It didn't matter, though. The cemetery, the roses, and Vivi herself—everything spoke of a deeper, eternal truth that no words could capture.

"You don't have to be alone," Emmeline whispered, stepping closer to Vivi. "I come here all the time. I feel like… you're not just guarding the dead. You're watching over people like me too."

Vivi's gaze softened, just for a moment, and Emmeline felt a flicker of warmth pass through her—a strange but comforting sensation. It was as if, for a brief moment, Vivi had acknowledged her, accepted her as part of the cemetery's ever-growing story.

Then, as quickly as she had appeared, Vivi began to fade. Her form flickered once more, the edges of her body dissolving into the night air, like smoke being carried away by the wind. Emmeline reached out instinctively, but she knew there was nothing to hold onto.

"Wait—" she started, but Vivi was already gone, her form dissipating into the darkness.

But the roses remained.

Emmeline stood in silence for a long time, the cool night air wrapping around her. She didn't know if she would ever see Vivi again, but she felt, deep in her bones, that the girl would always be there, in some way. Not just in the cemetery, but in the stories they shared, the people she had touched, the legacy of protection she had left behind.

The world outside the cemetery continued on, oblivious to the quiet guardian that watched over the dead and the living alike. But within those grounds, the roses would bloom, and the story of Vivi, the goth girl who had sacrificed everything to protect the balance, would never fade.

Emmeline smiled softly, the heavy sense of isolation she had carried for so long beginning to lift. She wasn't alone. Not really.

And neither was Vivi.

The balance remained, fragile yet unbroken. And the roses, dark and beautiful, would continue to grow, their roots tangled deep in the soil, nurtured by the quiet, eternal presence of a girl who had become more than just a guardian—she had become the heart of the cemetery itself.

As the years rolled on, the cemetery began to attract a different kind of attention. It wasn't just the quiet whispers of legends that surrounded it anymore; there was something more palpable, more mysterious that drew people in. Ghost hunters, curious locals, and spiritual seekers all ventured to the cemetery, each hoping to catch a glimpse of the ghostly figure that wandered the grounds or to feel the strange energy that seemed to radiate from the soil.

The dark roses had flourished, now growing in clusters throughout the cemetery, their deep crimson hue a stark contrast to the grays and blacks of the tombstones. Emmeline, who had become a frequent visitor, always noticed how the roses seemed almost alive in ways that were hard to explain. They grew in the oddest places, wrapping gently around statues, gravestones, and along the old wrought-iron fence that encircled the cemetery. It was as if they were trying to reach something, to connect to a deeper power that lay just beyond the grasp of the living.

One evening, as autumn set in, Emmeline found herself drawn to the cemetery once more. The air was colder than usual, and the sky was a deep violet as the sun dipped below the horizon. The place felt different tonight—tense, almost expectant, as though something was about to happen. The wind whispered through the trees, carrying with it the familiar scent of earth and roses.

She made her way to the center of the cemetery, where the oldest gravestones stood like silent sentinels, watching over the land. As she approached, Emmeline noticed something strange— an area of the cemetery, near the spot where she had first seen Vivi, was shrouded in mist, thicker than the usual evening fog that sometimes rolled in.

Her heart quickened. This wasn't normal.

As she stepped closer, the mist parted slightly, revealing a figure standing in the center of the clearing. It was Vivi.

But something was different this time. Vivi wasn't just flickering at the edges of existence like before. She looked more real, more solid than Emmeline had ever seen her. Her long black hair flowed gently behind her, and her pale face was more visible in the dim light, her eyes dark but filled with a kind of clarity that hadn't been there before.

"Vivi?" Emmeline called out, her voice soft but steady.

Vivi didn't respond with words, but she turned toward Emmeline, her gaze intense. There was something in her eyes— an urgency, as though she was trying to communicate something important, something that couldn't be spoken aloud.

Emmeline stepped forward, but as she did, the ground beneath her began to tremble slightly. The mist swirled more violently around them, and a low hum filled the air, as if the cemetery itself was awakening to something long dormant.

And then, Emmeline saw it.

At the far edge of the clearing, where the old mausoleums stood, the earth began to crack open. It wasn't like the small fractures that had appeared during the sealing of the darkness years ago. This was different. The cracks were jagged, deep, and pulsed with an eerie glow—a faint red light that seemed to come from far beneath the surface.

Vivi turned to face the cracks, her posture tense, and for the first time, Emmeline saw real fear cross her face.

"What's happening?" Emmeline asked, panic creeping into her voice.

Vivi remained silent, but her body language told Emmeline everything she needed to know. Whatever was happening here, it wasn't supposed to. The darkness that Vivi had once sealed away was stirring again, and this time, something was pushing it back to the surface.

Emmeline's heart raced as she moved to Vivi's side. "What do we do? How do we stop it?"

Vivi looked at her, and for the first time, her lips parted. Her voice, when it came, was soft and distant, like a whisper carried on the wind. "You…"

Emmeline blinked, unsure what she meant. "Me? I'm not —"

Vivi held out her hand, palm up, as if offering something invisible. Emmeline stared at it for a moment, confusion swirling in her mind. But then, without fully understanding why, she reached out and placed her hand in Vivi's.

The moment their hands touched, Emmeline felt a surge of cold energy rush through her, like icy water filling her veins. Her vision blurred, and for a split second, she saw flashes of something—memories, maybe, or visions of a world far different from her own. She saw the cemetery as it had been long ago, before Vivi's sacrifice, vibrant and alive with unseen forces. She saw the moment Vivi had sealed the darkness, felt the weight of her decision, the pain of leaving the world of the living behind.

And then, she saw something else. A force, ancient and malevolent, buried deep beneath the cemetery—something that had never truly been sealed. It was the darkness, yes, but it was more than that. It was a hunger, a void, something that had been waiting for centuries to break free.

The vision snapped away, and Emmeline gasped, pulling her hand back from Vivi's. Her body shook with the force of what she had just seen, and her mind reeled from the knowledge that had been imparted to her.

"Why me?" Emmeline asked, her voice trembling. "What am I supposed to do?"

Vivi's eyes softened, and for the first time, a faint, almost imperceptible smile crossed her lips. "You're part of it now," she whispered. "The balance. The roses… they've chosen you."

Emmeline stared at her in shock, but before she could respond, the cracks in the earth began to widen, the glow intensifying. The cemetery trembled violently, and from the depths of the cracks, tendrils of shadow began to rise.

"No," Emmeline breathed, instinctively stepping back. "We can't let it out."

Vivi's form flickered, becoming less solid once more, and she glanced at Emmeline with a look of quiet determination. Emmeline knew, in that moment, what had to be done. Vivi had given everything to protect the world from the darkness, and now… it was her turn.

Without hesitating, Emmeline stepped toward the cracks, her heart pounding in her chest. She could feel the pull of the darkness, the same insidious force that had almost consumed the cemetery all those years ago. But she also felt something else—a warmth, a strength that came from the earth beneath her feet, from the roses that had bloomed in the wake of Vivi's sacrifice.

She knelt down, placing her hands on the cold, cracked earth, just as Vivi had done before. The tendrils of shadow twisted around her, cold and sharp, but she didn't flinch.

"I understand now," Emmeline whispered, her voice steady. "I'm not afraid."

The roses around her began to glow faintly, their deep crimson petals pulsing with life. The ground beneath her hands vibrated, and Emmeline could feel the cemetery responding to her, as though the land itself was alive, waiting for her to take the next step.

With a deep breath, Emmeline closed her eyes and let the energy of the cemetery flow through her, just as Vivi had done. She could feel the darkness resisting, trying to break free, but she pushed back with everything she had. This time, there would be no cracks, no imbalance. She wasn't sealing the darkness away— she was becoming part of the balance, just like Vivi.

The ground trembled one last time, and then, with a final surge of power, the cracks closed, the tendrils of shadow dissolving into the earth. The eerie glow faded, and the cemetery fell silent once more.

Emmeline opened her eyes, breathing heavily. The roses around her still glowed faintly, and the air was thick with the scent of earth and flowers. She stood up slowly, her body aching but her mind clear.

Vivi was gone.

But Emmeline didn't feel alone. She could feel her presence, deep in the earth, woven into the fabric of the cemetery. She was part of it now, just as Vivi had been. The guardian of the dead, the keeper of the balance.

And as she stood there, surrounded by the quiet night and the glowing roses, she knew that the cemetery—and the world—was safe. For now.

But the balance was delicate, and Emmeline understood, as Vivi had before her, that the darkness would always try to rise again.

And when it did, she would be ready.

Chapter 15

After that night, Emmeline found herself changed.

The weight of what she had done, of the mantle she had accepted, stayed with her like a whisper in her mind, ever present. She was now part of the cemetery, woven into its ancient rhythms and mysteries just as Vivi had been. Her senses sharpened—she could feel the subtle energy of the land, hear the quiet whispers of the wind as it rustled through the dark roses, and sense the spirits that lingered there, peaceful but watchful.

The cemetery had a pulse, a life force of its own, and she could feel it now, beating in time with her own heart. The roses, dark and beautiful, continued to bloom in greater numbers, spreading their roots deep into the soil. Wherever Emmeline went, they seemed to follow, like living shadows, silent sentinels watching over the graves.

Word of the roses began to spread, and with them, stories about the new guardian of the cemetery—a young woman, pale and dark-haired, who wandered among the graves late at night. People who visited the cemetery claimed they felt something different now. It wasn't just the somber quiet of a resting place for the dead—it was a sense of protection, as if the cemetery itself had come alive, sheltering those who visited with the respect it demanded.

Emmeline became a myth in her own right, just as Vivi had before her.

She didn't shy away from her new role. On the contrary, she felt more at home in the cemetery than she ever had anywhere else. In life, she had always felt out of place, a misfit wandering through a world that didn't quite understand her. But here, in the quiet of the graveyard, she felt grounded, connected to something older and more profound than anything she had known before.

The cemetery became her sanctuary.

Still, the memory of that night—the cracking earth, the darkness rising—haunted her. Though she had managed to seal the darkness once again, she knew it was only a matter of time before it stirred again. The balance between life and death was delicate, and the ancient force buried beneath the cemetery was patient, biding its time, waiting for the right moment to try and break free again.

It was a burden she carried with her, but she wasn't afraid. Not anymore.

One evening, as autumn began to deepen, Emmeline sat by the old tree in the cemetery's heart, staring out at the gravestones bathed in the pale light of the rising moon. The air was cold and still, but it was the kind of stillness that felt alive, like the cemetery was watching, waiting.

She ran her fingers through the grass, feeling the life pulsing beneath her fingertips, and closed her eyes. As the guardian, she had come to understand the rhythms of the cemetery in a way that no one else could. The land spoke to her in its own quiet language, telling her when the balance was shifting, when something was wrong.

And tonight, something was different.

A chill ran down her spine, and she opened her eyes, scanning the cemetery. The mist had begun to roll in again, thick and heavy, curling around the gravestones like tendrils of smoke. The moonlight seemed dimmer, and the wind carried an unsettling whisper.

Emmeline stood, her senses on high alert. She could feel it now—a disturbance, something wrong beneath the surface of the cemetery. The earth trembled slightly beneath her feet, a faint but unmistakable vibration.

"No," she whispered, her heart racing.

The darkness was stirring again.

She moved quickly, making her way to the center of the cemetery where the cracks had appeared before. As she approached, the mist grew thicker, swirling around her like a living thing. The ground trembled more violently now, and a faint red glow began to seep through the cracks in the earth, just as it had that night with Vivi.

Emmeline's breath caught in her throat. This time, it felt stronger, more urgent, as if the darkness was pushing harder, trying to break free with renewed force.

She knelt down, placing her hands on the ground, just as she had done before. The roses around her glowed faintly in the mist, their dark petals shimmering with a strange, otherworldly light. She could feel the energy of the cemetery pulsing beneath her hands, but it was chaotic, unbalanced, like a storm brewing beneath the surface.

Closing her eyes, Emmeline reached out with her mind, trying to connect with the land, with the balance she had sworn to protect. She could feel the darkness pushing against her, trying to force its way through, but she pushed back with all her strength, focusing on the life around her—the roses, the trees, the spirits of the dead who rested peacefully in the cemetery.

But this time, it wasn't enough.

The ground beneath her split open, jagged cracks tearing through the earth. The red glow intensified, and from the depths of the cracks, tendrils of shadow began to rise, swirling and twisting through the air. The darkness had found a weakness, a way through the barrier that Emmeline and Vivi had fought so hard to maintain.

Emmeline gritted her teeth, refusing to give in to the fear that threatened to overwhelm her. She couldn't fail—not now. Not after everything.

But just as she felt herself weakening, struggling to hold back the force rising from beneath the cemetery, she felt a presence beside her.

Vivi.

Her form was faint, more of a shadow than a solid figure, but Emmeline could feel her strength, her determination. Vivi knelt beside her, placing her hands on the earth, and for a brief moment, their energies combined. The cemetery responded, the ground humming with power, and the darkness recoiled, retreating slightly.

"Together," Vivi whispered, her voice soft but firm.

Emmeline nodded, drawing strength from Vivi's presence. Together, they pushed back against the darkness, their combined will forcing it down, sealing the cracks in the earth once more.

The red glow faded, and the tendrils of shadow dissolved into the mist.

The ground trembled one last time, then fell still.

Emmeline opened her eyes, breathing heavily. The mist was beginning to clear, and the cemetery was silent once more. She turned to Vivi, who was still kneeling beside her, her form flickering in and out of focus.

"Thank you," Emmeline whispered, her voice hoarse.

Vivi met her gaze, and for the first time, she smiled—a real, genuine smile, filled with warmth and understanding. Then, slowly, she began to fade, her form dissolving into the night air.

Emmeline watched her go, her heart heavy but filled with a deep sense of peace. Vivi's spirit had been with her all along, guiding her, helping her to protect the balance. And though she was gone now, Emmeline knew that Vivi's legacy would live on, in the cemetery, in the roses, and in her.

The darkness had been sealed once more, but Emmeline knew it wasn't gone forever. The balance was fragile, always shifting, always threatened by forces older than time itself. But now, with Vivi's guidance and her own growing strength, she was ready.

She would stand watch, just as Vivi had done before her. She would protect the cemetery, the souls who rested within it, and the balance between life and death.

And when the darkness rose again, she would be there to face it.

Chapter 16

In the months that followed, Emmeline adjusted to her new life as the cemetery's guardian. The weight of her duty was no longer a burden but a part of her, woven into her very soul. She spent most of her days tending to the cemetery, caring for the roses that now flourished in every corner of the graveyard, their dark crimson petals a silent reminder of the power that lay beneath the earth.

But she was not alone.

Vivi's presence lingered, not as a ghost or a vision, but as a quiet force that Emmeline could feel whenever she needed guidance. The cemetery was more alive than it had ever been, a sanctuary not just for the dead, but for Emmeline herself. She had found her place, her purpose, and though the shadows of the past still loomed large, she no longer feared what lay ahead.

One evening, as the sun dipped below the horizon, casting long shadows over the gravestones, Emmeline felt a familiar stirring in the air. The temperature dropped, and the wind picked up, carrying with it the scent of roses and something else— something darker, more ancient.

She stood at the edge of the cemetery, watching as the mist began to roll in from the woods. It wasn't the thick, ominous fog that had accompanied the darkness before, but something gentler, almost inviting. Still, Emmeline knew better than to let her guard down.

Her heart quickened, and she moved toward the center of the cemetery, where the oldest graves lay. The ground was cool beneath her feet, the roses rustling softly in the wind. As she approached the ancient tree that stood like a sentinel in the heart of the graveyard, she saw something—or someone—standing there.

At first, she thought it might be another spirit, perhaps one of the lost souls that sometimes wandered the cemetery at night. But as she drew closer, she realized it was something different.

The figure was tall and shrouded in dark robes, their face hidden beneath a hood. They stood perfectly still, their presence unnerving yet strangely familiar.

Emmeline stopped a few feet away, her hand instinctively reaching for the earth, ready to call upon the power of the cemetery if needed. "Who are you?" she asked, her voice steady despite the tension in the air.

The figure remained silent for a moment, and then, in a voice as ancient as the wind, they spoke. "I am the one who watches."

Emmeline's brow furrowed. "Watches what?"

"The balance," the figure replied, their voice soft but laced with power. "As you do now."

A chill ran down Emmeline's spine. "Are you here to help or to hinder?"

The figure tilted their head slightly, as if considering the question. "Neither. I am a witness. The balance has always been, and will always be. It is not my place to interfere."

"Then why are you here?" Emmeline asked, her fingers brushing against the cold earth beneath her feet.

The figure was silent for a moment, and then they spoke again, their voice heavy with meaning. "The balance you protect is but one of many. There are others—guardians, like yourself, in places far and near. Each of you holds a piece of the whole, but none can hold it forever."

Emmeline's heart raced. "What do you mean?"

"You are not the first guardian, and you will not be the last," the figure said, their tone almost regretful. "The darkness you faced—what you call 'the darkness'—is not unique to this place. It exists in many forms, in many places, always seeking to break free."

Emmeline swallowed hard, her mind racing. "Are you saying it will rise again?"

The figure nodded slowly. "It always does. But each time, a guardian rises to meet it. That is the way of things."

She felt a mix of dread and acceptance settle over her. "And when it rises again, I'll be ready."

The figure inclined their head, as though in acknowledgment. "Perhaps. But the time will come when the balance will shift beyond your control. When that day comes, you must be prepared to pass the mantle to another, just as it was passed to you."

Emmeline's breath caught in her throat. "To another?"

"All things change," the figure said, their voice softer now. "Even guardians."

For a moment, Emmeline felt the weight of her role settle heavier on her shoulders. She had become part of something much larger than herself, something that stretched far beyond the boundaries of this cemetery. She wasn't just protecting this place—she was part of a larger tapestry, one that stretched across time and space, connecting all who had come before and all who would come after.

The figure began to fade into the mist, their form dissolving like smoke on the wind. But before they disappeared completely, they left her with one final message.

"Remember, Emmeline: the darkness will always rise. But so will the light."

And then, they were gone.

Emmeline stood in the quiet of the cemetery, her mind spinning with the weight of what she had just learned. She wasn't alone in her fight. There were others like her, guardians of other places, other balances. The knowledge gave her a sense of comfort, but it also filled her with a quiet determination.

She knelt down, her hand brushing against the roses that grew at the base of the ancient tree. They glowed faintly in the moonlight, their petals soft and cool to the touch. The cemetery was peaceful again, the balance restored—for now.

But Emmeline knew the peace wouldn't last forever. The darkness would rise again, just as it always had. And when it did, she would be ready to face it.

For now, though, she would watch over this place, tending to the roses and the spirits who called the cemetery home. She would guard the balance, just as Vivi had before her, until the day came when she would pass the mantle to someone else.

Until then, the cemetery—and the world beyond it—was safe.

Chapter 17

As the days turned into weeks, Emmeline settled further into her role, becoming one with the cemetery's rhythms. The nights were colder now, and the air carried the bite of the approaching winter. The dark roses continued to bloom despite the chill, their petals vibrant against the frost-laden ground. Visitors to the cemetery became fewer as the season deepened, and Emmeline found solace in the quiet stillness of the graves.

But the figure's words stayed with her. "You will not be the last." She had never considered the possibility of someone else taking her place, of a future beyond her own guardianship. It made her wonder who that next person might be—and if she would recognize them when the time came.

One night, while walking the familiar path between the gravestones, Emmeline felt a subtle shift in the air. It wasn't the stirring of darkness, nor the presence of a spirit seeking peace. It was something else, something softer and more human. Her senses, now finely attuned to the energy of the cemetery, picked up on it immediately.

Someone was watching her.

She turned slowly, scanning the shadows cast by the towering monuments and ancient trees. At first, she saw nothing but the pale glow of the moonlight reflecting off the gravestones. But then, near the far edge of the cemetery, she spotted movement—a figure standing near the old iron gate, partially hidden in the mist.

They were young, perhaps around her age, dressed in black and draped in layers that fluttered in the wind. Their face was partially obscured by the shadows, but Emmeline could make out the glint of dark eyes watching her intently. Whoever they were, they didn't seem afraid—if anything, they seemed drawn to the cemetery, much like she had once been.

Emmeline's heart quickened as she approached, her steps slow and deliberate. The figure didn't move, though their posture was tense, as if waiting for her to make the first move.

"You're not lost, are you?" Emmeline asked, her voice breaking the silence.

The figure stepped forward, their boots crunching softly against the frost-covered ground. Now that they were closer, Emmeline could see more clearly—a girl, probably not much younger than herself, with jet-black hair and a pale face framed by the hood of her oversized coat. There was something familiar about her, a kind of quiet intensity that reminded Emmeline of her own younger self.

"No," the girl replied softly. "I came here on purpose."

Emmeline studied her for a moment, sensing something unusual beneath the surface. "Why?"

The girl hesitated, her eyes flickering over the graves around them. "I've been coming here for a while, just... watching. I didn't think anyone else noticed."

"I notice everything in this place," Emmeline said, her tone gentle but firm. "What is it you're looking for?"

The girl shifted uncomfortably, then met Emmeline's gaze with a mixture of curiosity and uncertainty. "I don't know exactly. I just... feel like I belong here. Like I'm supposed to be here."

Emmeline's heart skipped a beat at the girl's words. She remembered that feeling—the inexplicable pull toward the cemetery, the sense of belonging in a place most people feared. It had been the same for her when she first stumbled into Vivi's rose garden. Could this be what the figure had meant? The one who would come after her?

"What's your name?" Emmeline asked.

The girl blinked, surprised by the question. "It's Mae."

"Mae," Emmeline repeated softly. She glanced down at the roses growing at her feet, the same ones Vivi had nurtured so long ago, and wondered if this was how it had all begun for her, too— an unspoken calling, a strange pull toward something greater than herself.

Mae shifted nervously, as if unsure of what to say next. "I don't mean to intrude. I just... feel like there's something here for me."

Emmeline felt a surge of recognition. "You're not intruding. This place has a way of calling to those who are meant to find it."

Mae's eyes widened slightly, her gaze darting from Emmeline to the dark roses. "You sound like you know a lot about it."

"I do," Emmeline replied, her voice calm but tinged with a deeper understanding. "This cemetery, these roses... they're more than just a resting place for the dead. They're part of something much older, something that needs protecting."

Mae's brow furrowed. "Protecting from what?"

Emmeline took a deep breath. "From the darkness that lies beneath. It's quiet now, but it won't stay that way forever. Someone has to watch over it, to keep the balance between life and death."

Mae was silent for a moment, processing Emmeline's words. Then, slowly, she nodded. "And you're the one who does that?"

"For now," Emmeline said, feeling the weight of the statement. "But there will come a time when I can't do it alone."

Mae's gaze lingered on the roses for a long moment before she spoke again. "What happens then?"

Emmeline met her eyes, a quiet certainty settling over her. "Then someone else steps in. Someone the cemetery calls."

Mae looked down, her expression thoughtful. "Do you think... it's calling me?"

Emmeline didn't answer right away. She wasn't sure if Mae was meant to be the next guardian, but there was no denying the connection the girl felt to the cemetery. Whether this was the beginning of something greater or just a moment of clarity for Mae, only time would tell.

"Maybe," Emmeline said softly. "But that's something only you can decide."

Mae looked up at her, and for the first time, Emmeline saw a flicker of hope in the girl's eyes. "How will I know?"

"You'll feel it," Emmeline replied. "Just like I did."

Mae nodded slowly, and for a moment, they stood in silence, the night air heavy with possibility. Emmeline could feel the cemetery's energy shifting, like the first stirrings of something new—something that might change the course of her guardianship forever.

Mae took a step back, her gaze lingering on the roses once more. "I think... I'd like to come back. If that's okay."

Emmeline smiled, a quiet, knowing smile. "You're always welcome here."

As Mae turned to leave, disappearing into the mist that clung to the edges of the cemetery, Emmeline felt a strange sense of peace settle over her. The figure's words echoed in her mind: *You will not be the last.*

Perhaps the next chapter was already beginning, written in the footsteps of a girl drawn to a place of shadows and roses, just as Emmeline had been before her.

The cemetery, as always, watched and waited.

Chapter 18

$\mathcal{In}$ the days that followed, Mae returned to the cemetery often, always at dusk when the world seemed to soften between light and shadow. She never said much, but Emmeline could sense the girl's curiosity growing with each visit. Mae would wander the paths between the graves, lingering by the dark roses, as if absorbing the quiet energy that pulsed beneath the surface of the land.

At first, Emmeline kept her distance, watching from afar as Mae explored. She knew this journey was something Mae had to take on her own—just as Emmeline had done before her. But it wasn't long before the two of them began to spend more time together, walking the cemetery grounds in silence, occasionally sharing brief conversations.

"Do you ever get scared?" Mae asked one evening as they stood beneath the ancient tree in the cemetery's heart, watching the mist roll in.

Emmeline glanced at her, then at the graves stretching out before them. "I used to," she admitted. "When I first started, I was terrified of what was out there. The darkness, the things I didn't understand. But over time, I learned to trust the cemetery, to trust myself."

Mae was quiet for a moment, her gaze fixed on the roses growing near the tree's roots. "What if I'm not strong enough? What if something happens and I can't stop it?"

Emmeline placed a hand on Mae's shoulder, her touch light but reassuring. "You are stronger than you think. The cemetery wouldn't have called you if you weren't."

Mae looked up, her expression a mixture of doubt and hope. "How do you know it called me?"

"Because I felt the same way when I first came here," Emmeline said. "Lost, unsure, like I didn't belong anywhere else. But the cemetery—it has a way of finding the right people, the ones it needs."

Mae nodded slowly, as if trying to absorb Emmeline's words. "I think I want to learn more."

Emmeline smiled softly, her heart warming at the thought. "Then I'll teach you. But understand this isn't just about learning spells or rituals. Being a guardian is about balance, about listening to the land and knowing when to act. It's about patience and trust."

Mae's eyes lit up, and for the first time, Emmeline saw a spark of determination there, the same spark that had driven her to become the cemetery's protector all those years ago. "I want to help."

And so, the lessons began.

Each night, Emmeline guided Mae through the cemetery, teaching her the old ways that Vivi had once taught her—the ways of the roses, of the spirits, and of the land itself. Mae was a quick learner, her natural connection to the cemetery growing stronger with each passing day. She learned how to listen to the whispers of the wind, how to sense when the balance was shifting, and how to draw strength from the earth beneath her feet.

But there were also harder lessons—lessons about the darkness that lurked beneath the surface, waiting for its chance to rise again. Emmeline told her everything, about the night she had faced the darkness with Vivi, and the figure's warning that the balance would one day shift beyond her control.

"That day will come," Emmeline said one night as they stood by the cracked earth where the darkness had once emerged. "But we don't know when. Until then, we watch, we learn, and we protect."

Mae stared at the ground, her expression serious. "And if the darkness rises again?"

Emmeline's voice was steady, though a hint of fear lingered in the back of her mind. "Then we'll face it together."

Mae nodded, her resolve hardening. There was a quiet strength in her that Emmeline recognized—the same strength that had carried her through her own trials as the cemetery's guardian. She knew that Mae had the potential to become a great protector, just as Vivi had seen in her.

One cold winter night, as a thick fog rolled in and the temperature plummeted, Emmeline felt the first stirring of something unsettling. It was faint, almost imperceptible, but her connection to the cemetery allowed her to sense it—something was wrong.

The mist swirled around the gravestones, unnaturally thick and cold, and Emmeline could feel the air grow heavy with tension. She glanced at Mae, who stood beside her, eyes wide with alarm.

"Do you feel that?" Mae whispered.

Emmeline nodded, her pulse quickening. "It's starting."

They moved quickly toward the center of the cemetery, where the oldest graves lay. The ground trembled faintly beneath their feet, and as they approached the ancient tree, Emmeline saw it—the red glow beginning to seep through the cracks in the earth.

The darkness was rising.

Emmeline's heart pounded in her chest, but she forced herself to stay calm. This wasn't the first time she had faced the darkness, and it wouldn't be the last. She turned to Mae, who was staring at the glowing cracks with a mixture of fear and determination.

"Stay close to me," Emmeline instructed. "We'll do this together."

Mae nodded, her hands trembling slightly as she knelt beside Emmeline. They both placed their hands on the ground, feeling the energy pulsing beneath the surface. The darkness was pushing harder this time, more forceful, more aggressive. It wanted to break free.

Emmeline closed her eyes, focusing her energy on the earth, calling upon the power of the cemetery to seal the cracks. The roses around them began to glow, their dark petals shimmering with an eerie light as they absorbed the energy of the land.

Beside her, Mae was struggling, her face contorted with effort as she tried to focus her energy. The darkness was strong, too strong for her to handle alone.

"I can't—" Mae gasped, her voice strained.

"You can," Emmeline said firmly. "Just breathe. Trust yourself. Trust the cemetery."

Mae took a deep breath, her hands steadying as she concentrated. Together, they pushed against the darkness, their combined will forcing it down, sealing the cracks in the earth once more. The red glow faded, and the ground fell still.

For a moment, there was silence. Then Mae let out a shaky breath, her face pale but triumphant. "We did it."

Emmeline smiled, pride swelling in her chest. "Yes, we did."

But even as the relief washed over her, she couldn't shake the feeling that this wasn't the end. The darkness had been sealed again, but it was growing stronger, testing the limits of the balance.

As they stood together in the quiet of the cemetery, Emmeline realized something: Mae wasn't just a potential guardian—she was part of the battle now, just as much as Emmeline was.

The cemetery had chosen her, just as it had chosen Emmeline. The time for passing the mantle had not yet come, but Emmeline knew that when it did, Mae would be ready.

For now, they would continue to watch, to learn, and to protect. Together, they would face whatever came next, the darkness and the light intertwined in an eternal dance that neither could escape.

And when the time came, Emmeline would pass the torch to Mae, knowing that the cemetery—and the world—would be in good hands.

Chapter 19

Winter deepened, and the cemetery felt more alive than ever. The roses, black against the frost, remained in full bloom, defying the cold. Every night, Emmeline and Mae worked together, growing closer as teacher and student, but also as friends bound by the gravity of their shared role.

One evening, when the moon hung low in the sky, casting long shadows across the cemetery, Emmeline noticed something different in the air. It wasn't the thick tension of the approaching darkness, nor the light pull of a wandering spirit seeking solace. It was something... quieter, softer, almost melancholic.

As Emmeline walked the familiar path along the oldest graves, she saw it: a faint, glowing figure standing near Vivi's rose garden, the place where Emmeline had first encountered her predecessor. The figure was tall, feminine, and wrapped in a translucent shroud that shimmered in the moonlight.

Emmeline's breath caught in her throat. It couldn't be.

But it was.

Vivi stood among the roses, her form ghostly but unmistakable. She looked as she had the last time Emmeline saw her—a shadow of the past, both haunting and beautiful.

"Vivi," Emmeline whispered, her voice trembling. She hadn't seen her since the night she had taken up the mantle of guardian. A surge of emotion hit her—a mixture of grief, longing, and reverence for the one who had guided her through the darkest of nights.

Vivi turned toward her, her ethereal face calm, though her eyes held the weight of countless years. "Emmeline," she said, her voice a soft echo on the wind.

Mae, who had been trailing behind Emmeline, stopped short when she saw Vivi. Her eyes widened in shock. "Is that...?"

Emmeline nodded slowly, her gaze never leaving Vivi. "Yes. This is Vivi. She was the guardian before me."

Vivi smiled faintly, her presence gentle yet commanding. "And now, you are the guardian," she said, her voice carrying a strange mix of pride and sorrow. "You've done well, Emmeline. The cemetery thrives under your care."

Emmeline swallowed hard, emotions swirling within her. "I couldn't have done it without you, Vivi. You saved me. You showed me the way."

Vivi's expression softened. "You were always strong, Emmeline. I only helped you see it."

For a long moment, they stood in silence, the weight of their shared history heavy between them. Mae, unsure of what to say, remained silent, though her gaze flickered between the two women with a kind of awe.

Finally, Emmeline broke the silence. "Why are you here, Vivi? Is something wrong?"

Vivi's gaze shifted to the roses, their dark petals glowing faintly in the moonlight. "The time is drawing near, Emmeline. The balance is shifting once more, and soon, it will no longer be yours to maintain."

Emmeline's heart sank. She had known this day would come, had even prepared herself for it, but hearing Vivi say the words made it feel real. "You mean... it's time to pass the mantle."

Vivi nodded. "Yes. The darkness grows stronger each day, and the cemetery will need a new guardian to face what's coming. You have trained Mae well. She is ready."

Mae's eyes widened in disbelief. "Me? But I—"

"You've felt the call, haven't you?" Vivi asked, her voice gentle but knowing. "The cemetery has chosen you, just as it chose Emmeline before you. You are meant for this, Mae."

Mae looked at Emmeline, her face a mixture of fear and uncertainty. "I don't know if I'm ready for that. I don't know if I can do what you do."

Emmeline stepped closer to her, placing a hand on her shoulder. "I felt the same way when Vivi passed the mantle to me. But you are ready, Mae. You've already shown your strength and your connection to this place. The cemetery chose you for a reason."

Vivi nodded in agreement. "Being a guardian isn't about being fearless, Mae. It's about standing in the face of fear, knowing that you're part of something greater than yourself. The balance is delicate, but you have the strength to maintain it."

Mae's hands trembled slightly, but she lifted her chin, her eyes meeting Emmeline's. "If you believe in me, then... I'll do it. I'll protect the cemetery."

A sense of peace settled over Emmeline. Mae was the right choice. She had seen it in her from the beginning, the quiet strength that had been waiting to be awakened. And now, as Vivi had once done for her, it was time to pass the mantle.

Vivi extended her hand, and from the mist, a single dark rose appeared, its petals shimmering with a deep, otherworldly glow. "The cemetery has always been tied to these roses. They carry its life force, its power. Take this, Mae. It will bind you to the land, just as it did for Emmeline and for me."

Mae hesitated for only a moment before reaching out and taking the rose from Vivi's ghostly hand. The moment her fingers touched the petals, a soft pulse of energy surged through the ground, and the cemetery seemed to exhale around them.

Emmeline watched as the roses bloomed brighter, their dark petals swaying gently in the wind. She felt the connection shifting, her bond with the cemetery loosening as Mae's grew stronger.

Vivi turned to Emmeline, her eyes filled with warmth. "You've done your part, Emmeline. The cemetery will always remember you."

Tears welled in Emmeline's eyes, but she smiled through them. "Thank you, Vivi. For everything."

Vivi gave her a final, knowing look. "Your journey doesn't end here, Emmeline. You've only just begun."

And with that, Vivi's form began to fade, her figure dissolving into the mist until she was nothing more than a faint memory among the roses.

Emmeline and Mae stood in silence for a long while, the weight of the moment settling over them. The cemetery felt different now—lighter, calmer, as if the transition had brought with it a sense of peace.

Mae clutched the rose in her hand, her expression thoughtful. "It's strange. I feel... connected. Like the cemetery is speaking to me."

"It is," Emmeline said, smiling softly. "It always will."

Mae looked at her, the uncertainty in her eyes replaced with quiet determination. "What about you? What happens now?"

Emmeline took a deep breath, the night air cool and crisp. "I'm not sure yet. But Vivi was right—my journey isn't over. I'll still be here, helping you when you need me. But the cemetery is yours now, Mae."

Mae nodded, a small smile playing on her lips. "I'll take good care of it."

Emmeline knew she would.

As they stood together beneath the ancient tree, the cemetery around them glowing with life, Emmeline felt a sense of closure, but also the beginning of something new. The mantle had passed, and with it, the balance had been restored.

For now, the darkness was quiet. But it would rise again, as it always did. And when it did, Mae would be ready.

And so would Emmeline, wherever her path might take her next.

The eternal cycle of guardianship continued, the roses blooming, the balance shifting, and the darkness waiting—but never for long.

Chapter 20

The following weeks were a quiet but profound shift for both Emmeline and Mae. The days seemed to pass slowly, yet the air was thick with change. Mae began her role as the cemetery's guardian, walking the grounds alone at dusk, her connection to the land deepening with each passing day. The roses bloomed brighter under her care, their dark petals pulsing with the life force of the cemetery. The spirits that once lingered near the edges of the graves now approached her more openly, as if recognizing their new protector.

Emmeline watched from a distance, allowing Mae the space to grow into her role. She still walked the cemetery often, but now, it felt different. She wasn't bound to it in the same way anymore. The cemetery still whispered to her, but the voice was softer, less urgent. Her purpose here was no longer to protect—it was to guide.

One evening, as the first snow of the season dusted the ground, Emmeline stood at the edge of the cemetery, gazing out over the rolling hills of graves and roses. The wind carried a familiar chill, one that had always signaled the presence of something more. But this time, it wasn't the darkness. It was a different kind of calling.

Emmeline closed her eyes, listening to the wind. It spoke of paths beyond the cemetery, of places she had yet to explore. For so long, her life had been tied to this place—to its rhythms, its spirits, its roses. But now, as the cemetery settled into Mae's hands, Emmeline felt the stirrings of a new journey ahead.

She wasn't sure where she would go or what she would find, but there was a certainty in her heart that the world had more to show her. She had been given a gift—a connection to the unseen, the ability to navigate the spaces between life and death. And now, she would take that gift and carry it with her beyond the cemetery's gates.

That night, she approached Mae as the young guardian tended to the roses near the ancient tree. The moonlight cast a silver glow over the cemetery, illuminating Mae's calm, determined face as she worked.

"How are they?" Emmeline asked, her voice soft.

Mae looked up, a small smile on her lips. "Stronger than ever. The cemetery... it feels more alive every day."

Emmeline nodded, her heart swelling with pride. Mae had grown so much in such a short time. She had found her place, just as Emmeline once had.

"Mae," Emmeline began, her tone more serious now, "I think it's time for me to go."

Mae's hands stilled, her smile fading. "Go? Where?"

Emmeline took a deep breath, choosing her words carefully. "I'm not sure yet. But the cemetery... it no longer needs me the way it did before. It's yours now. And I feel like there's something out there for me, beyond these gates."

Mae's brow furrowed in confusion and worry. "But... what if something happens? What if the darkness rises again?"

Emmeline smiled gently. "You've already proven you can handle it. You sealed the cracks. You felt the pull of the land. You've become a part of the cemetery in a way that I never could. And I'll always be here if you need me. But it's time for me to find my own path."

Mae's gaze dropped to the ground, her hands tightening around the stem of one of the roses. "I don't know if I'm ready to do this alone."

"You're not alone," Emmeline said, stepping closer and placing a reassuring hand on Mae's shoulder. "The cemetery is with you. The spirits, the roses, the land—they will guide you, just as they guided me. And I'll never be far if you need me."

Mae nodded slowly, though the uncertainty still lingered in her eyes. "I'll miss you."

"I'll miss you too," Emmeline admitted, her voice thick with emotion. "But this isn't goodbye forever. It's just... a new chapter."

They stood in silence for a moment, the weight of the moment settling between them. Then, with a final, lingering glance at the roses, Emmeline turned and walked away, her footsteps light on the frost-covered ground.

As she passed through the cemetery's gates, a sense of freedom washed over her—a freedom she hadn't felt in years. The world beyond the cemetery was wide and unknown, but Emmeline was no longer afraid of the unknown. She had faced darkness and come out stronger. She had found her strength, her purpose.

And now, it was time to find herself.

In the weeks that followed, Mae continued to care for the cemetery with quiet determination. She learned to trust the land, to listen to its whispers, and to sense when the balance shifted. She was still young, still learning, but the cemetery had accepted her, and that acceptance gave her the confidence to face whatever challenges lay ahead.

The darkness did not rise again—not yet. But Mae knew it would one day. The balance was delicate, always teetering between light and shadow. But Mae was ready. She had Emmeline's teachings, Vivi's wisdom, and the strength of the land behind her.

And so, the cemetery thrived under Mae's care, the roses blooming darker and more vibrant with each season. The spirits found peace, the graves stood undisturbed, and the darkness waited, as it always did, for its time to come.

But Mae would be ready.

And somewhere, out in the world, Emmeline walked her own path, guided by the same whispers of fate that had once led her to the cemetery. She was no longer bound to the graves and the roses, but her heart would always carry the weight of her time as guardian.

For the cycle continued, and though the names and faces of the guardians changed, the cemetery remained eternal.

And so did the roses.

Chapter 21

As winter melted into spring, the cemetery bloomed with renewed life. The dark roses stood tall, their petals unfurling in rich shades of black and violet, contrasting against the vibrant greens that spread through the cemetery. Mae had settled into her role as the cemetery's guardian, and though the weight of responsibility often lingered on her shoulders, she carried it with quiet strength.

The spirits, once restless, grew calm under her care, and the delicate balance between life and death seemed to hold steady. Yet Mae knew better than to let her guard down. The darkness was always waiting, lurking beneath the surface, and though it had not stirred since that winter night, she could feel its presence—its hunger.

One evening, as twilight cast long shadows over the graves, Mae felt a shift in the air. It was subtle at first, like a low hum vibrating through the earth. She paused in her work, kneeling by a freshly dug grave, and closed her eyes, letting the energy of the cemetery wash over her. There it was again—a disturbance, faint but undeniable.

Mae stood and turned toward the ancient tree, where the darkest roses grew. The mist had begun to roll in, thickening around the gravestones like an ominous veil. Her heart quickened as she made her way toward the center of the cemetery, her instincts sharpening with each step.

When she reached the tree, she saw it: a small crack in the earth, barely visible, but glowing faintly with a dull, red light. The sight sent a chill down her spine.

The darkness was trying to break through again.

Mae knelt beside the crack, placing her hands on the ground, just as Emmeline had taught her. She closed her eyes, focusing her energy on the earth, willing the crack to seal. But something was different this time—something was resisting her.

The darkness was stronger.

Mae's pulse quickened, but she didn't allow herself to panic. She dug deep, pulling from the strength of the cemetery, from the roses and the land itself. Slowly, she began to feel the earth respond to her, the crack shrinking under her touch. It was a struggle, but Mae held her ground, determined not to let the darkness win.

Suddenly, a sharp gust of wind whipped through the cemetery, howling like a scream. Mae's eyes flew open, her focus faltering. The crack widened slightly, and the red glow intensified, casting eerie shadows across the gravestones.

Panic surged in Mae's chest. She could feel the darkness pushing back, more forceful than ever before. For a moment, doubt crept in. Was she strong enough? Could she really hold it back on her own?

And then, a familiar voice echoed in her mind, soft but steady.

"Trust the cemetery. Trust yourself."

Emmeline's words, spoken to her so many times, anchored Mae. She took a deep breath, grounding herself. The darkness was stronger now, yes, but so was she.

Mae pressed her hands harder against the earth, channeling every ounce of energy she could muster. The cemetery pulsed beneath her, responding to her call, and the roses around her began to glow with an ethereal light. Slowly, the crack began to seal again, the red light dimming.

But just as it seemed like the darkness was retreating, a voice—a deep, rasping whisper—crept into her mind.

"You can't hold me forever."

Mae froze, her heart skipping a beat. The voice was different from the spirits that wandered the cemetery. This voice was ancient, malevolent, and filled with a cold, dark promise.

She didn't respond, but her resolve wavered for a split second, just long enough for the crack to glow brighter again. The ground beneath her trembled.

"The balance will break."

Mae gritted her teeth, forcing the voice out of her mind. She couldn't let it distract her. She focused harder, drawing strength from the roses, from the very land she had sworn to protect.

And then, with one final surge of energy, the crack sealed completely. The red glow faded, and the cemetery fell silent once more.

Mae collapsed to her knees, her breath coming in ragged gasps. Her entire body ached, the strain of holding back the darkness weighing heavily on her. But she had done it. She had sealed the crack.

For now.

As she knelt there in the quiet of the cemetery, Mae couldn't shake the words the darkness had whispered to her. **"The balance will break."** What did that mean? How much stronger would it become the next time it tried to rise?

She knew she couldn't ignore the warning. The darkness was growing, and eventually, it would find a way to break free. She would have to be ready for it.

The following night, as Mae walked the cemetery under the pale light of the moon, she heard a familiar voice call out to her from the shadows.

"Mae."

She turned to see Emmeline standing at the edge of the cemetery, her face illuminated by the soft glow of the moon. Mae's heart lifted at the sight of her former mentor.

"Emmeline," Mae breathed, hurrying toward her. "I'm glad you're here. Something happened."

Emmeline's expression was calm but serious, as if she already knew. "I felt it. The darkness—it's growing stronger, isn't it?"

Mae nodded, her voice tinged with worry. "I sealed the crack, but it was harder this time. And it... spoke to me. It said the balance will break."

Emmeline's eyes darkened with concern. "The balance is always fragile. But if the darkness is speaking now, it means something has shifted. We'll need to be prepared."

Mae felt a knot tighten in her chest. "What if I'm not enough to hold it back?"

Emmeline placed a hand on Mae's shoulder, her touch firm and reassuring. "You are enough, Mae. You've proven that time and again. But you don't have to do this alone. I'm still here, and the cemetery is always with you."

Mae nodded, drawing strength from Emmeline's words. But deep down, she knew that the coming battle would be unlike anything they had faced before.

The darkness was no longer content to linger in the shadows. It was preparing to rise, and when it did, Mae would need every ounce of strength she had to keep the balance intact.

As the two women stood together beneath the moonlight, the wind rustling the petals of the dark roses around them, Mae felt a sense of determination settle in her bones.

The darkness would rise again.

But so would she.

And when the balance was threatened, Mae would be ready.

Chapter 22

As the weeks passed, the foreboding presence of the darkness lingered in the back of Mae's mind, like a shadow she couldn't shake. The cemetery itself felt uneasy—restless. The spirits grew quieter, almost hiding, as if sensing the encroaching threat. The roses, once in full bloom, began to wither, their petals darkening further, almost to the point of decay.

Mae spent long nights walking the grounds, her connection with the cemetery deepening with every step, but so did her anxiety. She could feel the darkness pulsing beneath the earth, waiting for its moment to break free again. The air was thick with a sense of impending doom.

One night, as she sat beneath the ancient tree, she felt the earth tremble. The crack that had once appeared near the tree had stayed sealed, but now, a low rumble moved through the ground, growing stronger. Her heart raced. The darkness was stirring again.

Without hesitation, Mae jumped to her feet and sprinted toward the center of the cemetery, where the disturbance felt strongest. The mist thickened around her as she ran, the wind whipping through the trees, carrying an eerie, hollow wail. She knew this was different from before. The darkness was pushing harder, testing her limits.

As she reached the heart of the cemetery, the ground beneath her split open once more. This time, the crack was larger —wider than before—and the red light that glowed from within was blinding. Mae could feel the darkness clawing its way out, like a beast trapped beneath the earth, desperate to be free.

She fell to her knees, pressing her hands against the ground as she had done before, but something was wrong. No matter how much energy she channeled into the earth, the crack wouldn't close. The darkness pushed back, more forceful, more alive than she had ever felt.

The voice came again, deeper and more menacing.

"You are not enough."

Mae's breath hitched in her throat. The voice was louder now, more present, as though it were standing right behind her, whispering into her ear.

"The balance will break, and you will fall."

Panic gripped her heart. For the first time, she wasn't sure if she could stop it. The ground beneath her trembled violently, the crack widening as dark tendrils of mist began to rise from the opening. The darkness was spilling into the world, and Mae was losing control.

She closed her eyes, digging deep, trying to pull strength from the cemetery, from the roses, from everything she had. But the darkness was stronger. So much stronger.

"Emmeline!" Mae screamed, her voice echoing through the cemetery. "Help me!"

For a moment, nothing happened. The wind howled, the ground shook, and the darkness rose higher, surrounding her like a thick fog. Mae's heart pounded in her chest as despair started to creep in. She couldn't do this alone. She wasn't strong enough.

But then, through the chaos, a familiar warmth filled the air. A gentle breeze brushed against her cheek, and a soft, calming presence enveloped her. She opened her eyes to see Emmeline standing beside her, her face illuminated by the glow of the dark roses.

"Mae," Emmeline said, her voice steady. "You are strong enough. You can do this."

Mae shook her head, tears stinging her eyes. "I can't. It's too strong. I'm not ready."

Emmeline knelt beside her, placing a hand on her shoulder. "You are ready. You've been ready. But you need to stop fighting it alone."

Mae looked at her, confused. "What do you mean?"

Emmeline's gaze softened. "The cemetery isn't just yours to protect. It's part of you, part of something much bigger. You can't fight the darkness by yourself. You need to trust the cemetery, let it guide you. It's not just a place—it's alive, and it's with you. Always."

Mae closed her eyes again, her mind racing. She had always tried to control the cemetery, to wield its power. But Emmeline was right. The cemetery wasn't something to be controlled—it was something to be connected with. To trust.

Taking a deep breath, Mae let go of her fear. She released the tight grip she had on the earth, and instead of pushing against the darkness, she let herself sink into the cemetery's energy. She felt the pulse of the land beneath her, the heartbeat of the roses, the spirits that wandered the graves. She was part of it all, and it was part of her.

Slowly, the trembling ground began to settle. The crack stopped widening, the red light dimming. Mae felt the darkness pushing against her, but now it wasn't overwhelming. It was something she could face—something she could contain.

The cemetery responded to her, the roses glowing brighter, their energy intertwining with hers. Together, they pushed back the darkness, sealing the crack once more. The red glow faded completely, and the ground grew still.

Mae exhaled shakily, her body trembling with exhaustion. But she had done it. The crack was sealed.

Emmeline smiled softly beside her. "See? You were never alone in this."

Mae looked at her, tears of relief filling her eyes. "Thank you."

Emmeline shook her head. "You didn't need me, Mae. You had the strength all along. You just needed to trust yourself—and the cemetery."

Mae stood slowly, her legs weak, but her spirit lighter than it had been in weeks. She had faced the darkness, and though it had been stronger this time, she had been stronger too. The cemetery had chosen her for a reason.

As they walked back toward the ancient tree, the mist began to lift, and the stars twinkled faintly in the sky above. The roses swayed gently in the breeze, their petals glowing with a soft, otherworldly light.

But even as the peace returned, Mae knew this wasn't the end. The darkness had been growing, and it would continue to do so. The balance was fragile, and every time the darkness tried to break through, it would be stronger.

Mae was ready, though. She had Emmeline's guidance, the cemetery's strength, and her own power. Whatever came next, she would face it head-on.

Because now, Mae understood something she hadn't before.

The darkness wasn't just something to fight. It was part of the balance. And so was she.

And as long as the cemetery lived, so too would the roses—and so too would the guardians who watched over them.

Together, they would keep the balance.

No matter how many times the darkness tried to rise.

Chapter 23

The days following Mae's battle with the darkness passed in a haze of calm, but Mae knew the peace was only temporary. The cemetery had settled, the roses blooming once again in their dark beauty, but the weight of what had happened still lingered in her mind. The crack had sealed, but the voice—its warning—echoed inside her.

"The balance will break, and you will fall."

Mae couldn't shake the feeling that something worse was coming, something the cemetery had never faced before. And while she had grown stronger, she knew the darkness was only biding its time, waiting for the right moment to strike again.

One evening, as the sun dipped below the horizon and shadows stretched across the cemetery, Mae found herself standing at the edge of the ancient tree once more. The roses swayed gently in the evening breeze, their petals glowing faintly in the twilight. She could feel the hum of the land beneath her feet, the energy of the cemetery always present, but tonight it felt... different. There was an uneasiness in the air, a tension that made the hairs on the back of her neck stand on end.

Mae crouched beside the tree, her fingers brushing the cool earth. She closed her eyes, trying to tune into the whispers of the cemetery, to sense what had changed. The ground was quiet, but there was something just beyond her reach, something faint, like a thread of shadow slipping through her grasp.

Suddenly, a cold breeze swept through the cemetery, carrying with it a sound—a distant, mournful wail. Mae's eyes snapped open, her heart racing. She stood and scanned the cemetery, her gaze darting between the gravestones, the mist beginning to rise from the ground.

The wind howled again, louder this time, and Mae felt the familiar pull of the darkness, but it wasn't coming from the crack in the earth. It was coming from the graves.

She moved quickly, weaving through the rows of gravestones, her instincts leading her toward the source of the disturbance. The mist thickened as she approached a cluster of older graves, the air growing colder with each step. Mae's breath fogged in front of her as she reached the center of the disturbance, and there, she saw it: a grave, untouched for centuries, now glowing faintly with the same red light she had seen before.

Her pulse quickened. The darkness wasn't just trying to break through the earth—it was rising from the dead.

As she stepped closer to the grave, the ground beneath her feet trembled. The tombstone—worn and covered in moss—began to crack, the earth shifting as something stirred beneath it. Mae's heart pounded in her chest as she knelt beside the grave, pressing her hands against the ground.

She could feel it—the darkness was spreading, taking root in the graves themselves.

"You cannot stop me," the voice whispered in her mind, louder now, filled with cold malice.

Mae gritted her teeth, pushing back with all the strength she had. She channeled the energy of the cemetery, the roses, the spirits that had once walked these grounds. But this time, the darkness was more insidious, spreading like a disease through the graves, turning the earth cold and lifeless.

As she fought to contain it, a shape began to form in the mist—a figure, dark and twisted, rising from the grave. Mae's breath hitched as she watched it take shape, its form tall and skeletal, draped in tattered shadows. Its eyes glowed red, the same menacing light that had spilled from the crack in the earth.

Mae stumbled back, her heart pounding in her chest. This wasn't just the darkness anymore—this was something worse, something alive.

The figure stepped forward, its movements slow and deliberate. Its eyes bore into Mae, filled with an ancient, malevolent hunger.

"You cannot hold me back forever," the figure rasped, its voice like a thousand whispers layered on top of each other. **"The dead will rise, and the balance will fall."**

Mae's legs trembled, fear clawing at her throat. She had never faced anything like this before. The spirits that roamed the cemetery had always been peaceful, quiet—this was something entirely different. This was darkness given form.

But even as the fear gripped her, Mae remembered Emmeline's words. **"The cemetery is with you. Always."**

She couldn't let the fear control her. She couldn't let the darkness win.

Mae stood her ground, her fists clenched at her sides. The figure loomed closer, its skeletal form towering over her, but she didn't back down.

"I'm not afraid of you," Mae said, her voice steady despite the fear coursing through her veins. "This cemetery is mine. These spirits are under my protection. You won't take them."

The figure laughed, a hollow, empty sound that sent chills down her spine. **"You are nothing compared to what I am. You are just a girl playing with powers you cannot control."**

Mae's jaw tightened. She could feel the pull of the cemetery, the energy of the land rising up to meet her. She wasn't alone in this fight.

With a deep breath, Mae reached out, channeling every ounce of energy she had into the earth beneath her. The roses responded immediately, their petals glowing brighter, pulsing with life. The spirits, once hidden in the shadows, began to emerge, their forms flickering in the mist.

The figure recoiled slightly, its red eyes narrowing. **"You think you can stop me with this? You are a fool."**

But Mae didn't waver. She felt the strength of the cemetery, the power that had been there all along, and for the first time, she truly understood what it meant to be the guardian of this place.

"I'm not fighting you alone," Mae said, her voice filled with determination. "This cemetery is alive. The roses, the spirits—they're with me."

The figure hissed, stepping back as the light from the roses grew brighter, surrounding Mae in a protective glow. The spirits began to circle the figure, their forms solidifying, pushing back against the darkness.

For a moment, the figure faltered, its form flickering, as though it were struggling to maintain its hold on the world.

Mae stepped forward, her eyes locked on the figure. "You will not break the balance. Not today."

With a final surge of energy, Mae pushed the darkness back, the roses flaring with brilliant light. The figure let out a guttural scream, its form dissolving into shadow as it was forced back into the grave. The red glow faded, and the ground stilled once more.

Mae collapsed to her knees, breathing heavily, the adrenaline slowly fading from her system. The cemetery was quiet again, the mist lifting as the spirits returned to their peaceful slumber.

She had done it. She had pushed the darkness back.

But as she sat there, the wind whispering through the trees, Mae knew this wasn't the end. The darkness had taken on a new form—one that would return, stronger than before.

The dead had begun to stir.

And Mae would need to be ready for whatever came next.

The following days brought an eerie quiet to the cemetery, a stillness that pressed on Mae's nerves. It was too calm, too peaceful—like the silence before a storm. The figure she had fought had been pushed back into the earth, but the feeling of something lurking beneath the surface remained.

Mae spent her days tending to the roses, her hands working the soil while her mind wandered, replaying the encounter with the dark figure over and over. She couldn't shake the memory of its red eyes, the way its form had risen from the grave like a creature torn from nightmare. Worse, she couldn't forget its parting words:

"You are nothing. The dead will rise, and the balance will fall."

The weight of those words clung to her like a shadow, a constant reminder that this battle was far from over. She had won a small victory, but the war was only beginning.

Late one evening, as the sun set and the moon began to rise, Mae found herself drawn to the ancient tree once more. The roses beneath its branches glowed faintly in the twilight, their petals shimmering with an almost ethereal light. Mae knelt beside them, letting the soft glow calm her restless thoughts.

As she traced her fingers along the edge of a rose petal, she felt a familiar presence approach. She didn't need to turn around to know it was Emmeline.

"You feel it too, don't you?" Mae asked, her voice barely a whisper.

Emmeline stepped beside her, her expression unreadable. "Yes. The darkness is growing. It's searching for a way back."

Mae swallowed hard, her hands curling into fists. "I don't know if I'm strong enough to face it. That... thing. It wasn't like the spirits. It was something else, something more powerful."

Emmeline knelt beside her, her gaze softening. "The darkness has always been a part of this place, Mae. But it's never taken form like that before. Something is changing—something is making it stronger."

Mae turned to look at her mentor, her heart heavy with worry. "What could be causing it?"

Emmeline was silent for a moment, her brow furrowing in thought. "I don't know for certain. But the balance is delicate. Any disruption—any shift—could give the darkness more power."

Mae's mind raced. She thought of the figure, the crack in the earth, the strange energy she had felt ever since she had taken on the role of guardian. It was all connected, but the pieces didn't quite fit.

"Is it possible that I'm the reason it's growing stronger?" Mae asked, the thought terrifying her. "Maybe I'm not doing enough. Maybe I've upset the balance."

Emmeline shook her head. "No, Mae. You've done more than enough. You've protected this place, kept the darkness at bay. But sometimes, forces beyond our control come into play. There are old powers here, older than you or I."

Mae felt a chill crawl down her spine. "Older than you?"

Emmeline smiled faintly. "Much older. This cemetery has existed for centuries. It has seen many guardians come and go, each facing their own battles. But something about this darkness feels different. It's as if it's waiting for something—biding its time."

Mae bit her lip, her thoughts swirling. "What if it's waiting for the balance to break? What if it's planning something bigger than just taking over the cemetery?"

Emmeline's eyes darkened with concern. "It's possible. The dead rising—that's a sign of something ancient. Something dangerous. If the dead begin to stir in large numbers, it means the barrier between life and death is weakening. And if that happens..."

"The balance will fall," Mae finished, her voice grim.

Emmeline nodded. "Yes. And if the balance falls, the darkness won't just be confined to this cemetery. It will spread, consuming everything in its path."

Mae's stomach twisted with dread. She had thought the cemetery was her only concern, but now it seemed the stakes were much higher. If she failed to contain the darkness, it wouldn't just be the spirits in the cemetery that were in danger. It would be the world beyond.

"What do we do?" Mae asked, her voice small.

Emmeline placed a hand on her shoulder, her grip firm and reassuring. "We prepare. We strengthen the cemetery's defenses. The spirits, the roses, the land itself—they can help you. But you'll need to call on them. You can't face this alone."

Mae nodded, feeling the weight of Emmeline's words settle over her. She had known for a while now that the darkness was growing, but this—this was something far worse than she had imagined. And she wasn't sure if she was ready.

But she had to be.

The cemetery depended on her. The balance depended on her.

As the days turned into weeks, Mae began her preparations. She spent every waking moment working with the spirits, fortifying the land, strengthening the bond between herself and the cemetery. The roses became her allies, their roots digging deep into the soil, creating a network of protection that spread across the cemetery grounds.

But even as Mae worked tirelessly, she could feel the darkness stirring beneath the surface, growing more restless with each passing day. The crack in the earth remained sealed, but the graves themselves had begun to whisper—faint murmurs that sent chills down her spine.

One night, as Mae patrolled the cemetery under a sky heavy with clouds, she heard something that stopped her in her tracks.

A voice. A voice that didn't belong to the spirits.

She turned, her heart pounding, and saw something that made her blood run cold.

A figure stood at the edge of the cemetery, its form cloaked in shadow. It was tall, unnaturally tall, and its eyes glowed red—just like the figure she had fought before.

But this time, there were more of them.

Three figures stood side by side, their red eyes piercing the darkness, their skeletal forms twisted and grotesque. They didn't move, didn't speak, but their presence was enough to send a wave of terror crashing over Mae.

They were waiting.

Mae's heart raced as she backed away slowly, her mind screaming at her to run, to flee. But she couldn't. This was her cemetery. She couldn't abandon it.

Taking a deep breath, she steeled herself and raised her hand toward the figures, calling on the power of the cemetery. The roses responded immediately, their petals glowing with a fierce light, casting the cemetery in a brilliant glow.

But the figures didn't move. They simply stood there, watching her with those cold, red eyes.

And then, as if carried on the wind, she heard the voice again.

"The dead will rise. The balance will fall. And you cannot stop it."

Mae's blood turned to ice as the figures began to fade into the mist, their forms dissolving like smoke.

She was out of time.

The dead were rising, and the darkness was coming for her.

And this time, Mae wasn't sure if she could stop it.

Chapter 24

The chill of the night clung to Mae as she stood alone in the cemetery, her eyes still fixed on the spot where the figures had vanished. The words echoed in her mind: **"The dead will rise. The balance will fall."** They haunted her, heavy with the weight of impending doom. The quiet of the cemetery was unsettling now, no longer a place of refuge, but a ticking clock.

She knew she couldn't hesitate any longer.

Mae hurried toward the ancient tree, the center of the cemetery's power. As she approached, the roses glowed faintly in the moonlight, their light pulsing in time with her quickening heartbeat. She knelt beside the tree, her fingers digging into the cool earth, trying to find any remnants of the presence that had visited her that night.

She closed her eyes and reached out, feeling for the pulse of the land, the heartbeat of the cemetery. It was faint but steady, like a flickering candle in the darkness. Mae focused, pushing deeper, trying to connect with the spirits, the roses, and the roots that lay beneath the earth.

After a few moments, she heard the familiar whisper of the spirits.

"Mae..."

It was a chorus, soft and distant, but comforting in its familiarity. The spirits were with her, though their voices were more subdued than usual. They, too, seemed to sense the growing danger.

"I need your help," Mae whispered, her voice trembling. "Something's coming—something I can't face alone. The darkness is rising, and I need to stop it before it's too late."

The whispers grew louder, swirling around her in the night air. The spirits were trying to guide her, but their voices were fragmented, difficult to understand. It was as though they, too, were being affected by the rising darkness.

A sudden gust of wind swept through the cemetery, causing the roses to tremble. Mae's eyes snapped open, and she felt a new presence. A heavy, oppressive energy, unlike anything she had felt before. The ground beneath her trembled, and a low, distant rumble echoed through the earth.

Mae stood up, her breath catching in her throat. She turned slowly, her eyes scanning the cemetery, searching for the source of the disturbance. The mist that had been hanging low now thickened, swirling ominously around the graves. The air grew colder, biting into her skin.

And then she saw it.

The graveyard was no longer empty.

Figures were rising from the earth, slowly emerging from the graves, their forms dark and skeletal, just like the ones she had seen before. But this time, there were dozens of them. Their red eyes gleamed in the mist, and their twisted, decayed bodies moved with a chilling grace, as if they had been waiting for this moment for centuries.

Mae's heart pounded in her chest. This was it. The dead were rising, just as the voice had promised.

The darkness had come.

Mae stumbled back, her mind racing. There were too many of them—far too many. She couldn't fight them all. Not like this.

She had to think. She had to remember what Emmeline had told her. **"You can't face this alone. You have to call on the cemetery—the spirits, the roses, everything. It's all part of you."**

Mae closed her eyes, forcing herself to focus. She couldn't panic. She couldn't let the fear take over. The cemetery was with her, she just had to trust in it. She just had to let go.

Taking a deep breath, Mae raised her hands, reaching out to the land beneath her feet, to the roots of the ancient tree, to the roses that bloomed all around her. She called on their strength, their energy, feeling it rise up from the earth and flow through her veins.

The roses responded instantly, their glow intensifying, spreading across the cemetery like wildfire. The petals pulsed with light, sending tendrils of energy through the ground, connecting to the graves, to the spirits, to everything that lay beneath the surface.

The skeletal figures hesitated, their red eyes flickering as the light from the roses surrounded them. They twitched, as though sensing the power Mae had called upon. But the darkness within them was strong, and they began to move again, their forms breaking through the mist, closing in on her.

Mae gritted her teeth, pouring more of her energy into the land. The ground beneath the graves began to shift and crack, the roots of the roses reaching out, wrapping themselves around the dead, pulling them back, trying to stop their advance.

But the darkness was relentless.

The figures fought against the roses, their skeletal hands clawing at the earth, their red eyes burning with a fierce hunger. One by one, they broke free, their movements quickening, their twisted forms dragging themselves toward Mae.

Her pulse raced, fear gnawing at the edges of her mind. There were too many. No matter how much energy she called upon, she couldn't hold them all back.

The dead were too strong. The darkness was winning.

Mae stumbled backward, her hands shaking as the figures closed in around her. She felt the weight of their presence pressing down on her, suffocating her, pulling her toward the edge of despair.

But then, in the distance, she saw a flicker of light.

Emmeline.

Her mentor stepped through the mist, her form glowing with the soft, ethereal light of the roses. She moved gracefully, as though the darkness couldn't touch her, and as she approached, the dead recoiled, their red eyes dimming.

"Mae," Emmeline called out, her voice steady and calm. "You're not alone. You've never been alone."

Mae's breath caught in her throat as she watched Emmeline raise her hands, her fingers glowing with the same light that pulsed through the roses. The dead hissed, retreating slightly, as if they recognized the power Emmeline wielded.

"You're the guardian of this place," Emmeline continued, her voice strong. "But you don't fight the darkness alone. The cemetery is alive, Mae. The roses, the spirits, the land—they're all part of you. And together, we can hold the darkness back."

Mae nodded, her fear melting away as she felt the energy of the cemetery surge within her. She was the guardian, but she wasn't just one person standing against the darkness. She was part of something much bigger—something ancient and powerful.

Taking a deep breath, Mae focused again, feeling the strength of the roses, the spirits, and the land flow through her. She raised her hands, just as Emmeline had, and together they channeled the full force of the cemetery's power.

The roses flared with brilliant light, their energy spreading like a wave, crashing over the dead. The skeletal figures let out a collective scream as the light engulfed them, their forms dissolving into shadow, one by one, until nothing remained but the faint echo of their cries.

The mist lifted, and the cemetery grew still once more.

Mae stood in the quiet, her chest rising and falling with labored breaths. She had done it. They had done it.

Emmeline smiled softly, stepping toward her. "The darkness will keep trying, Mae. It won't stop. But neither will you."

Mae looked up at her, the weight of her responsibility settling on her shoulders, but this time it didn't feel so heavy. She wasn't afraid anymore.

"I know," she said quietly. "But as long as the cemetery is with me, I can face it."

Emmeline nodded, her eyes filled with pride. "And I'll be here to guide you. But remember, Mae—the cemetery chose you for a reason. You're stronger than you think."

Mae looked out at the roses, their soft glow filling the night with a sense of peace. The darkness was still out there, waiting, watching. But for now, the balance held.

And Mae would be ready when it tried to rise again.

Chapter 25

In the days following their victory over the dead, Mae found herself in a strange state of quiet unease. The cemetery had returned to its usual peacefulness, the graves undisturbed, the roses blooming with an otherworldly beauty. Yet, despite the stillness, Mae could feel the darkness lurking beneath the surface, ever present, ever waiting. She had faced the rising dead and pushed them back with Emmeline's help, but deep down, Mae knew that it wasn't over.

The cemetery had become her entire world, and the responsibility weighed heavier on her now than ever before.

One evening, as the sun dipped low and the shadows stretched long across the graves, Mae stood by the ancient tree, her fingers lightly brushing the petals of a black rose. The connection between her and the land had grown stronger after the battle. She could feel the pulse of life beneath the soil, the spirits drifting through the air like whispers on the wind. It was a comfort, but also a reminder that she was never truly alone.

But something was different that night.

The wind stirred in a way that made her skin prickle. It was subtle at first, like a shift in the air, but then she felt it: a tremor in the ground, a soft thrum of energy that rippled through the earth beneath her feet. It was faint, but unmistakable. Something was stirring again, something deep and powerful.

Mae knelt beside the tree, pressing her hands into the cool earth, trying to feel for the source of the disturbance. The energy was erratic, pulsing in short bursts, as if the land itself was trying to communicate with her.

"Mae..." The voice of the spirits drifted to her, barely a whisper, but filled with urgency. "Below... something... ancient."

Mae's breath caught. Something ancient. Could it be older than the cemetery itself? She had always known that the cemetery was built on hallowed ground, that its power ran deeper than she could understand. But this... this felt different. Darker.

Her thoughts were interrupted by the sound of footsteps approaching from behind. She turned to see Emmeline emerging from the mist, her expression grave.

"You feel it too," Mae said, her voice steady despite the unease gnawing at her.

Emmeline nodded, her eyes narrowing as she glanced at the ground. "The land is restless. Something is waking up beneath the cemetery."

Mae stood, brushing the dirt from her hands. "What could it be? We sealed the crack, stopped the dead from rising. What else is down there?"

Emmeline's gaze shifted to the tree, her expression unreadable. "The dead that rose before—they were just a warning, Mae. A prelude. The true darkness lies deeper, beneath the surface, bound for centuries."

Mae's heart skipped a beat. "Bound?"

Emmeline nodded, her voice quiet. "The cemetery is built on ancient ground, long before it became a place of rest for the dead. There were rituals here, long forgotten, used to bind something powerful. Something that should never be released."

Mae felt a chill crawl down her spine. "What is it? What's down there?"

Emmeline hesitated, her eyes darkening with something like fear. "I'm not sure. But I believe it's something older than even the spirits that guard this place. Something that has been waiting for the right moment to break free."

Mae clenched her fists, her mind racing. She had fought the dead, faced the darkness, but this—this felt different. More dangerous. If there was something ancient and powerful beneath the cemetery, waiting to be released, then everything she had done so far had been just the beginning.

"How do we stop it?" Mae asked, determination hardening her voice.

Emmeline shook her head slowly. "I don't know if we can stop it, not entirely. The binding that holds it has weakened, and the land is shifting. We may only have one choice."

Mae's stomach twisted. "What choice?"

"We may need to go beneath the cemetery," Emmeline said softly. "To the source of the disturbance. We need to find out what's causing the awakening before it's too late."

Mae's pulse quickened. Beneath the cemetery. The thought alone sent a wave of unease through her. She had never ventured that far down, had never even considered that there was something more than the graves and the spirits. But now it seemed that there was an entire world beneath the surface, hidden from her view, waiting for her.

"I'll go," Mae said, her voice steady.

Emmeline studied her, a hint of pride flickering in her eyes. "You're brave, Mae. But this won't be like anything you've faced before. Whatever is down there—it's not like the spirits, or the dead that rose from the graves. This is older, darker, and far more dangerous."

Mae swallowed hard, but she didn't waver. "I know. But I have to go. The cemetery depends on it."

Emmeline nodded slowly. "I'll guide you as far as I can, but beyond that... you'll be on your own."

Mae took a deep breath, the weight of her decision settling over her like a heavy cloak. She had chosen to become the guardian of this place, and now she had to face whatever lay beneath it. There was no turning back.

That night, under the pale light of the moon, Mae and Emmeline made their way to the heart of the cemetery. The roses swayed gently in the breeze, their petals glowing softly, as if they were watching over her. The spirits whispered in the air, their voices filled with a mixture of concern and warning.

Emmeline led her to a secluded part of the cemetery, far from the graves and the familiar paths. The ground here felt different, almost hollow, and the energy that pulsed beneath the earth was stronger, more chaotic. It thrummed beneath Mae's feet, like a living heartbeat.

"This is the entrance," Emmeline said quietly, her hand resting on a stone that jutted out from the earth. It was old, ancient even, covered in symbols that Mae couldn't read. "Beyond here lies the passage to whatever is stirring below."

Mae stared at the stone, feeling the weight of its presence. This was it. The threshold between the world she knew and the unknown that waited beneath.

She took a deep breath and stepped forward.

As she crossed the threshold, the air grew colder, and the world seemed to shift around her. The cemetery above faded into the distance, and the ground beneath her feet gave way to stone steps, descending deep into the earth.

The passage was dark, the walls close and suffocating, but Mae pressed on, her heart pounding in her chest. She could feel the pull of the darkness, the weight of something ancient and terrible drawing her deeper and deeper.

And then, at the bottom of the stairs, she saw it.

A door.

It was massive, carved from black stone, and covered in symbols that pulsed with a faint, eerie light. The energy that radiated from it was overwhelming, like a tidal wave of darkness pressing down on her.

Mae stepped closer, her hand trembling as she reached for the door.

Whatever lay beyond it, she knew it was the source of the disturbance. The source of the darkness.

And she was the only one who could face it.

With a deep breath, Mae placed her hand on the door and pushed.

The darkness welcomed her.

The door groaned under the pressure of Mae's hand, the ancient stone grinding against itself as it slowly gave way. As it creaked open, the temperature plummeted, a biting cold that felt like it pierced straight through her skin and into her bones. The air that rushed out from beyond the door was heavy with a stale, oppressive weight, as if it had been sealed for centuries, waiting for someone to unleash it.

Beyond the threshold was a vast chamber, its walls lined with jagged, black rock. The floor sloped downward into a deep, cavernous pit, at the center of which stood a towering monolith, carved with the same symbols that had adorned the door. They pulsed faintly with an unnatural light, casting long, distorted shadows across the chamber.

The pit itself seemed to be alive, an abyss of writhing darkness that shifted and coiled like a mass of serpents. It churned in a slow, ominous rhythm, its depths whispering secrets too ancient to understand. Mae could feel its pull—an almost magnetic draw toward the center, toward the monolith that loomed above it all.

She swallowed hard, her breath coming in shallow, controlled bursts. Every instinct told her to run, to turn back before the darkness could consume her. But she couldn't. Not now.

Emmeline had been right. This wasn't just the dead rising from their graves. This was something far more ancient, far more powerful, and Mae was the only one who could stop it from breaking free.

Steeling herself, Mae descended the steps into the pit, her hand gripping the side of the wall for balance. As she neared the bottom, the symbols on the monolith grew brighter, their light flickering as if reacting to her presence. The air grew heavier, and with each step, she felt the weight of the darkness pressing down on her chest, making it harder to breathe.

But she pressed on.

When she reached the center of the pit, she stood before the monolith, staring up at its immense height. The symbols were glowing now, a sickly, pulsating light that filled the chamber with an unnatural hum. Mae raised her hand, reaching toward the stone, her fingers trembling.

The moment her hand touched the cold surface, the chamber shuddered violently.

The darkness in the pit roared to life, swirling faster and faster, as if it had been waiting for this moment. The monolith pulsed with energy, the symbols burning brighter and brighter until the entire chamber was bathed in their eerie glow.

Mae staggered back, her heart racing. The darkness in the pit surged upward, a mass of twisting, shadowy tendrils that reached for the monolith, for her. It was like the cemetery above, only this time, the dead weren't rising. This was something older, something more primal.

Something that had been sealed away for a reason.

The ground beneath her feet trembled as the tendrils of darkness writhed and lashed out, their movements chaotic, frenzied. Mae's eyes darted around the chamber, searching for some way to stop the monolith, to stop whatever was trying to break free.

"You are too late."

The voice was deep and guttural, like the earth itself had spoken. It echoed through the chamber, resonating with a power that sent chills down Mae's spine.

She turned, her heart pounding, and saw a figure emerging from the shadows at the far side of the chamber. Tall and cloaked in darkness, its face hidden beneath a hood, the figure radiated an aura of ancient malevolence.

"You've come all this way, only to fail," the figure said, its voice a low, mocking growl. "The binding is broken. The darkness will rise, and there is nothing you can do to stop it."

Mae's throat tightened as she stared at the figure. "Who are you?" she demanded, her voice trembling but defiant.

The figure stepped closer, its form shifting and distorting as it moved, as if it were made of the shadows themselves. "I am the one who was cast aside, bound to this pit for eternity. But that time has ended. I am free once more, and the world above will fall into darkness."

Mae felt a surge of panic rise in her chest, but she fought to push it down. "I won't let that happen," she said, her voice stronger now. "The cemetery chose me to protect it, and I won't let you destroy everything."

The figure laughed, a hollow, sinister sound that echoed through the chamber. "You think you can stop me? You are nothing but a child playing with forces beyond your comprehension. The dead rose because of me. The cemetery's power comes from me. You have no idea what you are dealing with."

Mae's heart raced as the figure's words sank in. If what it said was true, then everything she had fought for—the spirits, the roses, the cemetery itself—was connected to this ancient power. But she couldn't believe that it was all tainted by darkness. There had to be something good left in the land, something worth saving.

"Maybe I don't understand everything," Mae said, her voice steady. "But I know this—there's more to the cemetery than just you. There's light here, too. The roses, the spirits—they're part of this place, just like the darkness. And I won't let you take that away."

The figure paused, as if considering her words. For a moment, the chamber grew still, the tendrils of darkness slowing their frantic movement.

And then, with a sudden, violent surge, the figure raised its arms, and the darkness in the pit exploded outward, filling the chamber with a deafening roar. The tendrils lashed out, striking at the walls, the monolith, and Mae herself. She ducked and dodged, her heart racing as she tried to avoid the onslaught of shadow.

"You cannot stop me!" the figure bellowed, its voice booming through the chamber. "The darkness is eternal!"

Mae gritted her teeth, her mind racing. She couldn't fight this thing head-on, not with the power it wielded. But she had something it didn't. The cemetery wasn't just a place of death and shadows. It was alive, connected to her, and to the light of the roses that bloomed in its soil.

Focusing her energy, Mae reached deep into the earth, calling on the power of the cemetery. She felt the pulse of the land, the life that thrummed beneath the surface, and the energy of the roses flowing through her veins.

The monolith pulsed in response, its symbols flaring with light. The tendrils of darkness hesitated, recoiling from the brightness.

Mae stood tall, her hands glowing with the energy of the cemetery. "You're wrong," she said, her voice unwavering. "The darkness isn't eternal. It's only a part of the whole. And I won't let it consume everything."

With a cry, Mae thrust her hands forward, sending a wave of energy through the chamber. The light of the roses erupted from her palms, bright and blinding, washing over the monolith, the tendrils of darkness, and the figure itself.

The figure screamed, its form disintegrating as the light tore through it. The tendrils shriveled and withered, the darkness receding back into the pit as the energy of the cemetery overwhelmed it.

The chamber shuddered one last time, and then, with a final burst of light, the darkness was gone.

Mae collapsed to the ground, her chest heaving with exhaustion. The monolith stood silent and still, its symbols dim and lifeless.

It was over.

For now.

Chapter 26

Mae lay on the cold ground for what felt like an
eternity, her body trembling with exhaustion. The light from the
roses had faded, and the chamber was once again bathed in
darkness, but it was different now—a peaceful darkness, not the
oppressive, malevolent force that had tried to consume her.

She took a deep breath, her lungs filling with the stale air
of the underground chamber. Slowly, she pushed herself to her
feet, her muscles aching with every movement. The weight of
what had just happened settled over her like a heavy shroud. She
had faced something ancient, something that had been sealed
away for centuries, and somehow, she had survived.

But even as the darkness retreated, Mae knew this wasn't
truly the end. Whatever power she had tapped into, whatever
force had connected her to the cemetery's energy, it was only part
of a larger whole. She could still feel the lingering presence of the
figure, its essence woven into the very foundation of the land.

The monolith stood before her, silent and unmoving, its
symbols now dark and lifeless. The pit at its base was still, the
writhing tendrils of shadow gone. But the chamber remained, a
testament to the ancient power that had been bound beneath the
cemetery. Mae could sense it all around her, in the stone, in the
air, even in the soil beneath her feet.

As she stared at the monolith, a thought began to form in
her mind—a realization that filled her with both dread and
determination. The figure had said that the cemetery's power

came from it. If that was true, then whatever force had once been bound here wasn't just an enemy. It was part of the balance that kept the cemetery alive, that kept the dead from rising again.

She couldn't destroy the darkness completely, not without risking everything else falling apart.

"I understand now," Mae whispered to the empty chamber. "You were part of this place, part of what makes it whole. But you tried to take too much."

Her voice echoed off the stone walls, but there was no answer. The figure was gone, for now, but Mae knew that the darkness would always remain beneath the surface, waiting.

She turned and began the slow ascent back to the surface, each step heavier than the last. Her mind swirled with questions. Who had bound that power? Why had it been left to fester beneath the cemetery? And what role was she truly meant to play in all of this?

When she finally reached the top of the stairs, the cool night air hit her like a breath of fresh life. She stepped out into the cemetery, the moon hanging low in the sky, casting its pale light over the graves. The roses in the garden swayed gently in the breeze, their petals glowing faintly in the moonlight.

Emmeline was waiting for her, standing near the tree where they had first sensed the disturbance. Her expression was unreadable, but there was a flicker of relief in her eyes when she saw Mae.

"You did it," Emmeline said softly, stepping forward. "I could feel the shift from up here. The darkness... it's receding."

Mae nodded, though her heart still felt heavy. "It's not gone. Not completely. But I stopped it—for now."

Emmeline studied her, her gaze piercing. "And you understand, don't you? The cemetery is more than just a resting place for the dead. It's a balance, a delicate one. The darkness is part of that balance, just as much as the light."

Mae let out a long breath. "I understand. But that doesn't make it any easier."

Emmeline placed a hand on Mae's shoulder, her touch warm and comforting. "No, it doesn't. But you're not alone in this. The spirits are with you. The land is with you. And so am I."

For the first time that night, Mae allowed herself a small smile. "Thank you."

They stood in silence for a moment, the wind rustling through the trees and the roses. The cemetery had returned to its usual stillness, but Mae could feel the subtle changes beneath the surface. The darkness had been pushed back, but it would always be there, waiting.

"Will it come back?" Mae asked after a while, her voice quiet.

Emmeline's gaze drifted toward the horizon. "It might. But now you know how to face it. And when it does, you'll be ready."

Mae nodded, her resolve strengthening. She had been chosen by the cemetery, not just to protect it from the dead, but to maintain the balance between the forces that governed it. It was a weighty responsibility, but it was hers to bear.

As the first light of dawn began to creep over the horizon, Mae turned to the roses, their petals still glowing softly in the dim light. They had always been her connection to the cemetery, to the spirits that lived within it, but now she understood their true significance. They weren't just flowers—they were a symbol of the delicate balance she was sworn to protect.

The sun rose slowly, casting a golden glow over the cemetery, and for the first time in what felt like a lifetime, Mae felt at peace.

She had faced the darkness and survived.

Now, she was the guardian of the cemetery.

And whatever came next, she would be ready.

As the sun crept higher in the sky, its warmth touching the gravestones and casting long shadows across the cemetery, Mae felt a profound sense of calm. The battle was over, but she knew the cemetery's mysteries were far from fully unraveled. There would be more to discover—about the land, about the spirits, and about herself.

After a quiet moment, Emmeline broke the silence. "You've done more than anyone could ask. But you should rest. The land is still recovering, and so are you."

Mae's exhaustion suddenly hit her, as though her body had just now realized the magnitude of what she had been through. Every muscle ached, and her thoughts felt muddled by fatigue, but she resisted the urge to collapse right then and there. There were too many questions still swirling in her mind, too many unknowns she had to understand.

"I will rest," Mae said softly, her voice tired but resolute. "But I can't leave the cemetery unguarded, not after everything that's happened."

Emmeline's gaze softened. "The spirits will watch over it for a time. The land will heal itself as long as the balance is maintained. You've already done more than enough."

Mae nodded, knowing Emmeline was right. The cemetery was a living thing in its own way, connected to forces that went far beyond her. She couldn't be its only protector forever. But it was still difficult to shake the feeling of responsibility that had settled into her bones. The land had chosen her, and she was bound to it now, inextricably linked to its fate.

Together, they walked through the rows of graves, the roses swaying gently in the breeze, their colors vibrant in the daylight. Mae reached out to touch one of the blossoms, its petals soft and warm under her fingers. The roses had saved her more than once, and now, she felt their quiet, calming energy radiating into her.

As they approached her small house on the edge of the cemetery, Mae paused at the gate, turning to Emmeline. "I know this isn't over," she said, her voice firm despite her weariness. "There's something else out there—something deeper. The darkness is part of the balance, but I feel like there's more to it than we understand."

Emmeline nodded, her expression thoughtful. "There is more. Much more. The history of this land goes back farther than anyone knows, and its secrets are buried deep. But you don't have to face it all at once, Mae. For now, you've earned some peace."

Mae gave a small, grateful smile. She knew Emmeline was right. Whatever other dangers lay ahead, they would reveal themselves in time. For now, she needed to gather her strength and find solace in the quiet.

She pushed open the gate and stepped inside her yard, the small patch of earth where she had first planted her own roses now blooming in full. Their deep crimson petals glistened in the sunlight, a reminder of the life she had brought into this place of death.

"You're right," Mae said finally, her voice soft. "I'll rest. But when the time comes, I'll be ready for whatever this place still has in store."

Emmeline gave her a knowing look. "And when that time comes, you won't be alone."

Mae watched as Emmeline faded back into the mist that still clung to the cemetery's far edges, her form growing more and more translucent until she was gone entirely. The spirits would guard the cemetery for now, watching over the land while Mae took the time she needed to recover.

Inside her house, Mae felt the weight of the last few days truly descend upon her. She sank onto her small, worn bed, her body aching and her mind buzzing with lingering questions. She knew she was now forever tied to the cemetery, to the delicate balance of light and dark that governed it. But for now, at least, the immediate danger had passed.

As she closed her eyes, the scent of roses filled the air, comforting and familiar. Her last thought before sleep claimed her was a quiet, unspoken promise—to the land, to the spirits, and to herself.

She would guard this place, no matter what came next.

The cemetery would be safe under her watch.

Chapter 27

Mae slept deeply, her dreams filled with visions of the cemetery—its graves stretching out into infinity, the roses blooming like bursts of red stars in the dark. In her dreams, she walked the rows of headstones, accompanied by ghostly figures whose faces were half-hidden in shadow. They whispered to her, fragments of forgotten languages and ancient warnings that slipped through her fingers like smoke.

But at the heart of her dreams was the monolith. Its towering form loomed in the distance, its once-glowing symbols now dark and lifeless. She could feel it calling to her, an unspoken pull deep in her chest, but as she moved toward it, the ground beneath her feet crumbled, and the shadows thickened, wrapping around her like vines.

When she woke, it was late afternoon. Sunlight filtered through the thin curtains of her small window, casting soft, golden light across the room. For a moment, she lay still, her body stiff and sore from the night before, her mind trying to hold onto the fleeting images from her dreams. There was something about the monolith—something she hadn't understood before.

Mae sat up slowly, wincing at the ache in her muscles. Her mind felt clearer now, but the lingering sense of unease from her dreams remained. She had stopped the figure in the underground chamber, but she hadn't destroyed it completely. The monolith still stood, and whatever ancient power it was tied to wasn't finished with her yet.

She dressed quickly, pulling on her usual black clothes and lacing up her boots, then stepped outside into the cemetery. The air was cool and fresh, and the sky was a soft shade of gray, as if the world were holding its breath. The roses in her garden swayed gently in the breeze, their colors rich and vibrant, but there was a quiet tension in the air that Mae couldn't shake.

She made her way through the cemetery, her feet following a familiar path as she moved past the old gravestones and crumbling mausoleums. The spirits were quiet today, though she could feel their presence lingering in the shadows, watching her with silent eyes.

As she walked, her thoughts returned to the monolith. There had to be more to it than just a symbol of darkness. It was connected to the land, just as she was, and she could feel its pull even now. But what did it want? What had been bound within it, and why had it been left there, buried beneath the cemetery for so long?

Mae stopped in front of a particularly old headstone, one that she had always felt drawn to but had never fully understood. It was covered in ivy, its inscription worn and faded by time, but there was something about it that called to her. She knelt down and brushed away the ivy, her fingers tracing the weathered stone.

"To the Guardian of the Rose and Shadow," the inscription read, barely legible beneath the moss and dirt.

Mae's heart skipped a beat. The words echoed in her mind, a title she had never heard before, yet somehow, they felt like they had always been meant for her. The Guardian of the Rose and Shadow—was that her? Was that what she had become?

She stood slowly, her mind racing. The monolith wasn't just a prison for darkness. It was part of a greater balance, something older and deeper than she had imagined. The cemetery's power wasn't simply about light or dark, life or death. It was both, intertwined, and she was its guardian now, tasked with keeping that balance in check.

But if she was the Guardian of both the roses and the shadows, then her role was far more complicated than she had thought. She wasn't just protecting the land from the darkness; she was meant to protect both sides, to ensure that neither overpowered the other.

The realization hit her with the force of a cold wind. She couldn't simply banish the darkness. It was necessary, just as the roses were. The cemetery's balance depended on both.

Mae's fingers tightened into fists at her sides. The weight of her new understanding pressed down on her, heavy and unrelenting. She had fought so hard to push back the shadows, to keep the darkness at bay, but now she realized that was only half of her task. She had to learn to live with the darkness, to accept it as part of the whole.

Her eyes drifted back to the old headstone. If there had been another Guardian before her, someone who had understood this balance, then maybe she could find answers in the past. There were secrets buried here—secrets that the spirits and the land themselves held. And Mae would have to uncover them if she was going to truly protect the cemetery.

Steeling herself, Mae turned and began walking toward the heart of the cemetery, where the oldest graves lay, and where the spirits of those long-dead still whispered. She needed guidance. She needed to know what had come before.

The path wound through tall, crooked trees, their branches swaying overhead like skeletal fingers. The shadows lengthened as she walked, and the familiar feeling of being watched crept over her again. The spirits here were older, their presence more intense. They had seen countless generations pass through these gates, and Mae could feel their weighty silence.

She approached the mausoleum at the center of the cemetery, the place where the oldest records of the land were kept. The stone structure loomed before her, its door half-hidden by overgrown vines and moss, but Mae pushed forward. She had been inside only once, when Emmeline had first guided her here. Now, she would have to enter alone.

Taking a deep breath, Mae pushed the heavy door open and stepped into the cold, musty air of the mausoleum. Dust floated through the dim light, and the walls were lined with stone shelves, each one holding ancient tomes and scrolls. This was where the history of the cemetery was kept—where the past Guardians, if there had been any, had left their records.

Mae ran her fingers along the spines of the old books, searching for something—anything—that might give her the answers she needed. Finally, she came upon a leather-bound journal, its cover cracked with age, and pulled it from the shelf. The pages were yellowed and fragile, but the writing was still legible.

The journal belonged to someone named **Isolde**, and as Mae flipped through its pages, she felt a jolt of recognition. Isolde had been a Guardian too, centuries ago. She had faced the same darkness that Mae had encountered, and like Mae, she had struggled to understand the balance between the light and the shadow.

But Isolde's story didn't have a happy ending.

The final pages of the journal were filled with desperate, hastily scribbled notes—warnings about the power of the monolith, about the danger of letting the darkness gain too much control. Isolde had fought to maintain the balance, but in the end, she had been consumed by the very force she had sought to contain.

Mae's hands trembled as she read the final entry: **"The Guardian cannot destroy the darkness, only hold it at bay. But if the balance is broken, all will be lost."**

The words echoed in Mae's mind, a chilling reminder of what was at stake.

She closed the journal and stood in the silence of the mausoleum, her heart heavy with the weight of the past. Isolde had tried and failed. Mae wouldn't make the same mistake.

She was the Guardian of the Rose and Shadow now.

And she would find a way to keep the balance intact—no matter what it took.

Chapter 28

Mae stood in the cold, musty silence of the mausoleum, the weight of the ancient journal heavy in her hands. Isolde's desperate words had left an imprint on her mind, a stark reminder of how precarious the balance between the light and darkness truly was. The Guardian before her had failed, consumed by the very forces she sought to control. Mae couldn't let that happen—not to her, and not to the cemetery.

But the shadows that clung to the cemetery felt different now, as if they were watching her with new interest. They knew she understood the truth of her role—she was not here to destroy them but to maintain the fragile balance that gave the cemetery its life.

Her eyes drifted to the door of the mausoleum. The daylight outside had dimmed, the sun dipping lower in the sky, casting long shadows across the land. Mae could feel the pull of the monolith in the distance, like a heartbeat thrumming beneath the earth. The journal had warned her, but it hadn't given her a solution.

If Isolde had failed, what chance did Mae have?

The thought gnawed at her, but she couldn't let it take root. She had faced the darkness once before and survived. Now, armed with the knowledge of her predecessors, she had to find another way to keep the balance without losing herself in the process.

Determined, Mae tucked the journal into her bag and stepped out of the mausoleum. The air was cooler now, and the sky had turned a deep shade of purple, the stars beginning to blink to life. The cemetery was quiet, but there was an energy in the air, a subtle hum that prickled the hairs on the back of her neck.

She didn't return to her cottage. Instead, her feet carried her toward the monolith, deep within the cemetery, where the veil between life and death felt thinnest. The pull grew stronger with each step, the heartbeat of the land vibrating in her bones.

When she finally reached the monolith, she stood before it in silence, its towering form casting a long, ominous shadow over her. The symbols etched into its surface were still dark, but she could feel the power radiating from it, pulsing in time with her own heartbeat. The air around it felt charged, thick with the energy of centuries past.

Mae knelt before the stone, her fingers brushing the cold surface. She didn't know exactly what she was looking for, but something told her the answers were here, buried within the monolith itself. If the monolith was the key to the cemetery's balance, then she needed to understand it—its origins, its purpose, and the darkness it contained.

Closing her eyes, she focused on the energy emanating from the stone, letting it wash over her. The ground beneath her feet seemed to hum with life, and as she concentrated, she felt something shift—a subtle but unmistakable movement, like a door opening in her mind.

Suddenly, Mae was no longer in the cemetery.

She found herself standing in a vast, empty space, a void of blackness stretching out in all directions. The air here was thick and heavy, and the only sound was the slow, steady thrum of the monolith's energy, pulsing in time with her heartbeat. In the distance, she saw a figure—vaguely human in shape but wreathed in shadows, its form shifting and flickering like a flame caught in a windstorm.

It was the same presence she had felt before, deep in the underground chamber—the same entity that had tried to consume her.

Mae's pulse quickened, but she didn't flinch. This time, she wasn't here to fight.

The figure approached slowly, its form solidifying as it drew closer. It was taller than she remembered, its shadowy limbs twisting and curling as though made of smoke. But there was something almost human in the way it moved, something ancient and familiar.

"You return," the figure said, its voice a low, echoing rumble that seemed to reverberate through the void.

Mae stood her ground, her voice steady. "I came to understand. You are part of this place, just like the roses. I know that now."

The figure's head tilted slightly, as though regarding her with curiosity. **"You speak of balance, yet you are afraid of what you do not know."**

Mae clenched her fists. "I'm not afraid. But I won't let the darkness take over. If you destroy the balance, everything will fall apart."

The figure seemed to shift, its form becoming more solid, more defined. It was almost humanoid now, its features sharpening into something that resembled a face—though its eyes were still nothing but empty voids. **"The darkness does not seek destruction, Guardian. It is only part of the whole. You, too, are part of it."**

Mae frowned, her breath catching in her throat. Part of the darkness? The idea felt foreign, but the more she thought about it, the more it made sense. She had always felt a connection to the shadows, to the cemetery's quiet, eerie energy. It wasn't just the roses that called to her—it was the darkness as well.

"But why fight me?" Mae asked, her voice quieter now. "Why try to take over?"

The figure's eyes glowed faintly, like embers in the dark. **"Because you do not yet understand. The balance is delicate, yes. But the Guardian must embrace both the light and the shadow. Only then can the land survive."**

Mae's heart pounded in her chest as the realization struck her. She had been fighting the darkness, pushing it away, but that wasn't the answer. She wasn't supposed to defeat it—she was supposed to become part of it. To wield both the light of the roses and the shadow of the monolith.

She took a deep breath, steadying herself. "I understand now. I've been trying to hold the balance from outside, but I'm part of it too. I can't keep the cemetery safe unless I accept both sides."

The figure seemed to nod, though its form remained as insubstantial as ever. **"You are beginning to see. But your journey is not yet complete."**

Mae took a step forward, her eyes locked on the shadowy figure. "Then show me what I need to do. I'm ready."

The figure extended a hand, its fingers long and clawed, but Mae didn't hesitate. She reached out, her hand closing around the shadow's. It was cold—like ice—but there was a strange comfort in the touch, a sense of understanding passing between them.

"You will face many trials, Guardian," the figure said, its voice softer now. **"But remember this: the light and the shadow are one. Only together can they sustain the land."**

Mae nodded, her grip tightening on the figure's hand. "I won't forget."

In an instant, the void dissolved around her, and Mae found herself back in the cemetery, kneeling before the monolith. The air was still, the sky darkening with the approaching night, but Mae felt different. Stronger. More complete.

She rose to her feet, her gaze lingering on the towering stone. The balance was more fragile than ever, but now she understood what had to be done. She was not just the Guardian of the roses. She was the Guardian of the shadow as well.

And whatever trials awaited her, she would face them—armed with the power of both light and dark.

The cemetery was her home. And she would protect it with everything she had.

The night crept over the cemetery, enveloping it in a cool, velvety darkness. The once-familiar landscape now seemed to breathe with a new intensity—each shadow was deeper, each whisper of wind more purposeful. Mae stood before the monolith, feeling a new energy coursing through her, a power she hadn't fully understood before.

For so long, she had feared the darkness. Now, she realized it wasn't something to be feared, but something to be embraced.

The roses in the cemetery still bloomed, their crimson petals vivid even in the twilight, but there was a shift in their energy as well. They no longer stood as symbols of protection alone; now they felt like sentinels, guardians of both the living and the dead. Mae could feel their strength, their quiet resilience, intertwined with the shadow that lived beneath the cemetery. The roses and the shadows were bound together, just as she was bound to both.

With a deep breath, Mae began walking through the rows of graves, her senses heightened. The spirits that had once felt distant now seemed closer, their presence more tangible. She could feel their eyes on her, not with malice, but with a sense of watchfulness, as if they too were waiting to see what she would do next. They were part of this balance as well, after all—tied to the land, tied to her.

As she walked, Mae's thoughts turned to Isolde. The former Guardian had fought the darkness and lost, consumed by the very thing she had sought to control. Mae wondered what had gone wrong. Had Isolde been too afraid of the shadows? Had she failed to see that the darkness wasn't an enemy, but a necessary part of the land's existence?

The journal in her bag felt heavier with every step. Mae knew she had to learn from Isolde's mistakes, to walk a different path. But there was still so much she didn't understand, and the burden of the cemetery's future weighed heavily on her.

As she approached the oldest section of the graveyard, where the headstones were worn and crumbling, a familiar chill ran down her spine. The shadows here were thicker, darker, as if they clung more fiercely to the ground. It was here that the cemetery's deepest secrets were buried—the ancient forces that had shaped this land long before Mae had ever set foot within it.

She stopped in front of an old, nearly illegible gravestone. The earth around it was cold and damp, and the wind seemed to still as she knelt before it. She had come here once before, long ago, guided by a sense of curiosity. But now, with the knowledge she carried, she realized that this grave might hold more answers than she had initially thought.

As she brushed away the moss and dirt that clung to the stone, faint symbols came into view—similar to the ones etched into the monolith, but older, more worn. They pulsed faintly with an energy that felt both familiar and foreign, as if they were remnants of a power long forgotten. Mae's fingers traced the carvings, a strange warmth spreading through her as she did.

Suddenly, the air around her grew colder, and the ground beneath her trembled. Mae stood, her heart racing, as the shadows began to stir. From the darkness, a figure emerged, its form hazy and indistinct, but unmistakably human. The spirit glided toward her, its presence calm but commanding.

Mae's breath caught in her throat. It was a woman, dressed in a long, tattered robe, her hair wild and unbound. Her eyes, though shadowed, held a strange light, and her face was both beautiful and haunted. Mae recognized her instantly.

"Isolde," Mae whispered, her voice barely audible.

The spirit of the former Guardian stood before her, silent and still, her eyes locked on Mae's. For a long moment, neither of them spoke. Mae could feel the weight of the past pressing down on her, the history of this place, and the responsibility that now rested on her shoulders.

Finally, Isolde spoke, her voice soft but clear. **"You have seen the truth. The balance cannot be broken."**

Mae nodded, her throat tight. "I know that now. But I don't know how to keep it. I don't know how to control both the light and the dark."

Isolde's gaze softened, and she took a step closer, her form flickering slightly as though it were made of smoke. **"Control is not the answer, Guardian. You cannot control what you are part of. You must become it."**

Mae frowned, confusion swirling in her mind. "Become it? What do you mean?"

The spirit extended a hand, the shadows around her swirling like mist. **"The darkness and the light are not separate, Mae. They are one. You are both the rose and the shadow, just as I was. But I failed to see that. I tried to fight the darkness, to push it away. In the end, it consumed me because I refused to let it in. Do not make the same mistake."**

Mae's heart pounded in her chest. She had thought she understood the balance, but now she realized there was still so much more to learn. The darkness wasn't something to be fought, but something to be accepted, to be woven into the very fabric of who she was.

She looked into Isolde's eyes, seeing the pain and regret that lingered there. The former Guardian had been alone in her struggle, unable to accept the full truth of her role. Mae wouldn't let that happen to her.

"I won't fight it," Mae said softly. "I'll embrace it. The roses and the shadows—they're part of me now."

Isolde nodded slowly, her form beginning to fade. **"Remember, Mae. The balance must be kept at all costs. The cemetery's fate rests in your hands now. Do not let the light or the dark overtake you."**

As Isolde's spirit dissolved into the night, Mae felt a strange sense of peace settle over her. She had been given the warning, but she had also been given the key. The balance wasn't about control—it was about acceptance. She had to let the darkness in, let it become part of her, just as the roses had. Only then could she truly protect the cemetery.

Mae stood in the quiet of the night, the wind rustling through the trees. She felt different now—stronger, more complete. She was no longer just the keeper of the roses. She was the Guardian of both the light and the dark, the protector of the cemetery's delicate balance.

And whatever came next, she would be ready.

The shadows around her stirred, and Mae felt them settle into place, as if they, too, had accepted her. The cemetery was alive with both light and dark, and for the first time, Mae felt truly at peace with the land she was sworn to protect.

With a quiet resolve, Mae turned and began walking back toward her cottage, the roses swaying gently in her wake. She had embraced her role as Guardian, and now, she would face whatever trials the cemetery had in store for her.

The balance was hers to keep. And she would keep it, no matter the cost.

198

Chapter 29

The night was alive with the interplay of shadow and starlight as Mae returned to her cottage, the ancient knowledge settling deeper within her. The cemetery had changed—though perhaps it wasn't the land itself, but rather Mae's understanding of it. The quiet hum of power, once a distant undercurrent, now vibrated closer to her very being. She had crossed a threshold, accepting her place as both the keeper of the roses and the companion of the darkness.

When Mae entered the cottage, the familiar scent of dried herbs and old books greeted her, grounding her in the present. The small space felt more like a sanctuary now than it ever had before. The flickering candlelight cast long, wavering shadows on the walls, but instead of feeling menacing, they felt like extensions of her—part of the tapestry that bound her to the cemetery.

She set the journal Isolde had left her on the table and poured over the remaining pages, reading with a new perspective. The words once drenched in fear and confusion now made more sense. Isolde had struggled because she believed the darkness was an adversary. But Mae had seen it for what it truly was: a partner in the balance. A necessary force.

As Mae read, a soft scratching at the window pulled her attention. She glanced up, and her breath caught. A figure stood outside the cottage—tall, wrapped in shadow, but unmistakably human in form. Unlike the hostile entity she had once encountered beneath the monolith, this presence felt familiar. Steady.

Mae rose slowly, her heart thudding in her chest as she moved to the door. She opened it with a creak, stepping out into the cool night air.

The figure waited just beyond the threshold, standing in the path that led through the garden of roses. As Mae's eyes adjusted to the darkness, she realized that it was the shadowy figure from her earlier vision—the one who had spoken to her in the void. But now, it was more solid, more present, and its features, though still blurred, seemed almost human.

"You have embraced your role, Guardian," the figure said, its voice smooth and calm. **"The cemetery recognizes you now."**

Mae stepped forward, her pulse steady. "I understand what needs to be done," she said, her voice resolute. "But I still don't know what comes next."

The figure's form shifted slightly, as though it was made of smoke and air, but its presence remained grounded. **"The balance has always been fragile, even before you. There are forces outside this cemetery, Mae—forces that hunger for what you protect. They will test you, just as they tested the Guardians before you."**

Mae's eyes narrowed. "Forces? What do you mean?"

The figure's eyes, hollow and deep, gleamed faintly in the moonlight. **"The darkness is not the only danger. There are those who seek power from the veil that separates life from death. They will come for the cemetery, for the monolith, and for you. You must be ready."**

Mae swallowed hard. She had known, on some level, that there were threats beyond the shadows she now understood. But hearing it spoken aloud sent a chill down her spine. "How do I protect it? How do I stop them?"

The figure's gaze seemed to soften, as though recognizing her fear. **"You have already taken the first step by accepting both the light and the dark. But there is more to learn, Guardian. There are others like you—Guardians of other sacred places. You must find them. Together, you can guard the veil, protect the balance."**

Mae felt the weight of the task settle on her shoulders. She wasn't just responsible for this cemetery. There were others, other places where the veil was thin, where the light and dark danced in delicate harmony. And she would have to find these places, find these other Guardians. But where would she start?

The figure began to fade, its form dissolving into the night air. **"Seek the crossroads, Mae. The answers lie there."**

And with that, the figure disappeared, leaving Mae alone beneath the stars, the roses whispering softly in the breeze.

She stood there for a long moment, letting the weight of what had been revealed sink in. The crossroads. Other Guardians. Forces that sought to disrupt the balance, to consume the power of the veil.

Her life had changed irrevocably. The quiet cemetery she had once known was only a part of something much larger, and her role in it was far more dangerous than she had imagined.

But Mae didn't feel fear—not like she once had. The darkness was no longer an unknown. She had felt its pull, understood its place, and now, it was part of her. The light and shadow within her worked in tandem, and that gave her strength.

With a deep breath, she turned back toward her cottage, knowing that the next steps of her journey would be far from easy. But she was ready.

She would seek the crossroads, find the other Guardians, and together, they would guard the veil that kept the living and the dead in their rightful places. The cemetery would remain a sanctuary, a place of balance.

And Mae, the Guardian of roses and shadows, would ensure it stayed that way.

The wind rustled through the trees, carrying with it the faintest of whispers—echoes of the forces that lay beyond, waiting. But Mae was no longer afraid.

She would face whatever came next, and she would not stand alone.

The morning sun broke over the horizon, casting long, amber rays across the cemetery. The roses, shimmering with dew, seemed to hum with quiet life, their petals catching the light. Mae stood by the window of her cottage, watching the sun push the shadows back, knowing that even in the daylight, the balance remained. She had a mission now—a greater one than she had anticipated.

The idea of the crossroads lingered in her mind, its meaning unclear, yet weighted with purpose. Isolde's warning echoed in her thoughts: *"Seek the crossroads. The answers lie there."*

Mae packed lightly, knowing that her journey would take her beyond the familiar confines of the cemetery. She gathered a small satchel with her essentials—Isolde's journal, a few herbs from her garden for protection, and a silver pendant she had inherited from her mother, its crescent shape gleaming softly. She felt a pang of nostalgia as she touched the smooth metal. Her mother had always told her stories of hidden worlds, veils between realms. Maybe she had known more than she ever let on.

With the last of her belongings secured, Mae stood before the roses one final time, their deep red blossoms vibrant against the cool morning air. She knelt by the largest rosebush, where the oldest of the flowers bloomed, and whispered a quiet promise: **"I'll return. I'll protect this place. But I have to find the others."**

The roses swayed gently, as though in acknowledgment, their leaves shimmering like dark silk in the soft breeze. Mae rose to her feet, casting one last look at the cemetery before heading toward the outer gates. Her steps were firm but heavy with the weight of uncertainty. She was leaving the only home she had ever known, stepping into a world that might be far more treacherous than she could imagine.

The town just beyond the cemetery had always felt distant, even when she visited its narrow, cobblestone streets for supplies. People there whispered about her, casting glances filled with suspicion or curiosity, as though they sensed she was something more than just a strange girl who tended to the dead. Today, those stares would be more intense, she knew. But Mae had no intention of lingering there.

She needed to find the crossroads, the point where the realms of the living and the dead intertwined. Mae knew that such places existed, ancient locations where the veil between worlds was thin, where forces—both light and dark—converged. They had been hidden from most, but Guardians like her could sense them, feel the pull toward them.

Leaving the town behind, Mae ventured into the dense forest that bordered the cemetery. The canopy above blocked most of the sunlight, leaving the path beneath her feet dappled in shadow. She could feel the forest's pulse, an energy similar to that of the cemetery, though wilder and less restrained. Every step forward seemed to take her deeper into a place untouched by time, where the boundary between reality and the unknown blurred.

Hours passed, and the deeper Mae went, the more the world seemed to change around her. The trees grew taller, their trunks twisted and knotted with age, and the air grew thick with the scent of earth and moss. There was a stillness here, a quiet that seemed both peaceful and unsettling. The crossroads couldn't be far now—she could feel the pull, an almost magnetic force guiding her forward.

Then, as the sun began to sink lower in the sky, Mae saw it.

A clearing opened before her, at its center a small stone altar, ancient and covered in ivy. Around it, the ground was bare, save for a circle of weathered stones, each etched with runes that glowed faintly in the dimming light. The air here felt charged, thick with energy, and Mae knew she had found it—the crossroads.

She stepped cautiously into the clearing, her breath catching in her throat. The moment she crossed the threshold of stones, the energy surged, a current that thrummed through her veins. The altar seemed to pulse with a quiet power, and Mae could feel the veil between worlds thin here, so delicate she could almost reach out and touch the other side.

Suddenly, the air shifted, and a low voice called out from the shadows. **"You've come."**

Mae's heart raced as a figure stepped forward from the trees, cloaked in black. The person was tall, their face obscured by a hood, but their presence radiated an unmistakable power. The energy that Mae had felt in the cemetery, in the monolith, now felt mirrored in this figure. They were like her—another Guardian.

"Who are you?" Mae asked, her voice steady despite the tension in the air.

The figure removed their hood, revealing a woman with pale skin and piercing green eyes. Her hair, long and black, cascaded over her shoulders like a dark river. She regarded Mae with a mix of curiosity and wariness.

"My name is Delphine," the woman said, her voice soft but commanding. **"And like you, I am a Guardian. I have watched this place for centuries, waiting for the others to arrive."**

Mae blinked, taken aback. **"The others? How many of us are there?"**

Delphine's gaze flickered with something unreadable. **"More than you realize. Fewer than we need. The balance is threatened, and those who seek to destroy it are growing bolder. The forces that hunger for the power of the veil know we are scattered. They are coming."**

Mae felt a chill run down her spine. She had sensed something was coming, but hearing it spoken aloud made the threat all the more real. **"What do we do?"**

Delphine stepped closer, her eyes intense. **"We protect the veil. But first, we must find the others. You are not the only one who has been called. There are Guardians in other places—remote places where the veil is thinnest. We must unite before the darkness overtakes us."**

Mae nodded, her resolve hardening. **"I'll help you. I'll find the others."**

Delphine smiled, though it was tinged with sadness. **"Good. But be warned, Mae. The forces that seek the veil will stop at nothing to break it. They will come for your cemetery, for your roses, and for you."**

Mae's heart pounded, but she stood tall. **"Let them come. I'll be ready."**

Delphine nodded, her expression unreadable. **"Then our paths are aligned. We leave at dawn. The search begins now."**

As the sun set behind the trees, casting the clearing in shadow, Mae knew this was only the beginning. She had found the crossroads, but her journey was far from over. Together, she and the other Guardians would protect the veil, no matter the cost.

And if the forces of darkness came for her, for her cemetery, they would face the Guardian of roses and shadows—one who had embraced both the light and the dark.

She would keep the balance. She had no other choice.

Chapter 30

The night settled over the clearing, cold and still.

Mae and Delphine stood side by side, their silent understanding bound by a shared purpose. As darkness wrapped itself around them, Mae felt the gravity of what lay ahead. The crossroads had revealed Delphine, but the journey to find the other Guardians and protect the veil was just beginning.

They camped by the stone altar, a small fire casting flickering shadows on the ancient stones. Delphine sat across from Mae, her face illuminated by the soft glow of the flames, her green eyes reflecting the depth of her knowledge and experience.

"There are places in this world," Delphine began, her voice low and steady, **"where the veil is so thin that the living and the dead are almost indistinguishable. These are sacred places, places of power. The monolith in your cemetery is one such place. There are others."**

Mae leaned forward, listening intently. **"How do we find them? How do we know where the other Guardians are?"**

Delphine drew a small, intricate map from her cloak and spread it out on the ground between them. It was old, worn at the edges, and marked with symbols Mae didn't recognize. **"This map,"** Delphine explained, **"was passed down from Guardian to Guardian. It marks some of the crossroads, the places where the veil is weakest. But many of the symbols are faded, lost to time. We must follow the signs, feel the pull of the land.**

The Guardians are tied to these places, as you are to your cemetery. If we listen, we will find them."

Mae studied the map, her eyes tracing the symbols and lines, some of which led into distant, unfamiliar lands. She knew this journey would take her far from the cemetery she had sworn to protect. But it wasn't just about her cemetery anymore—this was a global fight, a battle to preserve the balance across many realms.

"How many Guardians are left?" Mae asked, her voice tinged with both hope and dread.

Delphine's eyes flickered, the firelight reflecting the weight of her answer. **"I do not know. Many have fallen over the centuries, either consumed by the darkness or lost in their isolation. The forces we face are cunning, patient. They have been eroding our numbers for centuries. But there are still some out there. We must find them before it's too late."**

The air grew thick with the seriousness of the task ahead. Mae realized the urgency of uniting the Guardians. They couldn't protect the veil alone. They needed strength in numbers, allies who understood the sacred duty they shared.

Mae's thoughts turned to the monolith, to the spirits she had encountered beneath the cemetery, to Isolde's mistakes and warnings. She understood now that her role wasn't just to tend to the dead—it was to ensure that the balance between life and death was never disturbed, that no one force overtook the other.

"What do these forces want?" Mae asked, her voice barely a whisper. **"Why are they after the veil?"**

Delphine stared into the fire for a long moment before answering. **"Power. Control. The veil separates life and death,**

and in that separation, there is balance. But if the veil is torn, if it is broken, the forces that dwell in darkness will consume both realms. The dead will walk among the living, and those who seek to exploit this power will reign over both. It's a chaos that cannot be undone."

Mae shivered, the weight of Delphine's words settling like a stone in her chest. She thought of her cemetery, the peaceful place where the dead rested, and the delicate thread that kept them from spilling into the world of the living. If that balance was shattered, everything she knew—everything she loved—would be consumed.

"How do we stop it?" Mae asked, her resolve strengthening.

Delphine looked at her, her expression fierce and determined. **"We find the other Guardians. We unite. And we fight. But first, we must find the places where the veil is weakest, where the forces of darkness are most likely to strike. Your cemetery is only one of many targets. We must stay ahead of them."**

The fire crackled between them, and the wind whispered through the trees. Mae could feel the land listening, the ancient power beneath her feet stirring in response to their conversation. It was as though the very earth understood the gravity of their mission.

As they prepared to rest for the night, Mae couldn't shake the feeling that something was watching them, lurking just beyond the edges of the clearing. She stood up, scanning the darkness. The shadows seemed to move, but when she blinked, they settled back into place.

"We aren't alone, are we?" Mae asked, her voice quiet but steady.

Delphine glanced at the surrounding forest, her eyes narrowing. **"No. We're never truly alone. The forces we face are always watching, always waiting. But they fear us, too. They know the power we wield as Guardians."**

Mae nodded, her hand instinctively reaching for the pendant around her neck. It had always been a symbol of protection, something her mother had given her for safekeeping. But now it felt like more—like a talisman connecting her to something larger, something ancient.

"Get some rest," Delphine said, her voice softer now. **"We leave at dawn. The road ahead is long, and we'll need all our strength."**

Mae lay down by the fire, her eyes closing as the flames crackled softly beside her. But sleep didn't come easily. Her mind raced with thoughts of the crossroads, the other Guardians, and the forces that threatened to unravel the world she knew.

As the night deepened, Mae finally drifted off, her dreams filled with visions of shadows creeping across the land, of roses blooming in graveyards, and of figures cloaked in darkness, watching, waiting.

And in the distance, she saw a great tear in the fabric of the world—a rip in the veil, where the living and the dead collided in chaos.

But standing at the edge of the rift were figures, Guardians like her, their hands outstretched, holding back the darkness.

She awoke with the dawn, the echoes of her dream still lingering in her mind.

It was time to find the others. Time to unite the Guardians.

The veil was weakening. The battle was coming.

And Mae would be ready.

The dawn broke over the horizon, painting the sky with streaks of gold and violet. Mae stood at the edge of the clearing, her gaze fixed on the dense forest that stretched beyond. She could feel the weight of her dreams from the night before—the creeping shadows, the rift in the veil, the distant Guardians standing together in defiance of the darkness.

Delphine was already awake, her cloak wrapped tightly around her as she studied the map by the fire's dying embers. The woman was a picture of calm focus, her green eyes sharp and thoughtful, scanning over the symbols that marked ancient places of power. When she sensed Mae's approach, she folded the map carefully and looked up.

"Did you sleep well?" Delphine asked, though her tone suggested she already knew the answer.

Mae shook her head, her thoughts still haunted by the images of chaos. **"No. But I saw something—something in my dream. A tear in the veil. And other Guardians… I could see them, trying to hold back the darkness."**

Delphine's gaze grew more intense, as if Mae's words had struck a chord. **"The veil is weakening faster than I thought. What you saw wasn't just a dream. It was a vision. The veil is calling to us, warning us. There's no more time to waste."**

Mae swallowed hard, her hand tightening around the pendant at her neck. She knew Delphine was right. Every second they delayed brought the forces of darkness closer to their goal. And the veil… she could feel it now, more fragile than ever, as if it were a thread being stretched too far.

"Where do we go first?" Mae asked, steeling herself for the journey ahead.

Delphine unfurled the map once more and pointed to a spot deep within the mountains to the north. **"There's a place, far from here, hidden in the highlands. An ancient tomb, older than any of the Guardians. It's said to be one of the original places where the veil was formed, one of the strongest points. If there's any hope of understanding how to stop this, it will be there. And with luck, we may find another Guardian."**

Mae studied the map, her finger tracing the path they would take through forests, over rivers, and up into the rugged mountains. It was a long journey—one that would take them far from the cemetery and deep into unknown territory. But she felt the pull, the same energy that had drawn her to the crossroads. The veil was calling her to the mountains, to the tomb that lay hidden in its peaks.

"How long will it take us?" Mae asked.

"At least a week, if we keep a steady pace," Delphine replied. **"But we can't afford to waste time. The forces we're up against… they already know what we're after. They'll be moving, too."**

Mae's heart quickened. The darkness had been watching them, always on the edges, waiting for a chance to strike. The closer they got to their destination, the more dangerous their path would become.

With no time to lose, they packed up the camp and set off into the forest. The morning air was crisp, the scent of pine and earth filling Mae's lungs as they made their way through the dense undergrowth. The forest was vast, its trees towering above them like ancient sentinels. Every rustle of leaves, every snap of a twig, felt heavy with meaning, as though the land itself was alive and watching.

For hours, they walked in silence, their focus on the path ahead. The further they went, the more Mae felt the veil's presence, a subtle but constant hum at the edge of her awareness. She could sense the places where the veil was strong, where the balance between life and death held steady. But in other places, she could feel the strain, as though the fabric of reality was being stretched too thin.

It wasn't until midday, when the sun was high overhead, that Delphine finally spoke. **"We're being followed."**

Mae froze, her heart pounding in her chest. **"Are you sure?"**

Delphine nodded, her hand already resting on the hilt of a dagger hidden beneath her cloak. **"I've sensed them for a while now. They're keeping their distance, but they're there. Watching. Waiting."**

Mae scanned the trees around them, her eyes searching for any sign of movement. But the forest was still, almost unnervingly so. **"What do we do?"** she whispered.

Delphine's expression was grim. **"We keep moving. But be ready. They'll make their move soon."**

They pressed on, their pace quickening as they left the thick forest behind and began to ascend into the foothills of the mountains. The landscape grew more rugged, the air colder, and the shadows deeper. Mae's senses were heightened now, every sound amplified, every movement in the periphery of her vision a potential threat.

By the time the sun began to set, casting a deep orange glow over the peaks ahead, Mae could feel it—a presence closing in on them. It was subtle at first, like a cold draft at the back of her neck, but it grew stronger with each passing moment.

Delphine's voice was low and urgent. **"They're here."**

Mae turned just in time to see the first of them emerge from the trees—a figure cloaked in darkness, its form shifting like smoke. It wasn't human, not entirely. Its eyes glowed with an unnatural light, and its movements were fluid, too fast, too smooth.

More figures appeared from the shadows, surrounding them. Their forms were twisted, part human, part something else —creatures born of the darkness that sought to tear the veil.

Delphine drew her dagger, the blade gleaming in the fading light. **"Stay close to me, Mae. These are shadowspawn, creatures from the void. They feed on fear, on chaos. But they can be destroyed."**

Mae's heart raced, but she didn't hesitate. She grabbed a branch from the ground, gripping it tightly like a makeshift weapon. **"How?"** she asked, her voice steady despite the fear gnawing at her.

Delphine smiled, a fierce, determined smile. **"You strike at their heart—their core of darkness. They'll try to**

overwhelm you with fear, but you have something stronger. You're a Guardian. You have the light."

The shadowspawn moved closer, their shapes writhing, their glowing eyes fixed on Mae and Delphine. The air grew colder, thick with an unnatural chill, and Mae could feel their darkness pressing against her, trying to seep into her mind, to drown her in fear.

But she stood tall, her grip tightening on the branch. The light, Delphine had said. The balance.

As the first shadowspawn lunged at her, Mae swung the branch, striking it hard across its chest. The creature hissed, recoiling as if burned, its form flickering like a dying flame. Mae felt a surge of energy, a warmth spreading through her veins—the same energy she had felt in the cemetery, in the presence of the roses and the monolith.

She wasn't afraid. Not anymore.

With a cry of defiance, Mae struck again, and this time, the shadowspawn dissolved into ash, its form disintegrating in the air.

Delphine fought beside her, her dagger slicing through the darkness with practiced ease. Together, they faced the creatures, their light pushing back against the encroaching shadow.

When the last of the shadowspawn fell, the night was eerily quiet. Mae stood, her chest heaving, the branch still clutched in her hand. She looked at Delphine, who was wiping the ash from her blade.

"That was only the beginning," Delphine said, her voice calm but firm. **"The real fight is still ahead of us."**

Mae nodded, her heart still pounding, but she was no longer afraid. She had faced the darkness, and she had survived.

The path ahead was long, and the forces they were up against were relentless. But Mae was ready.

She was a Guardian.

And she would protect the veil, no matter the cost.

216

Chapter 31

As the night deepened, a cold wind swept down from the mountains, chilling Mae and Delphine to the bone. The shadowspawn had been destroyed, but the air still felt heavy, as if the darkness they had fought clung to the very land. The quiet was unsettling.

Mae glanced at Delphine, who stood alert, her eyes scanning the forest as if expecting another attack. The map had shown a long, dangerous path ahead, and the encounter with the shadowspawn had only confirmed that the forces of darkness were growing bolder. They wouldn't stop—they'd keep coming, and Mae knew this was only the beginning.

"Do you think more will come tonight?" Mae asked, her voice hushed.

Delphine sheathed her dagger, her face grim. **"They won't stop coming, not until the veil is secure. But we've sent a message tonight—they know we're not easy prey."** She glanced toward the mountains, their peaks sharp and jagged against the night sky. **"We should find shelter for the night. The highlands are unforgiving, and we'll need our strength for the climb."**

Mae nodded, exhaustion finally creeping into her bones. They had to stay ahead of the darkness, but without rest, they wouldn't stand a chance. Together, they moved deeper into the foothills, the ground beneath them turning rocky and uneven. The forest gave way to a more barren, windswept landscape as they ascended into the mountains.

After an hour of walking, they found a small cave nestled in the side of a cliff, its entrance hidden behind a tangle of dead vines. It wasn't much, but it would provide shelter from the biting wind. Delphine lit a small fire, its flames casting flickering shadows on the cave walls. Mae sat close to the warmth, her muscles aching from the fight, her mind still racing with thoughts of the shadowspawn.

"What are they, exactly?" Mae asked, breaking the silence. **"The shadowspawn… I've never seen anything like them."**

Delphine's gaze was distant as she poked at the fire with a stick. **"They're creatures of the void, born from the spaces between worlds. The veil keeps them at bay, but as it weakens, they slip through the cracks, drawn to places of power like your cemetery. They thrive in chaos, in the fear and despair of the living. They serve the greater darkness, the force that seeks to tear the veil apart and consume both the living and the dead."**

Mae shuddered, the weight of Delphine's words settling over her like a heavy cloak. **"And who controls them? Who's behind all of this?"**

Delphine's eyes darkened, and for a moment, she looked far older than her years. **"There are many forces at play, but there's one in particular we need to worry about—a being older than time itself, a creature that feeds on the death of worlds. It goes by many names, but most call it *The Hollow One*. It's been trying to break the veil for centuries, using**

218

shadowspawn and other dark creatures to weaken its defenses."

Mae's blood ran cold. **"The Hollow One..."** She had never heard the name before, but it carried a weight that made her stomach churn. **"If it breaks through... what happens?"**

Delphine's voice was barely a whisper. **"The world will be consumed. The Hollow One feeds on the essence of life and death, drawing power from both realms. If it tears the veil, it will feast on everything—the souls of the living, the spirits of the dead, and the very fabric of reality itself. There will be nothing left but emptiness, an eternal void."**

A heavy silence fell between them, broken only by the crackling of the fire. Mae stared into the flames, her mind racing with the enormity of what they were up against. It wasn't just about protecting her cemetery anymore—it was about stopping a force that could end all life, everywhere.

"How do we stop something like that?" she asked, her voice trembling slightly. **"How do you fight something that ancient, that powerful?"**

Delphine's expression softened slightly, a flicker of sympathy in her eyes. **"It's not just about fighting it. It's about maintaining the balance. The veil exists for a reason—it keeps the realms of life and death separate, preventing any one force from overwhelming the other. As long as we can protect the places where the veil is strongest, we can keep The Hollow One at bay."**

She paused, then added, **"And there's still hope. The Guardians have always been the protectors of the veil, and though our numbers are few, we are not powerless. The**

ancient places of power—like the tomb in the mountains—
hold secrets, knowledge that might help us strengthen the veil
and stop The Hollow One before it's too late."

Mae nodded, though a pit of fear remained lodged in her
chest. The road ahead was long, and the forces they were up
against seemed impossibly strong. But she had come this far, and
she wasn't about to turn back now.

"We'll find the tomb," she said, more to herself than to
Delphine. **"And we'll find the other Guardians. We'll stop
this."**

Delphine smiled, though it didn't quite reach her eyes. **"I
believe in you, Mae. You're stronger than you know."**

They sat in silence for a while longer, the fire keeping the
chill at bay as the wind howled outside the cave. Eventually,
exhaustion overtook them, and they lay down to rest.

But even in sleep, Mae's dreams were haunted by
shadows. She saw the cemetery again, the roses blooming under a
darkened sky, their petals falling like blood onto the gravestones.
And beyond the cemetery, she saw a figure cloaked in black,
standing at the edge of the world, its face hidden in the darkness.

The Hollow One.

It turned, its empty gaze falling on her, and Mae felt the
cold void reach out, pulling her toward it. She tried to scream, but
no sound came.

She woke with a start, her heart pounding, the fire now
reduced to embers. Delphine stirred beside her, but Mae didn't
wake her. She sat up, clutching the pendant around her neck, the
weight of her dreams pressing heavily on her chest.

The Hollow One was out there, waiting. And it wouldn't stop until it had torn the veil apart.

But Mae was a Guardian. And she wasn't going to let that happen.

With a deep breath, she lay back down, determined to face whatever came next.

At dawn, they would continue their journey into the mountains. Toward the tomb. Toward the answers they needed.

And toward the fight of their lives.

The dawn arrived with an eerie stillness, the light pale and fragile as it filtered through the cave's entrance. Mae sat up, her muscles still sore from the battle the night before. She felt as though the weight of her dream had carried over into the waking world—the Hollow One's presence lingering in her mind like a shadow that refused to dissipate.

Delphine was already awake, crouching near the remnants of the fire. She met Mae's gaze with a look that spoke volumes: the time for rest was over.

"We need to keep moving," Delphine said, her voice low but urgent. **"The tomb is still days away, and the shadowspawn will likely track us again."**

Mae nodded, gathering her things, her resolve hardening. There was no time for fear or doubt. The veil was in danger, and they were its last line of defense.

As they packed up and began their trek through the foothills, the landscape around them grew more barren. The forest had vanished entirely, replaced by jagged rocks and steep cliffs. The wind howled, carrying with it a chill that bit into Mae's skin.

Every step felt heavier than the last, not just because of the rough terrain but because of the growing sense of urgency. Mae could feel it in the air—the tension, the weight of what was coming. The veil's fragility was palpable, a constant hum in the back of her mind, growing louder the closer they got to the tomb.

Delphine walked ahead, her eyes scanning the path for any signs of danger. But Mae's thoughts drifted back to her dream, to the Hollow One. She could still feel its gaze on her, the emptiness it brought with it. The memory of the cold, all-encompassing void made her stomach twist.

"Delphine," Mae called, quickening her pace to walk beside her companion. **"The Hollow One… I saw it. In my dream. It was standing at the edge of the world, like it was waiting for something. Watching me."**

Delphine's expression darkened. **"The Hollow One is always watching. It knows who the Guardians are, and it knows we're getting closer to finding the tomb. The closer we get, the more dangerous it becomes."**

Mae swallowed hard. **"But why? Why does it want to destroy the veil so badly?"**

Delphine hesitated, her brow furrowed in thought. **"The veil wasn't always there. Long ago, before time as we know it, the realms of the living and the dead were one and the same. Chaos ruled then, a world where death could walk alongside life. The Hollow One thrived in that chaos—it fed on it, drew its strength from the endless cycle of death and destruction."**

She glanced at Mae, her eyes serious. **"But then, the veil was created by the first Guardians, separating the realms and restoring balance. The Hollow One has been seeking to tear it** down ever since, to return the world to that primal state of disorder. If the veil falls, it will be free to feed on everything—living and dead alike. And it will grow more powerful than ever before."

Mae's heart sank. **"So we're not just trying to protect the veil. We're trying to stop the end of everything."**

Delphine nodded grimly. **"Yes. That's why the Guardians were created, to maintain the balance. And that's why you were chosen, Mae. The veil called to you because it knows you're strong enough to protect it."**

Mae wanted to believe that. But the weight of her responsibility pressed down on her, making it hard to breathe. She had never asked for this power, never asked to become a Guardian. But here she was, standing on the brink of a battle that could determine the fate of the world.

They continued their climb in silence, the path becoming steeper and more treacherous as the day wore on. The air grew thinner, colder, and Mae's legs burned from the effort. But she pushed forward, knowing they couldn't afford to stop.

By late afternoon, they reached a narrow ledge overlooking a vast, snow-covered valley. Delphine paused, her eyes narrowing as she studied the landscape below.

"We're getting close," she said, pointing to a jagged peak in the distance. **"The tomb is at the base of that mountain."**

Mae followed her gaze, her heart skipping a beat. The mountain loomed like a great stone sentinel, its slopes covered in ice and snow. It was an ancient, forbidding place, the kind of place that seemed to hold secrets older than time itself.

"It's hidden," Delphine continued, "buried beneath the ice. The tomb was sealed long ago, but there's a way in—a path known only to the Guardians. We'll need to find it."

Mae shivered, though it wasn't from the cold. The thought of what lay ahead filled her with a deep, gnawing dread. But she steeled herself. There was no turning back now.

As they descended into the valley, the sky began to darken, thick clouds rolling in from the north. The wind picked up, carrying with it the scent of snow.

Suddenly, Delphine stopped, her hand shooting out to grab Mae's arm. "Wait," she whispered.

Mae froze, her heart pounding. She followed Delphine's gaze and saw them—figures moving through the snow, barely visible against the white expanse. They were distant, but there was no mistaking their purpose.

"More shadowspawn," Delphine said, her voice tense. "They've found us."

Mae's pulse quickened. The creatures were closing in, their forms shifting like shadows against the snow.

"We can't fight them out in the open," Delphine said, her eyes scanning the landscape for cover. "There's a cave up ahead. We'll make our stand there."

Without another word, they broke into a run, the shadowspawn drawing closer with each passing second. Mae's breath came in ragged gasps as she struggled to keep pace, the cold air burning her lungs. The cave loomed ahead, a dark gash in the side of the mountain.

They reached the entrance just as the first of the shadowspawn emerged from the snow, its glowing eyes fixed on Mae. Delphine turned, her dagger flashing in the fading light as she prepared to fight.

"Get inside!" she shouted.

Mae hesitated for only a moment before diving into the cave, her heart racing. The air inside was cold and damp, the darkness oppressive. She could hear the sounds of the battle outside—Delphine's blade striking against the creatures, the hisses of the shadowspawn as they closed in.

Then, suddenly, the noise stopped.

Mae's blood ran cold. **"Delphine?"** she called, her voice trembling.

A shadow moved at the entrance of the cave, and Delphine stepped inside, her face pale, her cloak torn.

"They're gone," she said, her voice shaking slightly. **"But we need to keep moving. They'll be back. And next time, there will be more."**

Mae nodded, though fear gripped her heart. The shadowspawn weren't going to stop until the veil was torn apart. And The Hollow One wouldn't rest until it had consumed everything.

As they ventured deeper into the cave, the air grew colder, and the darkness thickened around them. Mae could feel the weight of the mountain pressing down, as if they were descending into the very heart of the world.

And somewhere, in that deep, suffocating darkness, the tomb awaited.

The answers awaited.

And so did The Hollow One.

The final confrontation was drawing near.

Chapter 32

The cave walls seemed to close in around Mae as they descended deeper into the mountain. The air grew colder, almost suffocating, and every sound echoed endlessly, amplifying the tension between them. Delphine walked ahead, her torch casting flickering shadows on the rough stone walls, while Mae kept her hand on the pendant around her neck, feeling the comforting pulse of its power.

But the pendant wasn't enough to quell the dread building in her chest. The weight of the mountain felt oppressive, as if the earth itself were trying to swallow them whole. The air was heavy with something ancient, a presence older than time, watching, waiting.

"How much farther?" Mae asked, her voice barely more than a whisper. It felt wrong to speak too loudly, as if the darkness itself would rise up and consume them if they disturbed it.

Delphine didn't turn around, her gaze fixed ahead. **"Not much. The tomb is buried deep, but we're close. I can feel it."**

Mae could feel it too—a strange, almost magnetic pull, like the very walls of the cave were drawing her toward something vast and terrible. The closer they got, the more she could sense the veil's weakness, its fragility pressing against her mind. It was like a web, frayed and torn, barely holding the two realms apart.

Then they came to a halt.

Ahead of them, the tunnel opened up into a massive underground chamber. The ceiling was so high it disappeared into darkness, and the walls were lined with ancient, crumbling carvings. At the center of the chamber, half-buried in ice, stood an enormous stone door—its surface covered in intricate symbols, glowing faintly with an otherworldly light.

Delphine stepped forward, her face illuminated by the eerie glow. **"This is it,"** she said softly. **"The Tomb of the First Guardian."**

Mae's breath caught in her throat. The door radiated power, but there was something else beneath it, something darker, as if the very ground beneath their feet was rotting away.

"What's behind that door?" Mae asked, her voice shaking. **"Is it… The Hollow One?"**

Delphine shook her head. **"No. This tomb is sacred. It was built to hold the secrets of the first Guardian—the one who created the veil. But if the veil is weak enough… The Hollow One will find its way in. We need to strengthen it before it does."**

Mae stepped closer to the door, feeling the ancient power emanating from it. The symbols carved into the stone seemed to pulse with life, reacting to her presence. She reached out, her hand hovering just above the cold surface.

Suddenly, a voice echoed through the chamber—low, rasping, and filled with malice.

"You're too late."

Mae's blood turned to ice. She spun around, her heart racing, but there was no one there. The chamber was empty, except for Delphine, who had drawn her dagger, her eyes scanning the darkness.

"Did you hear that?" Mae whispered, her voice trembling.

Delphine nodded, her expression grim. **"It's here."**

The Hollow One.

The darkness around them seemed to thicken, the air growing impossibly cold. A deep, rumbling sound echoed through the cave, like the very mountain was groaning in pain. Mae felt it—a presence so vast, so ancient, that it defied comprehension. It was everywhere, pressing in on them from all sides, and yet, it was nowhere to be seen.

"We need to open the tomb," Delphine said, her voice urgent. **"It's the only way to strengthen the veil."**

Mae's hands were shaking as she turned back to the stone door. She could feel the Hollow One's presence growing stronger, like a great tidal wave of darkness crashing toward them. There was no time to waste.

With a deep breath, she placed her hands on the door.

The moment her palms touched the stone, the symbols flared to life, glowing brighter and brighter until the entire chamber was bathed in blinding light. The door shuddered, and with a deafening groan, it began to open, revealing a narrow passage leading deeper into the tomb.

Delphine moved quickly, stepping into the passage, and Mae followed close behind. As soon as they crossed the threshold, the door slammed shut behind them, sealing them inside.

The passage was narrow and winding, the walls lined with more of the strange, glowing symbols. The air here was even colder, filled with the scent of ancient stone and decay. Mae's heart pounded in her chest as they descended deeper into the tomb, the Hollow One's presence lingering just behind them, like a shadow at the edge of her vision.

Finally, they reached the heart of the tomb—a small, circular chamber with a stone pedestal at its center. On the pedestal rested an ancient, weathered book, its pages glowing faintly with the same otherworldly light as the symbols on the walls.

Delphine approached the pedestal, her eyes wide with awe. **"This is it,"** she whispered. **"The First Guardian's Codex. It holds the knowledge we need to restore the veil."**

But as she reached for the book, a deep, mocking laugh echoed through the chamber.

"Fools."

Mae's blood ran cold.

From the shadows at the edge of the chamber, a figure emerged—tall, cloaked in black, its face hidden beneath a hood. The air around it seemed to warp and twist, as if reality itself was being bent by its presence.

"You cannot stop what is already in motion," the figure hissed, its voice like the rustling of dead leaves. **"The veil will fall, and I will feed on everything that remains."**

The Hollow One.

Mae's heart pounded in her chest. She could feel its power radiating from the figure, a force so vast and terrible that it threatened to consume her whole. She reached for her pendant, drawing on its power, but the Hollow One laughed again, the sound filling the chamber with a sickening sense of dread.

"You think you can resist me, little Guardian?" it sneered. **"Your power is nothing compared to mine. The veil is already crumbling. You are too late."**

Mae's hands trembled, but she forced herself to stand tall, facing the Hollow One. **"We're not too late,"** she said, her voice steady. **"We can still stop you."**

The Hollow One's laughter died, replaced by a low, menacing growl. **"Then come, Guardian. Let us see if you have the strength to defy me."**

The air in the chamber grew impossibly cold, and Mae felt the weight of the Hollow One's power pressing down on her, suffocating, crushing. But she wouldn't back down. She couldn't. The fate of the veil—and of the world—depended on her.

She glanced at Delphine, who nodded, her dagger at the ready.

Together, they would face the darkness.

Together, they would fight.

And somehow, against all odds, they would win.

With a deep breath, Mae drew on the power of the pendant, its light flaring to life in her hand. The Hollow One hissed, recoiling from the light, and Mae stepped forward, her heart pounding with determination.

This was it.

The final battle had begun.

Chapter 33

The chamber seemed to tremble as the Hollow One recoiled from the flare of Mae's pendant, its shadowy form writhing like smoke caught in a wind. Its presence was overwhelming, a suffocating darkness that clawed at the edges of her mind, trying to consume her will. But Mae held firm. The light from the pendant radiated outward, casting long, sharp shadows across the stone walls, and she felt the ancient power of the Guardians flowing through her.

Delphine stepped to her side, her dagger glowing faintly in the light. **"Whatever happens, don't stop,"** Delphine said through gritted teeth. **"The Hollow One is strong, but it feeds on fear. Stay focused, and we can push it back."**

The Hollow One's voice slithered through the chamber, its words dripping with malice. **"Push me back? You naive children. You are mere insects, crawling through the last moments of your existence. I have waited millennia for this moment, and nothing—nothing—will stop me now."**

With a violent screech, the Hollow One surged forward, its dark tendrils lashing out, seeking to extinguish the light Mae held. The air grew thick with malevolent energy, and Mae could feel it, the raw hunger of the creature, an endless void that sought to devour everything in its path.

But as the darkness closed in, Mae didn't falter. She raised her pendant higher, its light intensifying, pushing back against the oppressive shadows. **"You won't destroy the veil,"** she said, her voice steady. **"I won't let you."**

Hollow One's tendrils collided with the light, recoiling as if burned. It screamed in fury, its form twisting violently, but still it advanced, relentless.

Delphine lunged forward, her dagger slicing through the air as she attacked the creature's shadowy limbs. With each strike, the Hollow One hissed, its form flickering like a dying flame, but it wasn't enough. Mae could see it now—despite their efforts, the Hollow One was too powerful. They were only delaying the inevitable.

Delphine, it's too strong," Mae shouted, her voice strained as she poured more energy into the pendant. The light flickered, the weight of the Hollow One's power pressing harder with each second.

Delphine's face twisted with frustration. **"We can't kill it outright—not without the Codex's power."**

Mae's eyes darted toward the pedestal, where the ancient Codex still rested. The book radiated with a strange energy, the glow of its pages pulsing in rhythm with the pendant's light. That was it. The Codex held the knowledge to restore the veil, to turn the tide. But how could she reach it while keeping the Hollow One at bay?

Another wave of dark energy surged from the Hollow One, knocking both Mae and Delphine off balance. Mae stumbled backward, her pendant flickering as the darkness pressed in closer, suffocating her. The cold was unbearable, like the weight of a thousand winters descending upon her at once.

The Hollow One's voice echoed through her mind. **"Give up, little Guardian. You are nothing. I have destroyed your kind before, and I will do it again. You cannot hope to resist me."**

Mae's heart pounded in her chest, fear clawing at her thoughts. For a moment, she wanted to believe the voice, to succumb to the endless void that the Hollow One promised. But then she remembered the dream—the vision of the world burning, the veil torn apart, and the Hollow One standing triumphant in the ruins.

No. She couldn't let that happen.

With a surge of determination, Mae focused on the pendant, pulling every ounce of power from it. The light intensified once more, blindingly bright, pushing the Hollow One back a few precious feet. **"Delphine!"** she shouted. **"I'll hold it off—get the Codex!"**

Delphine didn't hesitate. She darted toward the pedestal, her movements quick and precise, as the Hollow One screeched in fury. Its dark tendrils lashed out wildly, trying to stop her, but Mae stood her ground, the light of the pendant forming a barrier between them and the creature.

Delphine reached the Codex, her fingers trembling as she grasped the ancient book. As soon as she touched it, the symbols on its pages flared to life, filling the chamber with a blinding white light. The air vibrated with power, and Mae could feel the energy coursing through the tomb, like the very bones of the earth were awakening.

The Hollow One howled, its form flickering violently as the light from the Codex grew stronger. **"No!"** it shrieked, its voice filled with fury and desperation. **"You cannot stop me! I am eternal! I am——"**

But its words were drowned out by the roar of the veil's power, surging from the Codex like a flood. The light engulfed the Hollow One, burning away its shadowy form, and for the first time, Mae heard something new in the creature's voice—fear.

"Now!" Delphine shouted, holding the Codex open. **"Mae, use the pendant—pour everything into it!"**

Mae didn't hesitate. She focused on the pendant, channeling all of her remaining strength into it. The light grew blinding, merging with the power of the Codex, until the entire chamber was filled with a radiant, searing brilliance.

The Hollow One screamed, its form disintegrating as the light tore through it, unraveling its very essence. Mae could feel it—the creature's power fading, its hold on the world slipping away. And then, with one final, piercing wail, the Hollow One was gone, its presence vanishing like smoke in the wind.

The chamber fell silent.

Mae collapsed to her knees, her body trembling with exhaustion. The light from the pendant flickered one last time before dimming, leaving only the soft glow of the Codex to illuminate the chamber.

Delphine stood beside her, her face pale but determined. **"It's over,"** she said softly, her voice filled with relief. **"We did it."**

Mae looked up at the Codex, its pages still glowing faintly. **"The veil... Is it safe?"**

Delphine nodded, her eyes filled with quiet triumph. **"For now. The Codex will restore the veil's strength, but we'll need to guard it. There will always be forces trying to tear it down. But as long as there are Guardians, the veil will hold."**

Mae felt a wave of exhaustion wash over her, but also something else—hope. The Hollow One was gone, defeated, and the veil was safe. For now, at least.

But as she stood in the heart of the ancient tomb, Mae knew that this was only the beginning. The darkness had been pushed back, but it would never be gone entirely. The battle would go on, for as long as there was light to protect.

And Mae was ready to face whatever came next.

Mae stood on her feet, the weight of the battle still heavy in her limbs. The chamber was quiet now, save for the soft hum of energy resonating from the Codex. Delphine stood nearby, her gaze fixed on the ancient book. Despite their victory, an unsettling tension lingered in the air, as though the Hollow One's presence had left a scar in the very fabric of the world.

Mae turned to Delphine, her voice weak. **"What happens now? Is it really over?"**

Delphine's expression was grave as she carefully closed the Codex. **"We've won this battle, but it's never truly over. The Hollow One is gone, but its influence lingers. There are other forces at play, Mae. Darker ones. And with the veil weakened, it's only a matter of time before something else tries to break through."**

Mae felt a chill run down her spine. She had hoped that defeating the Hollow One would bring peace, but Delphine's words confirmed what she had feared all along: their fight wasn't over. The veil, though temporarily restored, was fragile. It had been weakened by centuries of neglect, and the world beyond it was full of horrors just waiting for a crack to slip through.

"How do we protect the veil for good?" Mae asked, her voice barely above a whisper.

Delphine looked at her, the weight of responsibility clear in her eyes. **"We don't stop. We train. We watch. We keep the Codex safe, and we make sure there are always Guardians ready to defend the veil. You and I, we're part of something much bigger than ourselves. This is a war that stretches across time, and we're just the latest soldiers."**

Mae's thoughts raced. She had been pulled into this world of Guardians and ancient magic so suddenly, and yet it felt like she had always been meant for this. But the idea of spending her life guarding against unseen horrors, always on edge, always preparing for the next battle—it was daunting.

"Do you think we'll ever be free from this?" she asked, looking at Delphine.

Delphine hesitated, her eyes dark with an unspoken truth. **"I don't know,"** she said finally. **"Maybe one day. But for now, we have a duty. As long as the veil exists, there will always be something trying to tear it down. We just have to be strong enough to stop it."**

Mae nodded, the weight of her new reality sinking in. But even as she felt the enormity of the task before her, a strange sense of calm washed over her. She had faced the Hollow One and survived. She had stood her ground against an ancient evil, and she wasn't alone. Delphine was by her side, and there were others out there—other Guardians, other protectors of the veil. Together, they could stand against whatever darkness came next.

"We need to get out of here," Delphine said, breaking the silence. **"The tomb will hold for now, but it's not safe to stay any longer."**

Mae nodded in agreement, her body still aching from the battle. As they made their way back through the narrow passage, the cold air seemed less oppressive, the weight of the tomb less stifling. The danger had passed, for now.

When they finally emerged from the tomb into the open night, Mae took a deep breath, the fresh air filling her lungs. The stars above them glittered in the dark sky, a stark contrast to the suffocating shadows they had faced underground. For a moment, everything was still, peaceful.

"We did it," Mae whispered, almost in disbelief.

Delphine turned to her, a rare smile crossing her face. **"We did. And we'll keep doing it. But now, we rest."**

Mae nodded, feeling the exhaustion of the day catch up with her. They began the trek back toward the cemetery where it had all begun, the strange sense of calm settling over her once again. But in the back of her mind, she couldn't shake the lingering dread—the knowledge that this victory was only temporary, and the darkness was always waiting.

Weeks passed, and life returned to a strange semblance of normality. Mae spent her days training with Delphine, learning the secrets of the Guardians and the history of the veil. The Codex had been hidden away in a safe place, its knowledge too dangerous to leave unguarded, and Mae had taken on the mantle of a Guardian, her role now clear.

But the nights… the nights were different.

Mae often found herself wandering the cemetery, drawn to the rose garden she had once tended with such care. The roses bloomed again, vibrant and alive, their petals glistening under the moonlight. But there was something darker in the air, something that tugged at the edge of her consciousness whenever she stood among the gravestones.

It was on one of those nights, as Mae stood silently in the center of the garden, that she felt it again—a faint ripple in the air, like a tear in the fabric of the world. Her hand instinctively went to the pendant around her neck, its pulse steady but faint.

"You feel it, don't you?" Delphine's voice came from behind her.

Mae turned to find Delphine standing at the edge of the garden, her expression serious.

"The veil," Mae whispered. "It's weakening again."

Delphine nodded, her eyes scanning the night sky. **"It's always weakening. That's why we have to stay vigilant. There will always be something trying to break through."**

Mae clenched her fists, determination hardening her resolve. **"Then we'll be ready. Whatever comes next, we'll be ready."**

Delphine smiled faintly. **"Good. Because something *will* come. And when it does, we'll face it together."**

Mae nodded, her gaze drifting back to the roses. Their beauty seemed eternal, but she knew the truth now—the world was fragile, and darkness was always lurking just beneath the surface. But as long as there were Guardians to protect it, the light would hold.

For now, that was enough.

The night stretched out before them, quiet and still, but Mae knew it wouldn't last. The battles were far from over. But with Delphine by her side, and the knowledge of the Guardians behind her, Mae was ready to face whatever the darkness had in store.

And she would keep fighting.

Chapter 34

As the nights grew longer, the weight of Mae's new reality settled in more deeply. Each evening, she could feel the veil subtly trembling, a reminder that the peace they had won was fleeting. Delphine trained her with an intensity that Mae had never known, pushing her to unlock the full power of her pendant and hone her skills as a Guardian. The rose garden, once her sanctuary, became a place of reflection and preparation—a silent reminder of what was at stake.

One evening, after an exhausting session of combat drills, Mae stood alone in the garden. The roses swayed gently in the breeze, their petals glowing faintly under the moonlight. But even here, surrounded by beauty, she could sense the tension in the air. The veil was fragile, like a spider's web stretched too thin. She knew that something was coming, something worse than the Hollow One.

A voice broke her thoughts. **"You feel it, don't you?"** It was Delphine, standing at the edge of the garden, her expression grave.

Mae didn't answer immediately. She didn't need to—Delphine could see it in her eyes. Instead, Mae knelt beside one of the roses, brushing her fingers over its soft petals. **"It feels like the world is holding its breath,"** she murmured. **"Like something's just waiting to break through."**

Delphine stepped closer, her face drawn with concern. **"You're right. There's something coming. I've been trying to track the energy surges, but they're erratic. It's not just the Hollow One's remnants—it's something else, something bigger."**

Mae stood, her gaze meeting Delphine's. **"What do we do?"**

Delphine hesitated, a rare uncertainty flickering across her features. **"We prepare. I've been in contact with other Guardians across the world. They're feeling it too. Whatever it is, it's not just here. It's everywhere."**

Mae's heart sank. The idea that this darkness wasn't localized, that it was creeping across the globe, made the task ahead seem even more daunting. But she refused to give in to fear. **"Then we'll fight it. All of us."**

Delphine smiled faintly, though her eyes remained troubled. **"Yes. But there's more. I've been doing research in the Codex. There are references to something ancient, older than the Hollow One. A force that predates the Guardians themselves. It's vague, but it sounds like—"**

"—like the Hollow One was just the beginning?" Mae finished for her.

Delphine nodded. **"Exactly. The Codex speaks of a greater darkness, one that's been dormant for eons. Something that once tried to consume the world, and it's waking up."**

Mae felt a shiver run down her spine. **"Do we know what it is? How to stop it?"**

"**Not yet,**" Delphine admitted. "**But we will. The Guardians are gathering what we can, pooling our knowledge. But this force—it's powerful, Mae. Far more than anything we've ever faced. We're going to need every advantage we can get.**"

Mae clenched her fists, determination flooding her veins. "**I'm ready. Whatever it takes, I'll be ready.**"

Delphine's gaze softened. "**I know you will be. But it's not just about strength. We'll need more than just weapons and magic to stop this. We'll need to unlock the full potential of the Codex, and that's something we can't do alone.**"

Mae furrowed her brow. "**What do you mean?**"

Delphine glanced back toward the tomb where they had defeated the Hollow One. "**The Codex is old, and it's incomplete. There are pieces missing, pieces that were lost over the centuries. We'll need to find them if we're going to stand a chance.**"

Mae's mind raced. "**So we need to search for these missing pieces. Do you know where they are?**"

Delphine shook her head. "**Not exactly. But there are clues. Old legends, hidden artifacts. The Guardians have been protecting some of them for generations, but others… others are lost to time.**"

Mae exhaled slowly. "**This is bigger than I thought.**"

"**It is,**" Delphine agreed. "**But we're not alone in this. The Guardians are mobilizing. We'll start searching for the lost pieces of the Codex, and with any luck, we'll find them before this darkness fully awakens.**"

Mae nodded, a mixture of dread and determination swirling within her. She had only just begun to understand her role as a Guardian, and already the stakes had risen far beyond anything she could have imagined. But she wasn't going to back down.

"So where do we start?" Mae asked, her voice steady.

Delphine gave her a small smile. **"We start with the first clue. There's an old ruin, deep in the mountains to the north. The Codex makes a cryptic reference to it, something about an ancient key hidden there. It's dangerous, and the path isn't clear, but it's our best lead."**

Mae's heart raced with anticipation. **"When do we leave?"**

"Tomorrow," Delphine replied. **"Rest tonight. You'll need your strength for what's coming."**

The following day, Mae and Delphine set out on their journey, leaving the familiar cemetery and the quiet town behind. The path ahead was long and treacherous, but Mae felt a strange sense of purpose. The weight of the world rested on their shoulders, but she wasn't afraid. Not anymore.

As they ventured deeper into the wilderness, the air grew colder, the trees taller and more ancient. There was a strange energy here, something old and forgotten, lurking just beneath the surface. Mae could feel it in her bones—a presence watching them, waiting.

"This place feels different," Mae said quietly as they hiked through the dense forest.

Delphine nodded. **"The mountains have always been a place of power. There are forces here older than the Guardians, older than the veil itself. We're walking through history."**

Mae felt a chill. **"Do you think the darkness we're facing comes from here?"**

Delphine's gaze was distant. **"I don't know. But I think we'll find answers soon enough."**

As they continued their ascent, the forest thinned, revealing jagged peaks in the distance. At the foot of one of the tallest mountains, nestled among the rocks, was the ruin Delphine had spoken of—a crumbling stone structure, its walls covered in ancient glyphs that pulsed faintly with a long-forgotten magic.

Mae's breath caught in her throat as they approached. **"This is it, isn't it?"**

Delphine nodded. **"Yes. Whatever we're looking for, it's in there."**

With a deep breath, Mae stepped forward, her heart pounding in her chest. The air around them seemed to hum with anticipation, as though the very ground was alive with the echoes of the past. She and Delphine exchanged a glance—one filled with unspoken resolve.

And together, they entered the ruin, stepping into the unknown.

The ruin was cold and dark, its ancient stones heavy with the weight of forgotten history. As Mae and Delphine stepped inside, their footsteps echoed through the cavernous space, disturbing the thick silence. The air was dense with an eerie stillness, and the faint glow from the glyphs on the walls provided little comfort. Mae felt as though the shadows were watching them, waiting for something.

"Stay close," Delphine whispered, her eyes scanning the room. **"This place has been abandoned for centuries, but that doesn't mean it's safe."**

Mae nodded, gripping her pendant tightly. The energy in the air was different here, more oppressive than anything she had felt before. The pendant pulsed faintly against her skin, as though it was responding to some unseen force. She couldn't shake the feeling that they were walking into something far more dangerous than they had anticipated.

At the center of the room stood a stone altar, worn by time but still intact. Carved into its surface were intricate symbols, the same ones that adorned the walls, though these seemed more elaborate. In the middle of the altar was a small, circular indentation.

Delphine approached the altar cautiously, her brow furrowed. **"This must be the key the Codex mentioned,"** she said, tracing her fingers over the glyphs. **"But it's missing something. The key itself."**

Mae stepped forward, her eyes drawn to the circular indentation. **"Could it be hidden somewhere in the ruin?"**

Delphine shook her head. **"No, I don't think so. I believe the key was taken long ago. Whoever built this place must have hidden it somewhere else to keep it safe."**

Mae's heart sank. **"So we came all this way for nothing?"**

Delphine's gaze remained fixed on the altar. **"Not for nothing. This place was meant to protect something, and we're closer to understanding what it is. But we'll need to find the key if we're going to unlock its secrets."**

Mae turned away from the altar, her mind racing. They had come so far, and yet it felt like they were still no closer to finding the answers they needed. **"So where do we go from here?"** she asked.

Delphine's eyes darkened as she looked at Mae. **"The Codex spoke of other locations—places where the pieces of the puzzle might be scattered. But there's something else. Something I've been hesitant to mention."**

Mae's stomach tightened. **"What is it?"**

"There's a legend," Delphine began, her voice low. **"One that predates even the Guardians. It speaks of an ancient order of beings who once protected the veil, long before humans ever became its defenders. They were known as the Watchers, and they wielded a power far beyond anything we've ever seen. But they vanished ages ago—disappeared without a trace."**

Mae frowned. **"The Watchers? Why haven't I heard of them before?"**

"Their existence was kept secret, even from most Guardians," Delphine explained. **"But I believe they hold the key to understanding this darkness we're facing. If we can find any trace of them, we might be able to unlock the full power of the Codex."**

Mae's mind raced with questions. **"Do you think the Watchers are still out there? That they could help us?"**

Delphine's expression was unreadable. **"I don't know. But if they are, they could be our only hope."**

The gravity of Delphine's words hung in the air, and Mae felt a mixture of fear and determination swell within her. The idea that there were ancient, powerful beings who had once guarded the veil was both awe-inspiring and terrifying. If the Watchers were still out there, hidden in the shadows of history, they could be the key to stopping the darkness. But finding them—if they even still existed—was a task that seemed impossible.

"Where do we start?" Mae asked, her voice steady despite the uncertainty she felt.

Delphine glanced around the ruin, her eyes lingering on the glyphs. **"The Codex hinted at a place, a temple hidden deep within the eastern desert. It's said to be one of the last remnants of the Watchers' presence in our world. If we're going to find any answers, that's where we need to go."**

Mae nodded, a sense of purpose igniting within her. **"Then let's go. We don't have time to waste."**

The journey to the eastern desert was long and perilous, taking them through rugged terrain and desolate landscapes. Days turned into weeks as they pushed forward, driven by the urgency of their mission. The further they traveled, the more Mae could feel the weight of the darkness pressing down on them. The air seemed heavier, the nights colder and more oppressive.

Finally, after what felt like an eternity, they reached the edge of the desert. The endless expanse of sand stretched out before them, the heat of the sun beating down relentlessly. In the distance, barely visible through the shimmering waves of heat, was a towering structure—an ancient temple, half-buried in the sands.

"That's it," Delphine said, her voice filled with both awe and trepidation. **"The Temple of the Watchers."**

Mae's breath caught in her throat as they approached the temple. It was massive, its stone walls etched with the same glyphs they had seen in the ruin. But there was something else—a presence, ancient and powerful, that seemed to emanate from the very stones themselves. The air around the temple buzzed with a strange energy, unlike anything Mae had felt before.

"Are you ready?" Delphine asked, her hand resting on the hilt of her sword.

Mae nodded, her heart pounding in her chest. **"Let's find the answers we need."**

Together, they entered the temple, stepping into the cool shadows of the ancient structure. The air inside was thick with dust and the scent of age, and the faint sound of wind echoed through the hollow halls. As they ventured deeper, the strange energy that had surrounded the temple grew stronger, almost palpable.

At the heart of the temple, they found what they had been searching for. In the center of a vast, circular chamber stood a massive stone obelisk, its surface covered in intricate carvings. At its base was an inscription, written in the ancient language of the Watchers.

Delphine approached the obelisk cautiously, her eyes wide with wonder. **"This... this is it. This is where the Watchers once stood."**

Mae followed her, her eyes scanning the inscription. **"Can you read it?"**

Delphine nodded, though her expression was tense. **"I can. It speaks of a prophecy… one that foretells the return of the darkness. It says that when the veil weakens, the Watchers will rise again to defend the world."**

Mae's heart raced. **"So they're still out there?"**

Delphine hesitated, her eyes dark with uncertainty. **"Maybe. But it also says something else. Something about a key, a way to summon the Watchers from wherever they are. It's tied to the Codex, Mae. The key we've been searching for… it's not just a physical object. It's a way to call them back."**

Mae's mind reeled. **"So we need to find this key to summon the Watchers?"**

Delphine nodded, her gaze fixed on the obelisk. **"Yes. And if we don't… we may not be able to stop what's coming."**

Mae felt a cold knot form in her stomach. The stakes had never been higher. The fate of the world rested on their shoulders, and the only way to save it was to find the key and summon the Watchers before the darkness consumed everything.

And time was running out.

Chapter 35

The weight of their task settled over them like a thick fog, and Mae struggled to keep her thoughts clear. Everything they had uncovered led to this moment: the Watchers, the key, the prophecy of the veil's collapse. And yet, the ancient temple only offered more questions—mysteries layered atop each other.

Delphine's eyes didn't leave the obelisk. **"We have to figure out what this inscription means, exactly. It's giving us more than just a warning."**

Mae stepped closer to the obelisk, her fingers grazing the weathered stone. **"What do you mean?"**

Delphine pointed to a series of smaller glyphs at the base of the inscription. **"These markings. They're directions—or more accurately, coordinates. The Watchers hid the key in a place they believed only a Guardian would ever find."**

Mae's heart thumped in her chest. **"Where?"**

Delphine's voice dropped to a whisper, her face growing more somber. **"It's beneath the earth, buried in a place called the Hollow Tombs. An ancient underground labyrinth where time itself warps and bends."**

Mae felt a chill race down her spine at the mention of the Hollow Tombs. The name conjured images of dark, endless corridors, of shadows lurking at every turn. **"How far are we from there?"**

Delphine sighed. **"Far. The Tombs are located in the frozen north, buried under miles of ice. No one's ventured there for centuries—not even the Guardians. There are rumors that time ceases to function properly within the labyrinth. People who enter it either disappear or... come out changed."**

Mae swallowed hard. **"And this is where the key is hidden?"**

Delphine nodded. **"Yes. It's the last place the Watchers hid their greatest secrets. If we're going to summon them, that's where we'll have to go."**

Mae turned, her eyes tracing the darkened halls of the temple around them. The oppressive energy of the place made her heart heavy. **"Do you think we're ready? We barely survived the Hollow One, and now... now we're talking about going up against something even older, even stronger."**

Delphine's expression softened as she looked at Mae. **"I don't know if we're ready, Mae. But it's not about being ready—it's about doing what we have to. The world is already unraveling. We can feel it in the air, in the growing shadows."** She paused, her hand resting gently on Mae's shoulder. **"We're Guardians. This is our fight. If we don't try, there might not be a world left to protect."**

Mae took a deep breath, letting Delphine's words settle into her bones. She wasn't just an ordinary girl who had stumbled into a war she didn't understand. She was a Guardian. She had inherited a responsibility that she could never have imagined, and now she was part of something far larger than herself. And while fear clung to her like a shadow, so did purpose.

"Then we go to the Hollow Tombs," Mae said firmly, her voice steady with resolve.

The journey north was grueling. As they moved from the desert heat into the icy wilderness, the temperature dropped dramatically, and the terrain became unforgiving. The frozen wasteland stretched out before them in every direction, and the relentless winds howled through the mountain passes like the cries of lost souls.

Mae and Delphine trudged forward, their breath visible in the frigid air, their cloaks wrapped tightly around them. Each step felt heavier than the last, as though the land itself wanted to push them back, to keep them from reaching their destination. But they pressed on, driven by the knowledge that time was running out.

After days of travel, they finally reached the entrance to the Hollow Tombs.

It was an unassuming crack in the side of a jagged mountain, barely visible beneath the snow and ice. But as Mae and Delphine stood before it, they could feel the ancient magic radiating from deep within. The air around the entrance was unnaturally cold, even for the frozen north, and a strange pressure pressed against their minds, as though the tomb itself were alive and aware of their presence.

"This is it," Delphine said, her voice barely audible above the howling wind. **"Once we enter, there's no turning back. The Tombs don't let anyone leave easily."**

Mae felt her heart hammer in her chest. **"What exactly happens in there?"**

Delphine hesitated, her eyes scanning the dark entrance. **"No one knows for sure. Some say time loops in on itself, trapping those who enter in endless cycles. Others say the Tombs show you visions of your worst fears, or pull you into dreams so real you can't tell what's true anymore."**

Mae's pulse quickened. **"But we have to go in, don't we? To get the key."**

"Yes," Delphine answered, her expression grim. **"The only way to stop this darkness is inside."**

With a final glance at each other, they entered the Hollow Tombs.

The moment they crossed the threshold, the world seemed to shift around them. The biting cold vanished, replaced by a strange, suffocating stillness. The walls of the tomb were smooth and polished, yet there was an oppressive sense of age, as though the place had existed since the dawn of time. A faint, ghostly light flickered along the walls, casting long, shifting shadows that seemed to dance and writhe like living things.

As they ventured deeper, the passages grew narrower, twisting and turning in ways that defied logic. Mae felt a disorienting sense of deja vu, as though they had walked these same halls before. Her pendant pulsed faintly against her chest, a reminder that something was very wrong.

"We have to stay focused," Delphine warned, her voice echoing strangely in the confined space. **"The Tombs will try to play tricks on us. Keep your mind clear, and don't let yourself get lost."**

Mae nodded, though her unease was growing. The deeper they went, the more the walls seemed to shift, as though the tomb itself was moving, reshaping itself around them. She could feel the pull of ancient magic in the air, a force that tugged at the edges of her mind, whispering to her in voices she couldn't quite understand.

Suddenly, the ground beneath them trembled, and the walls rippled like water. Mae gasped, grabbing onto the nearest stone for support as the tomb seemed to twist around them. The passage in front of them collapsed, sealing them in.

"What's happening?" Mae shouted, her voice shaking.

Delphine's face was pale. **"The Tombs are waking up. We have to move quickly—before they trap us for good."**

Without warning, a low, rumbling voice echoed through the air, its sound vibrating through the stone walls.

"Who dares enter the Hollow Tombs?" the voice growled, ancient and filled with malice.

Mae's blood ran cold. **"What is that?"**

Delphine's eyes were wide with fear. **"I don't know… but it knows we're here."**

The voice spoke again, louder this time. **"The key you seek is not for the living. Turn back now, or face eternity in the dark."**

Mae exchanged a panicked glance with Delphine. **"We can't turn back. We need the key. We need to find the Watchers."**

Delphine drew her sword, her grip tight. **"Then we keep going. Whatever that voice is, it's trying to stop us. But we don't have a choice."**

As they pressed forward, the walls continued to shift, the air growing colder with every step. The voice rumbled again, now filled with fury.

"Very well.

The voice's deep growl reverberated through the twisting tunnels of the Hollow Tombs, vibrating in Mae's bones and sending a pulse of dread through her veins.

"Very well," it rumbled again, louder, colder. **"You have chosen your fate."**

Suddenly, the walls themselves seemed to close in, twisting into sharp angles, narrowing the passageway as if the tomb were alive and reshaping itself to trap them. The floor beneath their feet trembled again, and from the shadows of the walls, dark figures began to emerge—twisted forms of smoke and shadow, their hollow eyes glowing with a faint, eerie light.

Mae's heart raced as she clutched her pendant tightly, its warmth now the only source of comfort against the oppressive cold. **"Delphine!"** she gasped, her voice laced with panic. **"What are those things?"**

Delphine's gaze hardened as she readied her sword. **"Specters,"** she muttered through gritted teeth. **"They're drawn to the power in this place. We can't let them touch us."**

The first of the specters lunged forward, its form shifting and elongating, reaching out with smoky tendrils that twisted unnaturally in the air. Delphine met it head-on, her sword flashing in the dim light as she slashed through its form. The creature let out a wail, disintegrating into mist, but more followed, their hollow eyes fixated on Mae and Delphine.

Mae stumbled backward, panic surging in her chest as another specter reached for her. She raised her hand instinctively, the pendant glowing brighter, and a burst of light shot from it, sending the creature retreating in a hiss of pain. The action startled Mae as much as the specter, but she had no time to process what had just happened.

"Mae, stay close!" Delphine called out, cutting down another specter as the walls around them seemed to twist and tighten. **"The Tombs are trying to disorient us. We need to find the central chamber—fast!"**

Mae nodded, forcing herself to focus, though her hands were shaking. Together, they pressed forward, battling through the shifting tunnels and the spectral creatures that swirled in the darkness. The Hollow Tombs were alive, ancient magic coursing through every stone, warping reality as they moved deeper. Time itself felt slippery, moments stretching and collapsing as if the tomb was trying to unmoor them from reality.

Mae's pendant pulsed again, and she felt a faint tug—a direction. **"This way!"** she shouted, pulling Delphine with her as they dodged another specter. The twisting passages seemed to part for a brief moment, revealing a narrow staircase that descended into the earth.

Delphine nodded without hesitation, and they hurried down the steps, the darkness swallowing them as the howling voices of the specters echoed behind them. As they descended, the air grew heavier, colder, until they reached a vast underground chamber, its walls lined with the same intricate glyphs they had seen in the temple.

In the center of the chamber stood a massive stone pedestal, and upon it, resting in a pool of faint, ethereal light, was the key.

It was not what Mae had expected. The key wasn't metal, nor was it shaped like any traditional key. It was a crystal, jagged and raw, pulsing with a deep, internal light. The energy it radiated was unlike anything Mae had ever felt—powerful, ancient, and alive.

"That's it," Delphine whispered, her eyes locked on the crystal. **"The Watchers' key."**

Mae stepped forward, her pendant glowing brighter as she approached the pedestal. She could feel the pull of the key, its magic calling to her, resonating with the energy inside her. But as she reached for it, the rumbling voice from earlier returned, louder and more menacing than before.

"You dare to claim what is not yours," the voice growled, and the ground trembled beneath them. **"This place is a tomb for the living. You will not leave."**

From the shadows, a colossal figure emerged—larger and more terrifying than the specters. It was a being of darkness and smoke, its form constantly shifting, eyes glowing red as it towered over them. The ancient guardian of the Tombs.

Mae froze, her heart hammering in her chest. **"Delphine —what do we do?"**

Delphine gripped her sword tighter, her eyes narrowing. **"We fight. We take the key, and we get out of here."**

The guardian moved with unnatural speed, lashing out with a massive arm of smoke. Delphine dodged, rolling to the side as the ground where she had stood cracked and crumbled. Mae felt the surge of power within her pendant once again, but this time, she didn't hesitate. She raised her hand, focusing on the energy coursing through her, and a bright beam of light shot from the pendant, striking the guardian.

The creature recoiled with a deafening roar, its form flickering as though the light were burning away at its very essence. But it was far from defeated. It lunged again, the shadows around it twisting and growing darker, more violent.

Delphine darted forward, her sword gleaming as she slashed at the guardian's limbs, but the creature's smoke-like form shifted, avoiding most of her strikes. Mae unleashed another burst of light, her pulse quickening as she realized the guardian was weakening, but not fast enough.

The ground trembled again, and Mae stumbled, her eyes flicking to the key still resting on the pedestal. The crystal seemed to pulse with urgency, as though it knew the battle's outcome hung in the balance.

"Mae, grab it! Now!" Delphine yelled, fending off another strike from the guardian.

Without thinking, Mae sprinted toward the pedestal, her hand reaching for the key. The moment her fingers touched the crystal, a surge of energy exploded through her, so powerful it nearly knocked her to the ground. The key glowed brighter, its light filling the chamber, and suddenly, the guardian froze, its form flickering violently.

The light from the key enveloped the creature, and with a final, ear-splitting wail, the guardian disintegrated, its dark form dissipating into nothingness.

The chamber fell silent.

Mae stood there, clutching the key, her heart racing and her body trembling from the intensity of the magic. She could feel the power of the Watchers coursing through the crystal, ancient and incomprehensible.

Delphine approached her, breathing heavily but smiling with relief. **"You did it,"** she said softly. **"You found the key."**

Mae looked down at the crystal in her hand, its light pulsing gently now, as though it were alive. **"I can feel them,"** she whispered, her voice filled with awe. **"The Watchers… they're out there, waiting."**

Delphine nodded, her expression serious once more. **"Then we have to summon them before it's too late. The darkness is growing stronger every day. We'll need their power to stop it."**

Mae took a deep breath, the weight of their mission settling over her once again. They had the key, but their journey was far from over.

The real battle was still ahead.

Chapter 36

The oppressive silence of the Hollow Tombs hung in the air after the guardian's destruction, like a lingering shadow. Mae could feel the ancient magic in the crystal pulsing through her hand, its rhythmic glow a stark contrast to the cold stone walls around them. As the adrenaline began to fade, exhaustion settled into her bones, but there was no time for rest.

Delphine sheathed her sword, her eyes locked on the key in Mae's hand. **"We have to leave before the Tombs shift again. If we get caught in another cycle, we might not be able to find our way out."**

Mae nodded, slipping the key into a pouch on her belt. **"Do you think the Tombs will still fight us, even with the key?"**

Delphine looked around warily, her expression grave. **"The magic here is ancient and unstable. The key has power, but the Tombs have a will of their own. It won't let us go easily."**

As they turned to leave the chamber, the ground beneath them trembled once more, and Mae felt that eerie, twisting sensation in her stomach, like reality itself was warping. The passage they had come through was gone, replaced by a solid stone wall.

"It's starting again," Mae whispered, her heart pounding. **"The Tombs are shifting."**

Delphine cursed under her breath, her eyes scanning the walls for any sign of an exit. **"Stay close to me. Whatever happens, don't lose sight of the key. We can't let it fall back into this place."**

Mae gripped her pendant, hoping it would guide them again like before, but the light that had pulsed within it seemed dimmer now, as though drained by the magic of the Tombs. The oppressive feeling of being watched returned, stronger than ever, and the walls around them seemed to pulse, as though they were alive.

Suddenly, a low, whispering voice filled the air, coming from nowhere and everywhere at once.

"You cannot leave."

Mae froze, her breath catching in her throat. **"Did you hear that?"** she whispered.

Delphine nodded grimly. **"The Tombs… it's aware of us. We have to move fast."**

They rushed down a narrow corridor, the walls shifting and reshaping with each step, the architecture impossibly fluid. The feeling of being trapped grew stronger, the labyrinth bending time and space to disorient them, as though the Tombs themselves were desperate to keep them imprisoned.

After what felt like hours, they finally stumbled into a large chamber, its ceiling high and vaulted, with ancient symbols etched into the walls. Mae's eyes widened as she recognized some of the glyphs—they were similar to those in the temple where they had first discovered the prophecy.

"Delphine, look!" Mae pointed to the far wall, where a series of symbols seemed to form a map.

Delphine approached it, tracing the lines with her fingers. **"This… this shows the entire layout of the Tombs,"** she said, her voice filled with awe. **"And here—this symbol. It's the exit. It's not far, but we have to go through the central crypt."**

Mae's stomach dropped. **"The central crypt? Isn't that… where the oldest spirits are buried?"**

Delphine's expression was grim. **"Yes. The most dangerous ones."** She glanced at Mae. **"But it's our only way out."**

Mae swallowed hard, fear gnawing at her insides, but there was no other option. They had come too far, and there was too much at stake.

"Let's go, then," Mae said, her voice steadier than she felt.

They hurried toward the crypt, the map etched into their minds. As they moved deeper into the Tombs, the air grew colder, thicker, and the light from Mae's pendant flickered weakly, as though the magic here was too dense, too ancient for it to pierce.

When they reached the entrance to the central crypt, a pair of massive stone doors loomed before them, covered in more of the intricate glyphs they had seen before. The air here felt heavy, almost suffocating, and Mae could sense the presence of something powerful behind those doors.

"Are you ready?" Delphine asked, her voice barely above a whisper.

Mae nodded, though every instinct screamed at her to turn back. But they had no choice.

Delphine pushed the doors open, and they creaked loudly, the sound echoing through the dark chamber beyond. The crypt was vast, its ceiling disappearing into shadow, and the walls were lined with stone sarcophagi, each one etched with the names of long-dead rulers and warriors. The air was thick with the scent of decay and ancient magic.

"We need to cross to the other side," Delphine said, her voice tight with tension. **"Stay close."**

As they made their way through the crypt, the temperature dropped further, their breaths visible in the cold air. The silence was suffocating, broken only by the soft sound of their footsteps on the stone floor.

Then, without warning, a loud crack echoed through the chamber, and one of the sarcophagi began to shake violently.

Mae's heart stopped. **"What's happening?"**

Delphine drew her sword, her eyes fixed on the trembling sarcophagus. **"The spirits are waking up."**

The stone lid of the sarcophagus slid open with a deafening scrape, and from within, a skeletal figure began to rise. Its bones were wrapped in tattered, ancient robes, and its hollow eyes glowed with an unnatural light. More sarcophagi began to stir, the dead awakening as if called by the presence of the key.

"Run!" Delphine shouted, grabbing Mae's arm as the skeletal figure stepped forward, its bony fingers reaching out.

They sprinted through the crypt, the undead rising all around them, their hollow voices filling the air with a cacophony of whispers. Mae's chest burned as she ran, her fear propelling her forward, but the exit was still too far away.

Suddenly, the ground beneath them trembled, and a massive crack split the floor. Mae stumbled, falling to her knees as the pendant around her neck flared with light.

"Mae!" Delphine shouted, reaching out for her, but before she could help, the floor gave way entirely, and Mae tumbled into the darkness below.

She fell for what felt like an eternity, the light of the pendant the only thing illuminating the inky blackness around her. When she finally hit the ground, the impact knocked the wind out of her, and she lay there, gasping for breath, her body aching.

The light from the pendant flickered weakly, and as Mae struggled to her feet, she realized she was alone. Delphine was nowhere in sight.

Panic surged through her as she looked around, but all she could see were shadows and the faint glow of the pendant. **"Delphine?"** she called out, her voice echoing in the darkness. There was no response.

Mae's heart raced as she clutched the key in her hand, its faint glow the only thing keeping the encroaching darkness at bay. She was trapped, lost in the depths of the Hollow Tombs, and the undead were closing in.

And this time, there was no one to help her.

Mae's heart pounded in the suffocating silence. The faint glow of her pendant barely illuminated the darkness around her, casting eerie, flickering shadows on the stone walls. Panic clawed at her throat, but she forced herself to breathe, steadying her trembling hands. She was alone now, lost in the bowels of the Hollow Tombs, and the only thing keeping the crushing weight of fear from overwhelming her was the small, pulsing crystal in her hand—the key to summoning the Watchers.

She had to keep moving. She couldn't let the fear consume her.

Mae pushed herself to her feet, ignoring the pain in her limbs from the fall. The air here felt different—thicker, as though something unseen was watching her every move. The cold seeped into her bones, and the soft, distant whispers of the undead stirred in the dark, echoing through the labyrinthine corridors.

"Delphine?" Mae called out again, her voice trembling, but the only response was the shifting echoes of the tomb.

The floor beneath her feet was uneven, covered in cracks and crumbling stone, as though this part of the tomb had been long forgotten, abandoned even by the spirits that roamed the upper crypts. Her pendant flared briefly, casting a weak light that revealed a narrow passage ahead, leading deeper into the earth. She had no other choice but to follow it.

Each step felt heavy, the weight of the ancient magic pressing down on her, making her legs feel like lead. The walls were lined with glyphs, symbols similar to those in the chamber where they had found the key, but older—more twisted, as though the magic here had decayed over centuries.

The whispers grew louder as she moved deeper into the passage, and Mae's heart raced. She could feel the presence of something—something ancient and powerful—lurking just beyond the veil of shadows. The darkness seemed to pulse, alive with energy, and Mae's pendant flickered weakly, struggling to maintain its glow.

Suddenly, the ground trembled again, a deep, resonant rumble that seemed to come from the very heart of the tomb itself. Mae stumbled, catching herself against the cold stone wall, and as the tremor subsided, a voice echoed through the darkness.

"You are not the first… to seek the key…"

The voice was low, distorted, as though it came from somewhere far away, yet it reverberated inside Mae's mind. She froze, her blood turning to ice. **"Who… who are you?"**

The darkness seemed to shift, coalescing into a faint figure, barely visible in the dim light of the pendant. It was a ghostly, shadowy form, its features indistinct but undeniably human—though twisted, as if it had been warped by centuries of being trapped in the tombs.

"The Watchers… they are not saviors," the figure whispered, its voice like dry leaves rustling in the wind. **"They are destroyers. They will bring only ruin to the world above…"**

Mae's grip tightened on the key. **"That's not true. The prophecy says the Watchers will help stop the darkness that's coming."**

The figure let out a hollow laugh, its form flickering like a dying flame. **"The prophecies are lies, twisted by those who seek power. The Watchers… they were sealed away for a reason. If you summon them, you will bring death upon us all."**

Mae shook her head, her heart pounding in her chest. **"You're lying. The darkness is spreading—we need the Watchers' power to stop it."**

The figure's hollow eyes bore into hers, filled with a cold, ancient wisdom. **"The darkness is their doing. They are not saviors, child. They are the ones who brought the curse upon this world, and you are playing into their hands."**

Mae's mind reeled. Could it be true? Was everything she and Delphine had fought for a lie? The key in her hand pulsed faintly, as though it were alive, its energy entwined with her own, and she could feel the weight of its power, ancient and terrible.

"What… what am I supposed to do then?" Mae whispered, her voice shaking. **"If the Watchers are the cause of the darkness, how do we stop it?"**

The figure seemed to shift, its form growing dimmer, as though it were fading from existence. **"There is no stopping it,"** it said softly. **"The only hope is to bury the key and let the darkness consume what it must. The world will suffer, but it will survive. The Watchers must never rise again…"**

Mae felt the cold grip of despair tighten around her heart. Bury the key? Let the darkness consume everything? It couldn't be the only way. Delphine had believed in the prophecy, in their mission. How could she betray that now?

Before she could speak, the ground trembled violently, and the passageway around her began to collapse. Stones fell from the ceiling, and the walls shook with the force of the quake. The figure before her vanished into the shadows, its parting words a whisper on the wind.

"Do not summon them…"

Mae stumbled backward as the ceiling above her began to cave in. She ran, her heart hammering in her chest, dodging falling debris as the passage crumbled around her. The tremors grew stronger, and Mae knew the Tombs were reacting to the key's presence, as if the ancient magic here was trying to bury it —bury her with it.

She could barely see through the dust and darkness, but ahead, she glimpsed a faint light—an opening. Summoning every ounce of strength, Mae sprinted toward it, her legs burning, the sound of the tomb collapsing behind her like a roaring beast.

At the last moment, she leaped through the opening, tumbling onto the cold stone floor of a vast chamber. The ground trembled one last time, then fell silent.

Gasping for breath, Mae slowly pushed herself up, her body aching, her mind spinning. She looked around, realizing she had fallen into another chamber—larger than any she had seen before. In the center, bathed in a cold, ethereal light, stood an ancient altar, its surface carved with the same twisted glyphs that lined the walls.

And there, resting on the altar, was another artifact— larger and more foreboding than the key. It was a dark, jagged shard, pulsing with a malevolent energy that made Mae's skin crawl.

She didn't know what it was, but she knew it had something to do with the Watchers. And with the darkness.

As she stood there, staring at the shard, a cold realization settled over her.

She wasn't just holding the key to summon the Watchers.

She was standing in the heart of the curse itself.

Chapter 37

Mae stood frozen before the altar, her heart racing as the dark shard pulsed with a sinister light. The air around it crackled with an energy that made her skin prickle, and she could feel the malevolent force it radiated—a power that seemed to echo the warnings of the ghostly figure.

"This… this is what caused it all," she whispered to herself, her voice barely audible in the heavy silence of the chamber. The shard seemed to pulse in response, as though it recognized her presence.

The whispers of the Tombs grew louder in her mind, filling her with a deep sense of dread. The walls seemed to close in, and Mae felt the weight of the ancient magic pressing down on her, suffocating her.

She clenched the key in her hand, her knuckles turning white. **"If the shard is connected to the Watchers, then maybe… maybe it can be destroyed."**

But how? Destroying something like this wasn't a matter of brute force. This was no simple object; it was a fragment of something ancient, something powerful. Whatever it was, it had the power to bring the world to its knees.

Mae's eyes flicked between the shard and the key. The two pulsed with a strange synchrony, as though they were parts of the same ancient magic. The Watchers and the shard—they were linked. Perhaps that was why the Tombs had shifted so violently around her. The shard wanted to be found.

But the question still loomed: could she trust the figure's words? Were the Watchers truly the cause of the darkness, or was that just another layer of deception? And if they were, what was she supposed to do with the key now? Everything she had believed—everything Delphine had believed—was unraveling.

The pendant around her neck flickered, its light dimming, as though it, too, was being drained by the presence of the shard. Mae felt her own strength waning, her breath growing shallow. The shard's power was immense, and it was suffocating her with its malevolent force.

Suddenly, a voice echoed through the chamber—clearer now, almost human. But it wasn't Delphine. It was something… older.

"You are too late."

The voice came from everywhere and nowhere, reverberating through the stone walls. Mae's heart skipped a beat. She turned around, scanning the chamber, but there was no one. The voice was disembodied, yet it felt as though it was inside her mind, pressing into her thoughts.

"The darkness has already spread. The Watchers will rise."

Mae stumbled back, gripping the key tighter. **"No… there has to be a way to stop it. There has to be…"**

The voice chuckled, a deep, sinister sound. **"You think you can stop what has already begun? You, a mere mortal, think you can alter the fate of the world?"**

Mae's breath quickened, panic bubbling up inside her. **"I don't care what you are. I won't let the darkness consume everything!"**

The voice grew louder, more oppressive. **"You are nothing but a pawn in a game older than your world. The Watchers will rise, and the shard will complete the cycle. You are powerless."**

Mae felt her resolve faltering. The weight of the shard's presence, the voice, the Tombs themselves—they all seemed to press down on her, filling her with a deep, suffocating despair. What was she supposed to do? She wasn't a hero. She wasn't even supposed to be here. Delphine had always been the strong one, the brave one. But now…

Delphine was gone.

A surge of anger cut through her fear. No. She couldn't give up now. Not after everything they had been through. She wouldn't let the darkness win.

"I'm not powerless," Mae whispered, more to herself than to the voice. **"I have the key."**

The voice hissed, as if recoiling from her defiance. **"The key is your doom, child. It is the lock and the chain. It will bind you to the Watchers' will."**

Mae looked at the key in her hand, the crystal glowing faintly. Could she trust it? Was it a tool to fight the darkness, or was it part of the curse, just like the shard? Her mind raced, and the weight of the decision pressed down on her like a physical force.

Then she remembered something Delphine had once told her, long before they had set out on this journey. **"The future is shaped by the choices we make, not by fate."**

She took a deep breath, her grip tightening on the key. Maybe the prophecy wasn't set in stone. Maybe she could change it.

But first, she had to destroy the shard.

Mae stepped forward, closer to the altar. The shard's malevolent energy seemed to pulse more violently now, as though it sensed her intentions. Her pendant flickered weakly, the light fading to almost nothing. The shard was trying to drain everything around it, to draw all the life and magic it could into itself.

She raised the key, holding it above the shard. The two pulsed in synchrony again, the light from the key growing brighter as it neared the dark shard. Mae could feel the tension between the two forces—the light of the key and the darkness of the shard—battling for dominance.

The ground trembled beneath her feet, the Tombs reacting to the magic. Dust fell from the ceiling, and the walls seemed to shift and groan, as though the entire structure was alive, and it knew what she was about to do.

"You cannot destroy it," the voice hissed, more urgent now. **"The shard is eternal. You will only doom yourself!"**

Mae gritted her teeth. **"I'm willing to take that chance."**

With a shout, she slammed the key down onto the shard.

A blinding light erupted from the altar, and Mae was thrown backward by the force of the explosion. She hit the ground hard, her vision going white as the energy from the shard and the key collided, filling the chamber with a deafening roar.

For a moment, there was only the sound of crackling magic, the violent clash of light and darkness. Mae's entire body felt like it was on fire, the energy tearing through her like a storm.

And then, as quickly as it had begun, it was over.

Mae lay on the cold stone floor, gasping for breath. The light had faded, and the air was still. Slowly, painfully, she pushed herself up, her body trembling from the effort.

The shard was gone. The altar was shattered, and the oppressive energy that had filled the chamber was gone with it. The Tombs were silent once more.

But as Mae looked at the shattered remains of the altar, she realized something terrible.

The key was gone too.

She had destroyed them both—the shard and the one thing that might have stopped the darkness.

And now, the world was on its own.

Mae sat on the cold stone floor, her breath shaky and her mind racing. The key was gone. The one tool she thought could stop the impending darkness was destroyed, and with it, so was any clear path forward. Silence pressed in around her, thick and suffocating, as if the Tombs were holding their breath.

She tried to gather her thoughts, but they scattered like dust in the wind. She had acted out of desperation, trusting her gut, trusting Delphine's belief that she could make a difference.

But now, looking at the shattered altar and the absence of the key, she wasn't sure if she had saved the world—or doomed it.

"What have I done?" she whispered, her voice barely audible in the eerie stillness.

For a moment, the chamber remained silent. Then, in the far corners of the dark room, the whispers began again—soft, ghostly voices that seemed to echo from the depths of the Tombs. They were different now, less menacing, but still otherworldly, as if the spirits that lingered here were stirred by the events that had just unfolded.

Mae pushed herself up, her body aching, but her mind sharper now. She couldn't stay here, wallowing in uncertainty. The shard was gone, and with it, the curse that had been woven into the Tombs. She didn't know if she had done the right thing, but there was no turning back now.

Slowly, she began to make her way out of the chamber, her footsteps echoing in the vast emptiness. The tremors that had once threatened to bury her alive had subsided, and the oppressive weight of the ancient magic had lifted. But as she moved, she couldn't shake the nagging feeling that something was still wrong —that something darker was lurking just beyond her sight.

When she reached the corridor that led to the surface, a familiar figure materialized out of the shadows.

Delphine.

But it wasn't her—at least, not anymore.

The sight of her friend stopped Mae in her tracks. Delphine stood there, her pale skin almost translucent, her eyes wide and unblinking. Her expression was calm, but there was something deeply unsettling about her presence, like she was there and not there at the same time.

"Mae," Delphine said softly, her voice hollow, like it was coming from a distant place.

Mae's heart skipped a beat. **"Delphine?"** She took a tentative step forward. **"Is it… is it really you?"**

Delphine smiled, but it didn't reach her eyes. **"You did it. You destroyed the shard."**

Mae swallowed hard, the weight of the moment pressing down on her. **"I did. But the key… it's gone too. I don't know if I've saved anyone."**

Delphine's form flickered, like a candle in the wind. **"The key was never meant to save anyone, Mae. It was a piece of the curse, just like the shard. You did what had to be done."**

Mae shook her head, confusion swirling in her mind. **"But the prophecy… the Watchers…"**

Delphine's expression darkened. **"The Watchers are real, Mae, but they're not the heroes we thought they were. They're part of the darkness. The prophecy was a trap—a way to lure people like us into freeing them."**

Mae's blood ran cold. **"What are you saying?"**

Delphine took a step closer, her form wavering. **"The shard was just the beginning. The Watchers have been waiting, gathering their strength. They feed off the chaos, off the fear. And now that the shard is gone, nothing stands between them and the world."**

Mae felt her stomach drop. **"No… that can't be true. I—
I thought destroying the shard would stop them."**

Delphine's eyes gleamed with something Mae didn't
recognize—something dark and unearthly. **"It was always too
late. The moment we entered the Tombs, we became part of
their game. They're coming, Mae. And there's nothing we can
do to stop them."**

The air in the chamber grew colder, and Mae could feel a
presence, something vast and ancient, lurking just beyond the
shadows. The whispers grew louder, more insistent, filling her
mind with dread.

"Delphine, please," Mae said, her voice trembling. **"We
have to do something. There has to be a way to fight them."**

Delphine's smile widened, but there was no warmth in it
—only a hollow, eerie calm. **"There is no fighting them, Mae.
The Watchers are eternal. They are the darkness that waits at
the edge of the world. All we can do now is prepare for their
coming."**

Mae felt her legs weaken, but she stood her ground. **"No. I
refuse to believe that. There's always a choice."**

Delphine's form flickered again, and for a brief moment,
Mae thought she saw a glimmer of her old friend behind those
cold, distant eyes. But then it was gone, replaced by something
darker, something ancient.

"Then make your choice," Delphine said, her voice like
the wind. **"But know this: whatever path you take, the
darkness will follow. The Watchers are coming, Mae. And
they will consume everything."**

With that, Delphine's figure dissolved into the shadows, leaving Mae standing alone in the cold, empty corridor. The silence that followed was deafening.

Mae clenched her fists, her heart racing. She didn't know what to believe anymore, but one thing was clear: the Watchers were real, and they were coming. Whether she had freed them or delayed them didn't matter. She had to find a way to stop them, or the world would fall into darkness.

But how?

The key was gone. The shard was destroyed. And Delphine… Delphine was lost to her, claimed by the very darkness they had sought to fight.

Mae turned and began walking toward the surface. The whispers still followed her, but she ignored them, focusing on one thought:

She would find a way to stop the Watchers.

Even if it meant facing the darkness alone.

Chapter 38

$\mathcal{M}ae$ emerged from the tombs, the cold night air hitting her like a shock. The moon hung low in the sky, veiled behind a thin layer of clouds, casting a pale glow over the cemetery. The wind carried the distant rustling of leaves, but the world felt eerily quiet, as if it, too, sensed the approach of something terrible.

She stood in the middle of the cemetery, the place where this all began—where she and Delphine had discovered the map that led them to the Hollow Tombs. Now, it seemed like a lifetime ago. Delphine was gone, taken by the darkness, and Mae had destroyed the key, the only thing she thought could help them. But instead of relief or closure, she felt a deepening sense of dread.

The Watchers were coming. She didn't know how long she had or how they would manifest, but Mae could feel the world teetering on the edge. The air felt charged, like the moments before a storm.

"I can't do this alone," Mae whispered to herself, the weight of the realization settling in her chest. She had no allies, no answers, and the forces she had unleashed were far beyond her understanding.

The whispers from the tomb still echoed in her mind, haunting her with Delphine's final words. **"They will consume everything."**

Mae's gaze drifted over the cemetery, the rows of graves stretching out in front of her. The graves felt different now—less like resting places and more like gateways, portals to the same darkness she had glimpsed below. It was as if the entire world had become a waiting room for something more sinister.

A movement in the shadows caught her eye, and Mae tensed. At first, she thought it was a trick of the light, the wind stirring the branches. But then she saw it again—a flicker of something moving, darting between the gravestones.

Her heart pounded in her chest as she reached for the dagger strapped to her belt. She hadn't thought she'd need it so soon, but old habits died hard. The blade felt cold in her hand, a small comfort as the shadow grew closer.

"Who's there?" Mae called out, trying to keep the fear from her voice.

The figure stepped into the moonlight—a tall, gaunt man dressed in tattered black robes, his skin pale and his eyes hollow. His movements were slow, deliberate, as if he were being drawn forward by some unseen force. His eyes locked on Mae, and for a brief moment, she saw a flicker of recognition in them.

"You've come from the tombs," he said, his voice low and gravelly. **"You've awakened them."**

Mae's grip tightened on the dagger. **"Who are you? How do you know about the Watchers?"**

The man let out a dry, humorless laugh. **"I've been watching. Waiting. The signs have been there for centuries, but no one ever listens to old prophecies until it's too late."** He took another step closer, his gaze piercing. **"I saw what you did. You destroyed the shard, but you've only made things worse."**

Mae's blood ran cold. **"Worse? How could it be worse? The shard—"

"—was a seal,"** the man interrupted, his voice harsh. **"A part of the curse, yes, but it was also holding back something far darker. You didn't free the world from the darkness, girl. You've opened the door for the Watchers to walk through."**

Mae felt her stomach twist. **"I didn't know. I thought I was stopping them—"

"—you've sped up their return."** The man's face twisted into a grim smile. **"But all is not lost. There may be a way to contain them. To stop the full awakening of the Watchers."**

Mae took a step forward, her mind racing. **"How? Tell me what I need to do."**

The man studied her for a long moment, his eyes dark and unreadable. **"There's another shard. The shard you destroyed was only one of many. The others are scattered across the world, hidden in places forgotten by time. If you can gather them before the Watchers fully awaken, you might be able to reseal them."**

Mae's heart skipped a beat. **"Another shard? Where? How do I find them?"**

The man reached into his tattered robes and pulled out a small, weathered scroll. **"This will guide you to the next shard. But beware—the closer you get, the stronger the darkness becomes. The Watchers will try to stop you. They know you're a threat now."**

Mae took the scroll, her hands trembling slightly as the weight of the task ahead sank in. **"Why are you helping me?"** she asked, her voice barely above a whisper.

The man's gaze darkened. **"I've seen what happens if the Watchers are fully released. I've lived long enough to know the cost of failure. I don't want to see the world burn."**

Mae nodded, her resolve hardening. **"I won't let that happen."**

The man gave her a final, piercing look. **"You've already taken the first step, but this journey won't be easy. The Watchers aren't the only ones who will try to stop you. There are others—those who worship the darkness, who believe the Watchers' rise is inevitable. They'll hunt you, just like the Watchers will."**

Mae clenched her jaw. **"Let them come. I'll find the shards, and I'll stop this."**

The man's lips curled into a grim smile. **"Good luck, girl. You'll need it."**

With that, he turned and disappeared into the shadows, leaving Mae alone in the cemetery, clutching the scroll in her hand.

She stared down at it, her mind racing. The Watchers were waking, the darkness was spreading, and now she was the only one who could stop it. The weight of that realization pressed down on her, but instead of fear, she felt something else growing inside her.

Determination.

Mae looked out over the graves, the wind tugging at her hair, the moon hanging low in the sky. She had lost Delphine, and the world was teetering on the brink of ruin, but she wasn't going to give up.

She unfolded the scroll, her eyes scanning the cryptic symbols that would lead her to the next shard.

It was time to finish what she and Delphine had started.

Mae took one last look at the tombs behind her and set off into the night. The darkness was closing in, but she wasn't running from it anymore. She was going to face it head-on.

And she was going to win.

Mae moved through the cemetery, the scroll clutched tightly in her hand. The night was still and thick with tension, as though the world itself knew the Watchers were stirring. Every shadow felt alive, every breeze a whisper of something ancient watching her. She knew now that the clock was ticking. The man had been right—she had accelerated their awakening, and there was no time to waste.

The scroll led her out of the cemetery and into the heart of the nearby town. Streets, usually quiet at this hour, now seemed deserted. Lamps flickered with an eerie, unnatural glow, casting long, distorted shadows across the cobblestone. Mae's footsteps echoed, her pulse quickening with every passing moment. She had no idea where she would find the next shard, but she had to believe the scroll would guide her.

She glanced down at the symbols scrawled across the ancient parchment, faintly glowing in the moonlight. The lines of the map shifted slightly as she moved, as though alive, responding to her steps. The symbols were unfamiliar, but they pulsed with a strange energy, drawing her toward her next destination.

As she walked, Mae couldn't help but feel the growing presence of something malevolent. The town felt wrong—like the world was holding its breath, waiting for something terrible to happen. There were no sounds of life, no murmurs from behind closed doors, no distant clatter from alleyways. Just silence.

Her mind raced. What had the man meant by "others"—those who worshipped the Watchers? She hadn't considered the possibility of enemies who weren't bound to the darkness but who *embraced* it. They could be anywhere, hidden in plain sight, waiting for the right moment to strike. She had to stay sharp, had to be prepared.

The map led her deeper into the town, to a part she had never ventured before. The buildings here were old, crumbling. The streetlamps cast an orange glow on weathered stone walls, and the air felt colder, heavier. Mae stopped in front of a large, ancient church at the edge of a desolate square. Its stone walls were cracked, vines snaking up its sides, and its windows were dark, their stained glass long shattered.

She hesitated at the entrance, feeling a surge of apprehension. The map had led her here, to this place. But there was something deeply unsettling about it, as though the church had been forgotten by time, abandoned by whatever forces once protected it.

Taking a deep breath, Mae pushed open the heavy wooden doors. They creaked loudly, the sound echoing through the empty halls. Inside, the church was just as decrepit as the outside. Dust motes danced in the moonlight streaming through broken windows, and the air smelled of decay and disuse.

Mae stepped carefully inside, her eyes scanning the large, empty nave. Rows of pews, long rotted and splintered, lined the room, and the altar at the far end stood covered in debris. She could feel the presence of the shard—its pull was faint but unmistakable, hidden somewhere deep within the church.

As she moved further in, the shadows seemed to grow darker, heavier. Every sound—every creak of the floorboards, every gust of wind—felt amplified, as though the church itself was alive, watching her.

Suddenly, a soft, distant whisper broke the silence. Mae froze, her heart racing.

"You're not alone, girl," a voice said from the darkness.

Mae spun around, her dagger at the ready, her pulse hammering in her ears. **"Who's there?"** she demanded, her voice steady despite the fear gnawing at her insides.

A figure emerged from the shadows, stepping into the faint light that filtered through the broken windows. It was a woman, tall and gaunt, dressed in tattered robes similar to the man she had met in the cemetery. Her eyes gleamed with an unnatural light, and her face was twisted into a cruel smile.

"We've been waiting for you," the woman said, her voice dripping with malice.

Mae took a step back, her grip tightening on the dagger. **"Who are you? What do you want?"**

The woman's smile widened, and her eyes flickered with dark amusement. **"We are the children of the Watchers. We've** watched your journey, girl. You've already played your part in waking them. Now, we've come to ensure you can't stop them."

Mae's blood ran cold. **"You're one of them. One of the ones who worship the Watchers."**

The woman let out a low, chilling laugh. **"We serve the true masters of this world. The Watchers will cleanse it, reshape it in their image. And you"**—she took a step closer, her eyes narrowing—**"you're just a foolish girl playing at hero."**

Mae's heart pounded in her chest, but she stood her ground. **"I won't let them take this world. I won't let them win."**

The woman's expression darkened, and in an instant, her hand shot out, sending a wave of dark energy hurtling toward Mae. She barely had time to react, throwing herself to the side as the force slammed into the ground where she had just stood, shattering the stone floor.

Mae scrambled to her feet, her mind racing. She had no time to think, no time to plan—only to fight. The woman moved with an unnatural speed, her hands crackling with dark magic as she advanced on Mae, her eyes gleaming with bloodlust.

Mae darted between the pews, using the broken furniture as cover as the woman's attacks tore through the church, leaving destruction in their wake. She couldn't fight this woman head-on —she was too powerful. But Mae had faced dark magic before. She had survived the Tombs, survived the destruction of the shard. She wasn't going to die here, not now.

With a quick, desperate move, Mae threw her dagger at the woman. It wasn't meant to be a fatal strike—just a distraction. The woman batted it away effortlessly, but it gave Mae the opening she needed. She lunged forward, grabbing a piece of broken wood from a shattered pew, and slammed it into the woman's side.

The woman let out a snarl of pain, stumbling back. Mae didn't hesitate—she grabbed her dagger from the floor and rushed toward the altar. She could feel the shard's presence now, stronger than ever, buried somewhere beneath the rubble.

The woman screamed in fury, her voice echoing through the church. **"You cannot stop them, girl! The Watchers will rise, and you will die with the rest of them!"**

Mae ignored her, her hands digging through the debris behind the altar. There—beneath the broken stones—she saw a faint, glowing light. The shard.

With a final burst of effort, Mae pulled it free, its dark glow filling the room. The moment her fingers touched it, the world seemed to shift, the air growing heavy with power.

The woman let out a piercing scream, and Mae spun around just in time to see her dissolve into a swirling mass of darkness, her form unraveling as the shard's energy consumed her.

Mae collapsed to her knees, clutching the shard in her trembling hands. The woman was gone, but the weight of what lay ahead pressed down on her.

There were more shards to find, more enemies to face. The Watchers were stirring, and she was their only obstacle.

But for now, she had won. And she would keep fighting until the end.

Chapter 39

Mae stared at the shard in her hands, its surface pulsing faintly, as though it contained a life of its own. She could feel its power, raw and ancient, flowing through her fingers. The moment she touched it, a wave of conflicting emotions surged within her—fear, dread, but also strength. This shard, dark and twisted though it was, was a weapon. If she could find the others, she might be able to stop the Watchers from fully awakening.

She rose shakily to her feet, her eyes scanning the now-ruined church. The encounter with the woman had left the building in shambles, but there was no time to dwell on that. She could feel it—the darkness was growing. The air felt thicker, heavier, like the world was teetering on the brink of collapse. Whatever time she had, it wasn't much.

Mae slid the shard into her satchel, careful to wrap it in cloth to avoid its unsettling touch. As she stepped toward the exit, her body ached from the fight, and exhaustion tugged at her limbs. But she couldn't stop now. She had a mission, and stopping meant certain death—for her and for the world.

Outside, the town was still deathly quiet. The wind had picked up, swirling fallen leaves in little eddies across the empty streets. Mae took a deep breath, trying to calm her racing heart. She couldn't stay here. The presence of that woman—the "child" of the Watchers—meant others would be coming soon. She needed to keep moving.

As she made her way through the town, the scroll's map glowed faintly from her satchel, guiding her forward. The next shard was out there, hidden in another forgotten place, another tomb or temple lost to time. She would find it. She had to. There was no other choice.

But as Mae passed through the empty streets, she felt a prickle at the back of her neck—a sense that she was being watched. Her grip tightened on the dagger in her belt. The woman's warning echoed in her mind: *You're not alone. Others are coming.*

She glanced behind her. At first, she saw nothing. Just the still, desolate streets. But then, from the corner of her eye, she saw movement. A shadow darting behind a building, quick and silent.

Mae's heart lurched. Someone—or something—was following her.

Without a second thought, Mae broke into a run. Her boots pounded against the cobblestone as she sprinted down the narrow alleyways, her breath coming in short, sharp bursts. She could hear footsteps behind her now, the sound of pursuit growing closer.

She turned sharply down an alley, ducking behind a crumbling wall, her pulse racing. She crouched low, straining to hear. The footsteps slowed, approaching cautiously. Whoever—or whatever—it was, they were close. Too close.

Mae gripped her dagger, holding her breath as she prepared to strike. But before she could make a move, a soft voice whispered from the shadows.

"Wait."

Mae froze. The voice was familiar. Slowly, she peered around the corner, her heart skipping a beat as she saw who it was.

A figure stepped into the faint light, their face pale and gaunt but unmistakable.

"Delphine," Mae whispered, her voice shaking.

Delphine's eyes glimmered in the moonlight, hollow and distant, as if she were a ghost. Her once vibrant face was now etched with sorrow and weariness, her lips pale and cracked. She looked like a shell of the person Mae had known.

"You're… alive?" Mae's voice trembled, torn between shock and disbelief.

Delphine didn't answer immediately. She took a step closer, her eyes locking onto Mae's. **"I've seen what they are, Mae. The Watchers… they're waking up. I tried to fight it, but…"** She trailed off, her voice filled with a haunting emptiness.

Mae stood slowly, her dagger still in hand. She wasn't sure whether to feel relief or terror. **"How are you here? I thought you were—"**

"—gone? I was," Delphine interrupted, her voice cold. **"But the darkness… it doesn't let go. It pulled me in. It's like a poison, spreading through everything. I tried to resist it, but it's too strong. I saw what's coming, Mae. It's worse than we thought."**

Mae's heart sank. **"You can fight it. You're still here. We can stop this together."**

Delphine shook her head slowly, her expression pained. **"It's too late for me. I'm already part of it. The Watchers…**

they want you, Mae. You're the only one standing in their way now." She paused, her gaze darkening. **"And they will stop at nothing to get to you."**

A chill ran down Mae's spine. **"Delphine, please—"**

"Run." Delphine's voice was suddenly sharp, her eyes wide with fear. **"They're coming for you, Mae. You have to run. Now!"**

Before Mae could react, Delphine's form began to flicker, her body dissolving into shadows as the air around them grew thick with an oppressive, malevolent energy. The ground beneath Mae's feet trembled, and a low, ominous hum filled the air.

The Watchers were near.

Mae turned and ran, her heart pounding in her chest as she raced through the streets. The world around her seemed to blur, the once familiar town now a twisted, nightmare landscape. The shadows moved and writhed, as if alive, reaching for her with clawed hands.

She could feel them—the Watchers. Their presence loomed over her, vast and overwhelming, like a storm on the horizon. They were waking, and with each step, they drew closer.

But Mae wasn't going to give up. Not now.

With every ounce of strength she had left, she pushed forward, her mind focused on one thing: finding the next shard. It was her only hope, her only chance to stop the darkness from consuming everything.

And she would not let the Watchers win.

Not while she still had breath left in her body.

Mae ran until her legs burned, the sound of her own breath harsh in her ears. The oppressive weight of the Watchers loomed behind her, an invisible force that pressed on her chest and clouded her mind. Every street, every alley, seemed to twist into unfamiliar shapes, as if the very town were warping in their presence. The map in her satchel glowed faintly, but she was too panicked to check it. Right now, all she could do was run.

Delphine… alive? But how? Mae's mind was reeling. The friend she had mourned, the girl she had fought beside, was now twisted by the same darkness she was fighting. What had happened to her? Had she been corrupted by the Watchers? The thought gnawed at Mae's insides.

The streets began to narrow, and the buildings around her felt like they were closing in. She had to get out of here, had to find a place where she could regroup. Her eyes darted to the dark horizon—a distant forest stood at the edge of town, its silhouette a sharp contrast against the flickering sky. If she could reach the cover of the trees, she might be able to hide, gather her thoughts, and plan her next move.

She forced herself to push on, ignoring the ache in her legs. As she neared the forest, the hum in the air grew louder, more ominous. The Watchers were getting closer, their presence warping reality itself. She could feel it, like a hand reaching out from beyond the veil of existence, threatening to pull her into the abyss.

Just as she reached the edge of the forest, the ground beneath her feet rumbled. Mae stumbled, barely managing to keep her balance as cracks began to spiderweb across the cobblestone. A deep, guttural sound echoed through the air, and the shadows around her began to writhe, taking form.

Tall, twisted figures emerged from the darkness, their bodies made of smoke and shadow. Their eyes—glowing with the faintest flicker of pale blue light—locked onto Mae. The Watchers had sent their servants, their twisted creations, to hunt her.

Mae's pulse quickened. She was outnumbered, and she knew she couldn't take them all on. Her only choice was to keep running. She bolted into the forest, the twisted figures following closely behind, their forms shifting and bending in the dim light.

The trees closed in around her, the canopy above blotting out the sky. Branches whipped against her face as she sprinted deeper into the woods. She could feel the shards pulsing in her satchel, as if they were reacting to the presence of the Watchers' servants. But the forest was thick, dense, and Mae hoped it would give her some time to think.

Her breath came in ragged gasps as she finally slowed, ducking behind a large, gnarled tree. She pressed her back against the rough bark, trying to steady herself. The forest was quiet—unnaturally so. No wind rustled the leaves, no animals moved in the underbrush. It was as if the entire world was holding its breath, waiting for something terrible to happen.

Mae pulled out the scroll, her hands shaking. She needed to know where to go next. The map shimmered faintly, the lines shifting and moving as it revealed her next destination. The path was leading her further into the woods, toward an old, forgotten ruin.

Of course, she thought grimly. *Another hidden place, another shard buried deep in the shadows.*

But before she could start moving again, a voice echoed through the stillness of the forest.

"You can't run forever, Mae."

Her heart stopped.

It was Delphine's voice, but twisted, hollow. Mae turned, her dagger drawn, scanning the shadows for any sign of her. But there was nothing—just the dark trees and the oppressive silence.

"You should stop fighting. They will find you. They will break you."

The voice seemed to come from everywhere and nowhere at once. Mae's grip on her dagger tightened, her mind racing. **"Delphine, if you can hear me—if there's any part of you left —fight it. Don't let them control you."**

A soft, bitter laugh echoed through the trees. **"It's too late for me, Mae. And soon, it'll be too late for you."**

A shape flickered at the edge of Mae's vision—a fleeting shadow that disappeared as soon as she turned toward it. She couldn't stay here. The forest wasn't safe. Nowhere was safe.

Pushing through the fear, Mae started moving again, heading deeper into the woods. The path became rougher, the trees thicker and more twisted. Every step felt heavier, as if the darkness itself was pressing down on her, slowing her down.

After what felt like an eternity, she reached the ruins. Ancient stone pillars jutted from the ground like broken teeth, half-buried beneath centuries of dirt and decay. Vines snaked over the crumbling walls, and the air was thick with the scent of damp earth and rotting leaves.

Mae could feel the shard's presence here, strong and pulsing. It was close, hidden somewhere within the ruins. But she wasn't alone. She could feel the eyes of the Watchers' servants, lurking just beyond the edge of her vision, waiting for the moment to strike.

With her heart pounding in her chest, Mae moved carefully through the ruins, her eyes scanning every shadow. She knew the shard would be guarded. It always was. But this time, it felt different. The air was thicker, heavier, as if the shard itself was calling to the darkness, feeding it.

As she stepped into what remained of an old stone chamber, the ground trembled beneath her feet. A low, guttural growl echoed through the air, and Mae froze.

From the shadows, a massive figure emerged. It was unlike anything she had ever seen before—a twisted amalgamation of stone, shadow, and bone. Its eyes glowed with the same pale light as the other servants of the Watchers, but this creature was different. It radiated a terrible power, its form shifting and bending unnaturally as it lumbered toward her.

Mae's breath caught in her throat. This wasn't just another servant. This was something far worse.

The creature let out a deafening roar, and Mae barely had time to dive out of the way as it swung a massive, clawed arm at her, shattering the stone wall where she had stood moments before. She scrambled to her feet, her mind racing. She couldn't fight this thing—not directly. But she had to get to the shard. It was the only way.

With a surge of adrenaline, Mae darted through the ruins, the creature in close pursuit. She could feel the shard's pull, guiding her deeper into the chamber. But the creature was relentless, its roars shaking the very ground beneath her.

Just as Mae reached the center of the chamber, her eyes locked onto the shard—buried within a stone pedestal, glowing faintly. But before she could grab it, the creature was upon her, its massive form looming over her like a living nightmare.

Mae gritted her teeth, her mind racing. She had one shot. One chance.

With all her strength, she lunged for the shard.

Mae's fingers closed around the shard, its cold surface pulsing with energy as soon as she touched it. For a moment, time seemed to freeze. The creature roared behind her, the sound deep and guttural, echoing through the ancient ruins like a death knell. But Mae felt a surge of power coursing through her as the shard reacted to her touch. It wasn't just a piece of stone—it was alive, in a way, an extension of something far greater than herself.

She barely had time to react as the creature lunged again, its massive claws tearing through the air. Instinct took over. Mae threw herself to the side, narrowly avoiding the blow that sent chunks of stone flying through the chamber. Her heart pounded in her ears, but she knew she couldn't keep dodging forever. This thing was too powerful to face directly, but she had the shard now. It had to mean something.

The shard throbbed in her hand, its energy building. Mae could feel it—an ancient, primal force stirring inside her, waking something deep within her soul. It was as if the shard was speaking to her, calling her to use its power.

She didn't know how, but she trusted it.

With a fierce cry, Mae raised the shard high above her head. The air around her crackled with energy, a low hum vibrating through the stone walls. The creature hesitated for the briefest of moments, as if sensing the change, and that was all Mae needed.

A burst of blinding light erupted from the shard, radiating outwards in all directions. The creature let out a blood-curdling scream as the light struck it, its shadowy form writhing and twisting in agony. The energy from the shard surged through the ruins, shattering the dark presence that clung to the air.

Mae could feel the power within her growing, expanding, until it felt like she was about to burst. She directed it all toward the creature, forcing the light to burn through its corrupted form. The ground trembled beneath her as the creature howled, its body breaking apart, dissolving into smoke and ash.

Finally, with one last, shuddering roar, the creature collapsed in on itself, disappearing into nothingness.

Silence fell over the ruins, broken only by Mae's ragged breathing. The shard in her hand dimmed, its light fading to a soft, steady glow. Mae stumbled forward, exhaustion crashing over her in waves. Her body ached, her muscles screamed in protest, but she had done it. The creature was gone.

She collapsed to her knees, clutching the shard tightly. It was still warm, its power pulsing faintly, but it no longer felt overwhelming. For a moment, she allowed herself to breathe, to take in the fact that she had survived. But the victory was short-lived.

From the shadows, a familiar voice whispered through the chamber.

"It won't be enough."

Mae's eyes shot open. Delphine's voice again. She struggled to her feet, her heart pounding in her chest. The chamber was empty, but she could feel Delphine's presence lingering, as if she was watching from just beyond the veil of reality.

"They'll keep coming," Delphine's voice said, low and sorrowful. **"You can't stop them, Mae. You can't stop the Watchers."**

Mae gritted her teeth, her hands shaking with both anger and fear. **"I have to try."**

"You don't understand. The shards… they're part of it. Every piece you find only brings them closer. You're not just fighting the darkness, Mae. You're feeding it."

The words hit her like a blow to the gut. Mae looked down at the shard in her hand, suddenly feeling a cold weight settle in her chest. Was it true? Were the shards part of the Watchers' plan all along? Was she unknowingly helping them wake?

But she couldn't let that be true. There had to be another way.

"I won't let them win," Mae whispered fiercely. **"I'll find another way. I'll stop them."**

There was a long pause, the air heavy with unspoken tension. Then, Delphine's voice came again, softer this time, almost sad.

"You're not alone, Mae. I wish I could help you. But they're too strong. You'll see soon enough."

And then, just like that, the presence was gone.

Mae stood there in the ruins, clutching the shard tightly. The world felt heavier, darker, and her path more uncertain than ever before. She had thought the shards were the key to stopping the Watchers, but now… Now, she wasn't sure what to believe.

But one thing was certain: she couldn't stop. She had to keep moving, had to keep fighting. Even if the shards were part of some larger, darker plan, they were her only chance. And she wasn't going to let the Watchers destroy everything she had left.

With a deep breath, Mae turned and left the ruins, the shard still pulsing faintly in her hand. The forest loomed ahead, dark and silent, but Mae was no longer the same girl who had fled into it. She had faced the darkness, and though it had nearly swallowed her whole, she had survived.

But the fight was far from over.

As Mae disappeared into the shadows of the trees, the distant hum of the Watchers echoed faintly in the wind, a reminder that they were always watching, always waiting. And the next time they came for her, they would be stronger.

But so would she.

Chapter 40

Mae moved swiftly through the forest, the pulse of the shard still faint in her hand. The wind had picked up, rustling the leaves above, sending shadows dancing across her path. Though her body ached and her thoughts swirled with doubt, she pressed on. She had no choice now but to keep moving.

Delphine's words echoed in her mind: *"The shards… they're part of it."*

Could it be true? Was she helping the very darkness she was trying to fight? Mae's grip on the shard tightened as she navigated the twisting paths of the woods. She had fought too hard to let that be true. The shards had saved her life more than once, had given her strength when she needed it most. But the thought gnawed at her—what if, with each shard she claimed, she was drawing the Watchers closer to awakening?

The map had gone dark again, but Mae knew where the next shard was hidden. She had memorized its location before her encounter with Delphine. It was buried in the southern mountains, in a forgotten temple lost to time. The journey would be long and perilous, but Mae knew she couldn't stop. The Watchers would never stop.

After hours of traveling through the dense forest, Mae finally came upon a small clearing. The trees opened up, revealing a stream that cut through the earth like a silver ribbon. The water shimmered under the pale moonlight, offering a momentary reprieve from the oppressive darkness that hung in the air.

Mae knelt by the stream, splashing her face with the cool water. She stared at her reflection, barely recognizing the girl who looked back at her. Her once pale skin was smudged with dirt, her dark hair tangled and wild. But it was her eyes that had changed the most—they were haunted now, filled with a kind of determination that came from being hunted by forces far beyond her control.

As she stared into the water, something moved in the corner of her vision. Mae tensed, her hand instinctively going to the dagger at her waist. But when she turned, there was nothing there. Just the rustling of the trees in the wind.

She was about to rise when a figure stepped from the shadows.

It was a man, cloaked in dark robes, his face hidden beneath a deep hood. He moved silently, almost as if he were part of the forest itself. Mae's heart raced, and she rose to her feet, her hand tightening around the dagger.

"Who are you?" she demanded, her voice steady despite the fear gnawing at her insides.

The figure didn't answer right away. He stepped closer, his movements slow, deliberate. When he finally spoke, his voice was low and rough, as if it hadn't been used in a long time.

"I've been watching you."

Mae's blood ran cold. **"Are you one of them?"**

The man chuckled softly, though there was no humor in it. **"No. I'm not a servant of the Watchers. But I know them. I've** felt their influence creeping across this land, just as you have." He paused, studying her. **"And I know you seek the shards."**

Mae narrowed her eyes. **"What do you want?"**

The man stepped closer, his hooded face still obscured by shadows. **"I want what you want. To stop the Watchers from awakening. But the path you're on is dangerous. More dangerous than you realize."**

Mae's heart pounded. **"Why should I trust you? How do I know you're not leading me into a trap?"**

The man pulled back his hood, revealing a face lined with age and sorrow. His eyes, though dark, were filled with a kind of pain that Mae recognized all too well. He had lost something— someone. The same way she had.

"Because I've seen what happens if the Watchers awaken," he said softly. **"And it's a fate worse than death. I was once like you—fighting to stop them. But I failed. And now… now I'm here to help you succeed where I could not."**

Mae didn't lower her dagger. **"How can you help me?"**

The man's gaze drifted to the satchel at her side. **"You already know the shards are powerful. But they are also dangerous. Every shard you collect binds you closer to the Watchers. They are pieces of them, after all. The more you carry, the more they can see you, feel you. You may think you are using their power, but in truth, they are using you."**

Mae's stomach twisted. **"Delphine said the same thing,"** she whispered.

The man nodded gravely. **"She wasn't wrong. But there's still a way to stop it. You don't need to gather all the shards. You only need one—the Heart Shard. It holds the key to their undoing. With it, you can destroy the Watchers once and for all. But finding it will be… difficult."**

Mae's mind raced. **"Where is it?"**

The man's eyes darkened. **"In the deepest part of the Watchers' realm. A place where time and reality bend. A place no mortal has ever returned from."**

Mae felt a cold dread settle in her chest. **"And you want me to go there?"**

"I don't want anything," the man said quietly. **"But if you want to stop the Watchers, it's the only way. The other shards will only lead to their awakening. The Heart Shard… that's your only chance to end this nightmare."**

Mae stared at him, her mind spinning. Could she trust him? What if this was all part of the Watchers' plan, another trap to lead her into their grasp? But what choice did she have? If the other shards were truly binding her closer to the darkness, then continuing on her current path would only hasten the end.

She took a deep breath. **"Tell me how to find it."**

The man nodded, his expression somber. **"I'll guide you. But know this—once you enter the Watchers' realm, there is no turning back. You will face horrors beyond your imagination. And even if you succeed, you may not survive."**

Mae's jaw clenched. **"I don't care. If it means stopping them, I'll do whatever it takes."**

The man's gaze softened for a brief moment, a flicker of admiration in his eyes. **"Very well. We begin at dawn. Rest now. You'll need your strength for what lies ahead."**

As the man melted back into the shadows, Mae sank to the ground by the stream, her mind heavy with the weight of the choices before her. She knew what she had to do, but the path ahead was darker than anything she had ever imagined.

Still, she had come this far. There was no turning back now. With or without the man's help, she would find the Heart Shard.

And she would end the Watchers, once and for all.

Chapter 41

As the first light of dawn broke through the twisted canopy of trees, Mae stirred from a restless sleep. Her body was heavy with exhaustion, but her mind was sharper than ever. The man's words haunted her dreams, and now they clung to her waking thoughts. The Heart Shard—the key to defeating the Watchers—was within her reach. But the price of reaching it would be steep.

The man appeared silently from the woods, his face stern and shadowed beneath his hood. His eyes flicked briefly to Mae's satchel, where the shard pulsed faintly. **"We have a long journey ahead of us,"** he said, his voice low. **"The Watchers' realm is not of this world. To enter, we must find the rift that bridges our reality and theirs."**

Mae nodded, pushing herself to her feet. Her muscles ached, but the weight of the shard and the mission ahead kept her moving. **"Where is this rift?"**

The man pointed toward the distant mountains. **"At the summit of the Forgotten Peaks. There is an ancient altar there, long abandoned by the living. The rift lies within."**

Mae swallowed hard. She had heard rumors of the Forgotten Peaks—tales of travelers who had ventured there, never to return. The mountains were treacherous, plagued by violent storms and haunted by creatures born of darkness. But none of that mattered now. She would face whatever lay ahead.

As they set off, the forest around them gradually gave way to jagged cliffs and rocky terrain. The air grew colder, the sky darker. The sun seemed reluctant to rise fully, as if even daylight feared what lay beyond the mountains. The journey was grueling, and as they climbed higher, the wind whipped viciously at their faces, biting through their cloaks.

For hours they climbed, the man leading the way in silence. Mae struggled to keep pace, her thoughts drifting to Delphine. What had happened to her old friend? Could there still be a way to save her, or was she too far gone, another pawn of the Watchers? The thought gnawed at her, but Mae forced herself to focus on the task at hand.

As they ascended, the path became steeper, the air thinner. By the time they reached the summit, Mae's lungs burned, and every step felt like a monumental effort. But when they finally crested the peak, what awaited them was both awe-inspiring and terrifying.

The altar was ancient, made of stone so old that it was crumbling at the edges. Strange runes were etched into its surface, glowing faintly in the dim light. And in the center of the altar was a swirling vortex of shadows, twisting and writhing as if alive. The rift.

Mae felt an icy chill crawl down her spine as she approached. The air around the rift seemed to warp and bend, distorting reality. It was like looking into a nightmare. Beyond the swirling darkness, she could see flickers of another world—a twisted, broken landscape where the sky bled and the ground writhed like a living thing. The Watchers' realm.

The man stood beside her, his gaze fixed on the rift. **"Once we enter, there will be no turning back. The Watchers will know we're coming. They'll send their most powerful servants to stop us. You must be prepared for what you'll face inside."**

Mae took a deep breath, steeling herself. **"I've come too far to stop now. Tell me what I need to do."**

The man's eyes met hers, filled with a mixture of sorrow and determination. **"The Heart Shard is kept in the Watchers' sanctum, deep within their realm. It's heavily guarded, and the closer we get, the more reality itself will twist against us. But you are bound to the shards, which means you have some control over their power. Use it wisely, and we may stand a chance."**

Mae nodded, gripping the shard tightly in her hand. The pulsing energy within it felt more potent now, as if it could sense the proximity of its kin.

Without another word, the man stepped into the rift. His form wavered for a moment, as though he were being pulled apart, and then he disappeared into the swirling darkness. Mae hesitated only for a second before following him, the world around her warping as she crossed the threshold.

The moment she stepped through, Mae felt as if the ground had been ripped out from beneath her. She tumbled through an endless void, the air thick and oppressive, suffocating her. Visions of twisted faces and dark, inhuman eyes flashed before her, and the distant hum of the Watchers' presence grew louder, a dull roar that filled her mind.

Then, with a sudden jolt, she landed hard on solid ground.

Mae groaned, pushing herself up to her knees. The air here was thick with mist, and the sky was a swirling mass of dark clouds that moved unnaturally fast. The ground beneath her feet felt wrong—soft, like flesh, pulsing faintly as though it were alive. Shadows slithered at the edges of her vision, and the whole place seemed to be shifting constantly, as though reality itself was unstable.

The man stood nearby, his face grim. **"Welcome to the Watchers' realm,"** he said quietly. **"From here, things will only get worse. Stay close, and don't trust what you see."**

They began to move through the strange landscape, every step feeling heavier than the last. The further they went, the more the air hummed with energy. Mae could feel it in her bones, the same dark force that had been chasing her since she first found the shards. Only now, it was all around her, pressing in from every direction.

Suddenly, a deep, echoing voice reverberated through the mist, sending chills down Mae's spine.

"So you've come at last, little thief."

Mae froze. The voice was all too familiar—it was the voice of the Watcher who had haunted her dreams since she first touched the shards.

"You think you can destroy us? Foolish girl. You are already part of us."

A shadow moved in the mist, a massive, looming figure with eyes that glowed like pale moons. Mae's heart raced as the creature stepped forward, its form monstrous and shifting, a swirling mass of darkness and flesh.

The Watcher.

Mae's grip tightened around the shard as she stood her ground, her mind racing for a plan. The man beside her drew his sword, his face set with grim determination.

"This is only the beginning," the Watcher growled, its voice shaking the very ground beneath them. **"The Heart Shard calls to you, but it will be your undoing. You will never leave this place."**

Mae raised the shard, its energy pulsing violently in response to the Watcher's presence. **"I'll destroy you,"** she said, her voice steady despite the fear coursing through her. **"Even if it costs me everything."**

The Watcher laughed, a deep, rumbling sound that seemed to echo from all directions. **"We'll see, little thief. We'll see."**

And then, with a deafening roar, the Watcher lunged, its massive form hurtling toward them.

Mae braced herself, the shard flaring with power in her hand. This was it—the final battle. The fight for the Heart Shard, for her world, for everything she had left.

And she wasn't going to lose.

The Watcher's enormous shadow surged toward Mae and the man, its mass twisting in the shifting mist. The ground beneath them pulsed like the very heart of the nightmare they had entered. Mae's breath caught in her throat as she felt the full weight of the Watcher's presence bearing down on her. Its eyes, burning like pale moons, locked onto her, and she could feel it probing her thoughts, searching for any crack in her resolve.

The man sprang into action, his sword gleaming with a strange light as he slashed at the darkness. His blade connected with the Watcher's form, but the creature merely laughed, its voice deep and mocking.

"You cannot cut what does not live, foolish mortal."

Mae felt the shard in her hand vibrate, resonating with the power of the Watcher. She realized in that moment that the creature wasn't lying—it wasn't just flesh and shadow. The Watchers were entities bound to this place, manifestations of the very fabric of this twisted reality. She couldn't defeat it through brute force. She needed to think.

"We need to get to the sanctum!" the man shouted, parrying another blow from the creature's shadowy appendages. **"We can't fight it here—it's too strong!"**

Mae nodded, adrenaline surging through her veins. She turned and bolted, her boots pounding against the pulsing ground as she ran. The mist seemed to thicken around her, slowing her down, but she pushed forward. The man followed close behind, his sword glowing brighter as he fought off the tendrils of darkness that reached for them from the edges of the mist.

Behind them, the Watcher's voice echoed in the shifting air, cold and taunting. **"Run if you wish, but you cannot escape me, little thief. This realm belongs to us. And soon, so will you."**

Mae ignored the voice, focusing on the faint glow in the distance. That had to be the sanctum—the heart of the Watchers' realm, where the Heart Shard was hidden. Every step she took felt heavier, as if the realm itself were pulling her back, trying to stop her from reaching her goal. But she couldn't afford to stop. Not now.

The air grew colder as they approached the sanctum, a towering structure made of the same dark, pulsing stone as the rest of the realm. Its walls twisted and spiraled upward, disappearing into the swirling clouds above. Massive doors, etched with more of the strange runes, stood before them, sealed shut.

"The Heart Shard is inside," the man said, his voice tight with urgency. **"But the doors—how do we open them?"**

Mae looked at the doors, her mind racing. She could feel the shard in her hand pulsing harder now, reacting to the proximity of the Heart Shard. It was connected to this place, to the Watchers themselves. She knew that much. And if the shard was a piece of them, then maybe…

Taking a deep breath, Mae pressed the shard against the stone door.

For a moment, nothing happened. Then, with a deafening rumble, the runes on the door flared to life, glowing with a deep, red light. The doors shuddered, then slowly began to creak open, revealing the dark, foreboding interior of the sanctum.

Mae stepped inside, the man following close behind. The moment they crossed the threshold, the air shifted. It was colder here, sharper, as if the very atmosphere was charged with the raw energy of the Watchers. The walls of the sanctum were lined with jagged, black stone, and at the far end of the room, floating above a dais, was the Heart Shard.

It was unlike any shard Mae had ever seen. Where the other shards were small, dim fragments, the Heart Shard was massive, glowing with a pulsating light that was both mesmerizing and terrifying. It throbbed with power, the same dark energy that flowed through the entire realm, and yet it called to Mae, like a piece of her soul that had been missing for as long as she could remember.

"We found it," the man breathed, his voice filled with awe and fear. **"But we're not alone."**

From the shadows of the sanctum, more figures began to emerge—servants of the Watchers, their bodies twisted and malformed, their eyes glowing with the same eerie light as the Watcher that had attacked them. They moved silently, their forms flickering in and out of the darkness, surrounding the dais and the Heart Shard.

Mae felt a wave of dread wash over her. There were too many of them, and they were too powerful. But she had no choice. The Heart Shard was right there, within her reach. If she could get to it, if she could wield its power, she might stand a chance of destroying the Watchers once and for all.

"Go," the man said, his voice steady. **"I'll hold them off. You have to get to the shard."**

Mae turned to him, her heart racing. **"You can't fight them alone. You'll—"**

"I know," he interrupted, a grim smile on his face. **"But this is what I was meant to do. I failed once before, but not this time. Go, Mae. End this."**

Mae hesitated for a split second, but the determination in the man's eyes pushed her forward. She sprinted toward the dais, dodging the shadowy figures as they lunged for her. The air crackled with dark energy, and every step felt like it was pulling her deeper into the abyss, but she kept moving.

The moment she reached the Heart Shard, its power hit her like a wave, nearly knocking her off her feet. It pulsed violently, its light growing brighter as she touched it. The energy surged through her body, overwhelming her senses. She could feel the Watchers watching her, their presence all around, but now she had the Heart Shard in her grasp.

Suddenly, the Watcher's voice echoed through the sanctum, filled with rage. **"NO! You are too late, little thief. The Heart Shard is ours. You cannot control it!"**

Mae gritted her teeth, feeling the shard's power coursing through her veins. The Watchers' energy flowed into her, threatening to consume her, to bend her to their will. But she wouldn't let them win. Not now. Not after everything she had sacrificed.

"You don't control me," Mae whispered, her voice trembling with the effort. **"I control you."**

With a scream, Mae poured every ounce of her will into the Heart Shard, channeling its dark power. The air around her rippled as the energy intensified, crackling with violent force. The Watchers' presence roared in her mind, but Mae pushed back, refusing to let them consume her.

And then, with a final surge of power, the Heart Shard exploded with light.

The entire sanctum shook as the force of the shard's energy tore through the realm, ripping at the very fabric of the Watchers' world. The servants of the Watchers disintegrated into shadow, their forms unraveling like smoke in the wind. The walls of the sanctum cracked and shattered, and the ground beneath Mae's feet trembled violently.

The Watcher's voice screamed in her mind, filled with fury and fear. **"NO! YOU CANNOT DEFEAT US! WE ARE ETERNAL!"**

But Mae didn't stop. She focused all of her energy into the shard, pulling on every last bit of strength she had left.

"Not anymore," she whispered.

And with that, the Heart Shard shattered.

The explosion of light and power ripped through the Watchers' realm, and for a moment, everything went silent. The mist, the shadows, the darkness—all of it disappeared in an instant, leaving nothing but an empty, desolate void.

Mae collapsed to the ground, her body trembling, her breath coming in ragged gasps. She had done it. The Watchers were gone. The nightmare was over.

But as the silence stretched on, Mae realized something else.

She was alone.

Chapter 42

Mae lay on the cold, pulsing ground, her body trembling as the aftershocks of the Heart Shard's power faded from her veins. Silence engulfed the realm, thick and oppressive, and the air felt strange—too still, too empty. Slowly, she forced herself to sit up, her limbs heavy and her mind foggy from exhaustion. The sanctum, once dark and twisted, was now eerily quiet, as if the realm itself had been gutted of life. The swirling clouds overhead were gone, leaving behind an endless, dark sky.

She turned, searching for the man who had fought alongside her, who had bought her the precious seconds she needed to destroy the Heart Shard. But there was no sign of him. Only an empty space where he had stood moments before. Panic flickered in her chest.

"Hello?" Mae's voice sounded small, swallowed by the vast emptiness around her. She staggered to her feet, searching the crumbling remains of the sanctum for any trace of him. Nothing. It was as if he had been erased along with the Watchers and their twisted minions. The realization hit her like a punch to the gut.

She was truly alone.

The void pressed in on her from all sides, a stark contrast to the chaos that had ruled only moments before. Mae's heart raced as she scanned the horizon, looking for any sign of the exit, the rift they had come through—but there was nothing. No swirling mist, no flickering shadows, only the cold, dead silence of a world that was no longer alive.

The weight of what she had done settled on her shoulders like a heavy cloak. She had destroyed the Heart Shard. She had destroyed the Watchers. But in doing so, she had also shattered the only bridge between their realm and hers. There was no way back. The man had been right—there was always a price to pay.

Mae's knees buckled, and she collapsed onto the ground, her fingers gripping the cold, lifeless stone beneath her. She had fought so hard, risked everything to free herself from the Watchers' grasp, and now... now she was trapped in their realm, cut off from the world she had once known. There was no escape.

For a long time, she sat in the silence, letting the despair wash over her. The weight of her exhaustion, both physical and emotional, was unbearable. She had won the battle but lost herself in the process.

As the minutes stretched into hours, Mae's thoughts began to drift. She thought of Delphine, her old friend, lost to the Watchers' influence. She thought of the countless lives affected by the shards, by the twisted magic that had bound them to this dark realm. Had she really saved them? Or had her victory come too late to make a difference?

"I did this for you," she whispered to no one. **"For all of you."**

Her voice was swallowed by the emptiness, and she wondered if anyone would ever know what she had done. If anyone would remember her sacrifice.

But even as the darkness closed in, Mae felt a strange sense of peace. She had broken free of the Watchers. She had shattered their hold on the world. And while she was trapped in their forsaken realm, at least the people she cared about were safe. At least her world would not suffer the same fate as this broken, twisted place.

As Mae sat there, lost in her thoughts, a faint light appeared on the horizon.

At first, she thought it was a trick of her tired mind, a flicker of hope conjured by her desperation. But as the light grew brighter, more distinct, she realized it was real. A small, glowing figure was approaching, walking slowly through the endless void.

Mae's breath caught in her throat as the figure drew nearer. It was not a shadow or a monster, but something else entirely. A figure dressed in white, its face hidden beneath a hood. The light that surrounded it was soft, almost comforting, and as it came closer, Mae felt a strange warmth in her chest, like a forgotten memory stirring to life.

The figure stopped a few feet away from her, its presence calm and steady. Mae stared up at it, unsure of what to say, unsure of what it was.

"You are not alone," the figure said, its voice gentle, almost familiar.

Mae blinked, her mind racing. **"Who... who are you?"**

The figure didn't answer immediately. Instead, it reached out, offering its hand to her. **"Come with me, Mae. Your journey isn't over yet."**

Mae hesitated, her heart pounding in her chest. She didn't understand what was happening. She didn't know if she could trust this stranger. But as she looked into the soft, glowing light that surrounded the figure, she felt a deep, unshakable sense of calm.

Taking a deep breath, Mae reached out and took the figure's hand.

The moment their fingers touched, a wave of warmth surged through her, and the empty, desolate realm around them began to fade. The cold stone beneath her disappeared, replaced by soft, warm grass. The darkness lifted, revealing a bright, star-filled sky above.

Mae gasped, her eyes widening as she found herself standing in a vast, open field. The stars above were brilliant, casting a soft glow over the landscape. The air was cool and fresh, and for the first time in what felt like an eternity, Mae felt alive again.

The figure stood beside her, its face still hidden beneath the hood, but now its light was softer, more human.

"Where are we?" Mae asked, her voice filled with wonder.

"A place beyond time and space," the figure replied, its voice still calm, still familiar. **"A place between worlds. You've done what you set out to do, Mae. The Watchers are gone. But your story doesn't end here."**

Mae's heart raced as she looked up at the figure, a thousand questions swirling in her mind. ****"What do you mean? I destroyed the shards. I—"**

"You broke their hold on your world," the figure interrupted gently. **"But there are other realms, other worlds,**

where darkness still lingers. And there are others, like you, who will need your help."

Mae stared at the figure, her mind reeling. **"You want me to... keep fighting?"**

The figure nodded. **"You have a gift, Mae. The power to bring light to the darkest places. You're not bound to this realm or any other. You're free to choose your path."**

Mae was silent for a long moment, her thoughts racing. She had spent so long fighting, so long struggling to survive. The idea of continuing that fight in other worlds, of helping others break free from the darkness, was both terrifying and exhilarating.

Finally, she looked up at the figure, a small, determined smile on her face.

"Then let's go."

The figure nodded, its light growing brighter as the stars above seemed to shimmer in response. **"Very well. Your journey begins anew."**

And with that, the figure turned, leading Mae into the starlit expanse, toward whatever awaited her next.

Mae took one last look at the field, at the stars shining brightly above, and then she followed, her heart lighter than it had been in a long time.

Her fight was far from over. But now, for the first time, she knew she wasn't alone.

As Mae followed the glowing figure through the starry field, she felt a strange mixture of excitement and apprehension. The weight of her past battles hung in the back of her mind, but there was also a growing sense of hope. Whatever came next, she wasn't bound by the shadows of the Watchers anymore.

They walked in silence for what seemed like hours, though time felt different here—fluid, as if they were moving between moments rather than within them. The stars above glimmered like a thousand eyes, watching, but not threatening. Mae kept her gaze ahead, her thoughts drifting to the life she had left behind, to the people she had fought for.

The glowing figure slowed and turned toward her, still hidden beneath its hood.

"You must be wondering why you were chosen," it said softly, its voice soothing, yet ancient. **"Why the shards found you, and why the Watchers were so drawn to your spirit."**

Mae furrowed her brow. The thought had crossed her mind countless times during her struggle. She had never understood why she, out of all people, had been the one to take on such a burden.

"Yes," she admitted. **"I've wondered about that since the beginning. I don't feel special. Just... trapped."**

The figure paused, then gestured to the stars around them. **"You were never trapped, Mae. You were chosen because of your resilience, your strength in the face of darkness. The shards sought you out because they needed someone who could withstand their power without succumbing to it. Many before you tried and failed. You succeeded where they couldn't."**

Mae looked down, her fingers curling into fists. **"It didn't feel like success. I lost so much along the way. And now... I don't know what's left for me."**

The figure's light pulsed gently, as if offering comfort. **"There is always something left, Mae. Even in the darkest times. Your journey may have begun with loss, but it doesn't have to end that way. You have the power to shape your own path now."**

Mae let the figure's words sink in. She had fought so hard to survive, to destroy the Watchers, but in the process, she had lost a part of herself. Maybe that was the real battle—the struggle to find purpose after the fight was over.

"What happens next?" she asked, her voice barely a whisper.

The figure lifted its head slightly, the light from beneath its hood intensifying. **"That is up to you. You can return to your world, but it will not be the same as you left it. Or you can choose to continue fighting—there are others, in other realms, who need your strength. There are still shadows that lurk in the corners of existence, waiting to consume the light."**

Mae felt her pulse quicken. The idea of returning home, of seeing what had become of the world she had left behind, was tempting. But something deep inside her knew that she wasn't ready for that. Not yet. There were too many unanswered questions, too much unfinished business. And if there were others who needed her...

She met the figure's gaze, her expression resolute. **"I'll keep fighting."**

The figure nodded, its light flickering with approval. **"Very well. Your choice is made."**

Suddenly, the ground beneath them shifted, and the stars above began to spin. Mae stumbled, feeling a rush of vertigo as the world around her warped and stretched, the peaceful field vanishing in an instant. Darkness closed in again, but it was different this time—no longer the suffocating shadows of the Watchers, but something else. Something deeper, more primal.

When the world settled, Mae found herself standing on the edge of a vast, crumbling city. The air smelled of dust and decay, and the sky overhead was a stormy grey, thick with swirling clouds. Towering structures, once majestic, now lay in ruins, their stone walls cracked and covered in vines. Fires burned in the distance, casting an eerie glow over the desolate landscape.

Mae glanced at the glowing figure beside her, who now seemed more solid, its features clearer in the dim light of this broken world.

"Where are we?" she asked, her voice tight with anticipation.

The figure's gaze swept over the ruined city, its tone solemn. **"This is the world of Elysar, a place once full of life and light. But the Shadows of Malek have taken root here, consuming everything in their path. The people of this land fought against them, but they were overwhelmed. Now, only a few remain, scattered and hidden, clinging to what little hope they have left."**

Mae's heart sank as she looked out at the destruction. Another world ravaged by darkness, another people fighting a losing battle. The weight of it all pressed down on her, but at the same time, she felt a fire ignite within her. She had faced the Watchers and won. She could do this. She had to.

"What can I do?" Mae asked, determination flooding her voice.

The figure turned to her, its light brighter than ever. **"You have the power to resist the Shadows, to drive them back. But you will need allies—there are others like you, scattered across this world, gifted with strength but unsure of how to use it. Seek them out. Unite them. Only together can you stand a chance against the darkness that consumes Elysar."**

Mae nodded, her jaw set with resolve. She had fought alone for so long, but now she understood. This wasn't just her fight anymore. It never had been. It was about something greater —about bringing light to the places that had lost hope.

"Where do I start?" she asked.

The figure pointed toward the distant horizon, where the fires burned brightest. **"There is a resistance, hidden deep within the ruins of the old city. They fight the Shadows every day, but their numbers are dwindling. Go to them. They will need your strength."**

Mae squared her shoulders, her eyes fixed on the distant glow of the resistance. She felt the shard's absence, but in its place, a new sense of purpose filled her. The fight wasn't over. It was just beginning.

As she started down the path toward the ruined city, the figure's voice called out to her one last time.

"Remember, Mae, the light is not something you carry alone. It is something you share. Let it guide you."

With those words, the figure vanished, leaving Mae alone in the shattered world of Elysar.

But this time, Mae didn't feel alone.

This time, she knew exactly who she was.

Chapter 43

Mae marched forward, her boots crunching over broken stones and shattered remnants of what must have once been a proud city. The silence of Elysar was heavy, broken only by the distant crackling of fire and the occasional distant rumble of thunder. The city's ruins loomed around her, casting long shadows that seemed to reach out as she passed.

Every step deeper into the crumbling streets brought with it an eerie sense of desolation. The air was thick with the weight of loss, the kind that clung to the bones of a place long after its people had been driven to despair. Mae's hand instinctively hovered near the hilt of her blade, a remnant of her past battles, though here it felt more symbolic than real. She knew the Shadows of Malek weren't creatures that could be cut down so easily.

As she approached what appeared to be the center of the city, the fires glowing brighter in the distance, Mae's thoughts turned to the others the glowing figure had mentioned. **Gifted ones like her, lost and scattered.** She wondered how many had fallen under the weight of their burden, just as she had nearly succumbed to the Watchers. Her chest tightened. This time, she would find them. This time, she wouldn't let anyone fight alone.

She moved swiftly but cautiously through the debris-laden streets, her eyes sharp and her senses attuned to any sign of life— or danger. It wasn't long before she heard it: the distant clatter of steel on steel, the unmistakable sound of combat. Mae's heart raced, and she quickened her pace, drawn toward the sound like a beacon.

As she rounded a corner, the scene unfolded before her. A small group of fighters—no more than five or six—were engaged in a desperate battle against a swirling mass of dark energy. The Shadows of Malek. The creatures were amorphous, shifting between solid and smoke, their forms flickering in and out of existence as they attacked with vicious tendrils. The fighters, though skilled, were clearly outmatched, their exhaustion evident in their ragged movements.

Mae's instincts kicked in, and without hesitation, she charged toward the fray.

"Get down!" she shouted, drawing her blade as she closed the distance. One of the fighters—a young man with bloodied armor—glanced at her in surprise, but obeyed, ducking just in time as Mae's sword slashed through the nearest shadow. The creature recoiled, shrieking as its form was momentarily disrupted, but it quickly reformed, hissing and lashing out at her.

Mae dodged the strike, rolling to the side as another shadow lunged at her. She fought with a fluidity that came from years of facing impossible odds, her movements sharp and deliberate. The Shadows of Malek were unlike the twisted minions of the Watchers, but their dark energy felt disturbingly familiar. She could feel their hunger, their desire to consume, to corrupt.

"Stay together!" she called out to the others. **"Don't let them isolate you!"**

The fighters, encouraged by her arrival, rallied around her, forming a tight circle. One by one, they struck at the shadows, their weapons glowing faintly with a strange light—a light that, Mae realized, wasn't just from their steel.

They were gifted, like her.

Mae felt a surge of hope as they fought side by side, their combined efforts pushing the shadows back. The creatures snarled and writhed, but the fighters' resolve, strengthened by Mae's presence, held firm. With a final, coordinated strike, the shadows dissolved into smoke, their forms dissipating into the air like mist burned away by the sun.

For a moment, there was silence.

Mae straightened, wiping sweat from her brow, her breath coming in heavy gulps. The fighters around her were panting, their faces a mixture of relief and disbelief.

One of them, the young man with the bloodied armor, stepped forward. His brown eyes, though weary, shone with gratitude.

"Who are you?" he asked, his voice hoarse but steady. **"We thought... we thought we were done for."**

Mae sheathed her sword and offered him a faint smile. **"I'm Mae. I've come to help."** She glanced around at the others, their wary but hopeful expressions telling her they were just as curious. **"The Shadows of Malek aren't going to stop unless we stop them together. I heard there was a resistance here."**

The young man exchanged a look with one of the others, a woman with short-cropped hair and a scar running down her cheek. The woman nodded, then turned to Mae.

"You're standing in it," she said grimly. **"Or what's left of it. We've been fighting the Shadows for months, but they**

keep coming. Every time we think we've pushed them back, they return stronger."

Mae frowned, her gaze drifting to the darkened skies overhead. **"There has to be a reason they're targeting this city. Something they're after."**

The woman crossed her arms, her expression hardening. **"There is. We've heard rumors of an artifact hidden deep within the ruins. Something powerful. The Shadows are drawn to it, but we haven't been able to find it. Not yet."**

An artifact. Mae's mind raced. It sounded dangerously similar to the shards she had destroyed in her own world. Could this artifact be another source of dark power, something that needed to be sealed away—or destroyed?

"Then we need to find it before they do," Mae said, her tone resolute. **"If we can destroy whatever's calling them, we might be able to stop the Shadows for good."**

The young man nodded, his expression determined. **"We've been searching the ruins for weeks, but we're running out of time. We'll take you to the heart of the city. That's where we think it is."**

Mae felt the weight of the responsibility settle on her shoulders, but she welcomed it. This was why she had come—to help, to fight back against the darkness. She wasn't alone anymore, and neither were they.

As the fighters gathered their weapons and prepared to move out, Mae couldn't help but glance back at the path she had come from. The glowing figure was gone, but its words echoed in her mind.

"The light is not something you carry alone. It is something you share."

Mae took a deep breath, her gaze forward now, focused on the road ahead.

"Let's finish this."

The group moved swiftly through the rubble-strewn streets of the ruined city, their footsteps careful yet urgent. The silence was palpable, broken only by the occasional crackle of distant flames or the creak of crumbling structures. The weight of impending danger hung in the air like a storm about to break.

Mae, at the head of the group, kept her eyes sharp, her senses attuned to the subtle vibrations of the Shadows of Malek. She could feel their presence, lurking just beyond sight, waiting for the right moment to strike again. But she wasn't going to let them catch her or these fighters off guard.

The young man, whose name she had learned was Kade, walked beside her. His armor, though dented and bloodied, reflected the warrior spirit still burning inside him. He glanced at her as they pressed on through the ruins, the tension clear in his voice.

"You fight like someone who's seen the worst of it," he said, a note of curiosity in his tone. **"Where did you come from? How did you know to find us?"**

Mae hesitated for a moment, her mind flickering back to the Watchers, the shards, and the endless battles she had fought before arriving here. **"I've been through something similar,"** she replied, keeping her words vague. **"A different kind of darkness, but no less dangerous. I wasn't alone then, either.**

But I lost people along the way. Too many." She glanced over at him, her gaze hard. **"I don't plan on losing anyone else."**

Kade gave a grim nod, understanding the weight behind her words. **"We've lost our share, too,"** he said quietly. **"This city used to be full of people. A thriving, beautiful place. But when the Shadows came, it all fell apart. We've been fighting ever since, but we're barely holding on. If we don't find that artifact soon..."** His voice trailed off, leaving the unspoken fear hanging between them.

Mae set her jaw. **"We'll find it. And we'll stop them."**

The group continued deeper into the heart of the city, where the buildings became more intact, though still ancient and worn by time. The streets were narrow here, and the shadows cast by the crumbling walls seemed to stretch longer, darker, as if the city itself was alive and watching.

Suddenly, a cold wind swept through the street, carrying with it a sense of dread that made Mae's skin prickle. She held up a hand, signaling the others to stop.

"They're close," she whispered, her voice low but urgent.

Kade tensed, gripping his sword tightly. The other fighters fanned out, their weapons drawn and eyes scanning the surrounding ruins. The silence deepened, becoming oppressive, suffocating.

Then, from the darkness ahead, came a low, inhuman growl.

Mae's pulse quickened as a figure emerged from the shadows. It was massive, far larger than the shadow creatures they had fought earlier. Its form was vaguely humanoid but twisted and deformed, its body made of shifting, swirling darkness that seemed to pulse with malevolent energy. Red eyes burned like embers in its face, staring directly at Mae.

"That's not just a shadow," Kade muttered, his voice tight with fear. **"That's one of the Malek themselves."**

Mae swallowed, her grip tightening on her sword. The Malek. She had heard stories of them—ancient beings of darkness that commanded the Shadows, feeding on the fear and despair of worlds like this one. This was no ordinary enemy. It was a creature of pure evil, and it was coming for them.

"Spread out!" Mae commanded. **"Don't let it focus on any one of us!"**

The group moved as one, fanning out to encircle the creature. The Malek's eyes flicked between them, its lips curling into a grotesque grin. It seemed to feed off their fear, growing larger, more solid as it advanced.

With a roar, the Malek lunged, its massive arm swinging toward Mae. She dodged, rolling out of the way as its fist smashed into the ground, sending shards of stone flying. Without hesitation, Mae retaliated, her sword slicing through the air and striking the creature's shadowy form. The blade cut through, but the wound closed almost instantly, the Malek barely reacting.

"It's not enough!" one of the fighters shouted as their own strikes had similar effects. **"Our weapons can't hurt it!"**

Mae gritted her teeth, frustration bubbling inside her. The Malek was too strong, too resilient. But as she dodged another strike, her mind flashed back to something the glowing figure had said—**"You will need allies."**

Her gaze shifted to the fighters around her, watching as their weapons flickered with that same faint glow she had noticed earlier. The light of their gifts. It wasn't just their physical strength that mattered—it was the power they carried within.

"Focus your energy!" Mae shouted. **"Channel it into your weapons! We need to hit it with everything we've got!"**

The fighters exchanged uncertain glances, but they didn't hesitate. One by one, they closed their eyes, concentrating on the light within them, the power that had drawn them to the fight in the first place. As they did, their weapons began to glow brighter, pulsing with energy.

Mae felt the surge of power, the same light stirring within her. She closed her eyes for a brief moment, letting the energy flow through her, into her sword. When she opened them, the blade gleamed with a radiant light, as if infused with the essence of her very soul.

The Malek, sensing the shift, roared in fury and charged again. But this time, Mae and the others were ready.

"Now!" Mae yelled, and together, they struck.

Their weapons, blazing with light, cut through the Malek's dark form with a force that sent shockwaves through the air. The creature howled in agony, its body disintegrating where their blades touched. Its red eyes flared one last time before it exploded into a cloud of darkness, vanishing into the ether.

For a moment, the group stood frozen, panting and bloodied but victorious. The oppressive darkness that had hung over them lifted, and the air felt lighter, cleaner.

Mae lowered her sword, the glow fading, and turned to the others. They looked exhausted, but there was something else in their eyes now—hope.

Kade approached, his expression awed. **"That was incredible. I don't know what you did, but..."** He shook his head. **"We've never been able to hurt them like that."**

Mae smiled faintly. **"It wasn't just me. It was all of us."** She sheathed her sword, glancing at the horizon where the distant fires still burned. **"But we're not done yet. If there are more Malek, we need to find that artifact before they do."**

The woman with the scar, who had been watching from the sidelines, nodded. **"You're right. The heart of the city isn't far. We'll find it, and we'll destroy it."**

Mae's gaze hardened as she looked at the others. **"Let's finish what we started."**

Together, they turned toward the heart of the city, the final battle still ahead of them. But for the first time, Mae felt a glimmer of confidence. They had the power, and now, they had each other.

Chapter 44

As they moved deeper into the heart of the ruined city, the tension mounted. Every shadow seemed to flicker with menace, and every gust of wind carried the faint whisper of something unnatural. Mae, Kade, and the remaining fighters pressed on, their pace quickening as they navigated the narrow, winding streets that led to the heart of Elysar.

The city's center loomed ahead—a massive cathedral-like structure made of black stone. Its towering spires reached into the sky like skeletal fingers, and though it was in a state of decay like the rest of the city, it exuded an ominous, almost magnetic pull. The fighters exchanged uneasy glances as they approached, the air growing colder with each step.

"That's it," Kade said, his voice barely above a whisper. **"The artifact's got to be in there."**

Mae felt a heavy presence emanating from the cathedral, an oppressive force that made her skin crawl. There was no doubt in her mind—the artifact was inside, and the Malek, or something worse, would be guarding it.

They reached the grand entrance, the massive iron doors standing slightly ajar, as if inviting them inside. Mae's hand instinctively went to her sword, her fingers brushing the hilt. **"Stay close. We don't know what we'll find in there."**

With a deep breath, Mae pushed open the doors, the heavy iron creaking loudly as they stepped into the cathedral's vast, cavernous interior. The air was thick with dust and decay, and the faint glow of moonlight filtering through the shattered stained glass windows cast eerie patterns across the stone floor.

The silence inside was deafening. The only sound was the faint echo of their footsteps as they moved through the rows of broken pews, their eyes scanning the shadows for any sign of movement.

At the far end of the cathedral, the altar stood beneath a large, crumbling statue of a robed figure. Behind it, nestled in the center of a massive stone dais, was the artifact—a dark, pulsating crystal, its surface swirling with ominous energy.

Mae's breath caught in her throat. The sight of it filled her with dread. She had seen power like this before—something that could corrupt, destroy, and consume whole worlds.

"That's it," she muttered, her eyes locked on the artifact. **"We have to destroy it before it can do any more damage."**

But before anyone could move, the ground beneath them began to tremble.

A deep, guttural laugh echoed through the cathedral, and the shadows around them shifted, coalescing into a massive, twisted figure—far larger than the Malek they had fought before. This one was different. Its form was more defined, its eyes glowing with an ancient, malevolent intelligence.

"You think you can stop this?" the creature snarled, its voice reverberating through the walls. **"You, who are nothing but fragile light in an endless sea of darkness?"**

Mae drew her sword, the faint glow of the fighters' energy pulsing through the blade. **"We've faced worse than you,"** she shot back, her voice steady despite the fear gnawing at her insides. **"And we're still here. You can't stop us."**

The creature laughed again, its form shifting and expanding, filling the cathedral with its presence. **"The light you wield is but a flicker in the dark. And I... I am the darkness itself."**

Mae could feel the oppressive weight of its words pressing down on her, trying to smother the hope they had fought so hard to cling to. But she wouldn't let it win. Not here. Not now.

"Together!" she shouted, rallying the fighters around her. **"We hit it with everything we've got. No holding back!"**

The fighters, their weapons glowing brighter with the power of their gifts, formed a tight circle around the creature. The air crackled with energy as they prepared to face the full force of the darkness that had consumed Elysar.

With a deafening roar, the creature attacked, lashing out with tendrils of dark energy. Mae barely had time to react, her sword flashing as she blocked the first strike. The force of the impact sent her staggering back, but she quickly regained her footing, charging forward to strike at the creature's core.

Her blade cut through the darkness, and for a brief moment, the creature recoiled, its form flickering. But it was far from defeated. The creature snarled and lashed out again, its tendrils wrapping around one of the fighters, pulling him into the shadows.

"No!" Mae shouted, but it was too late. The fighter was gone, swallowed by the darkness.

The loss hit hard, but Mae couldn't afford to let it shake her. She gritted her teeth, her grip on her sword tightening. **"Keep fighting! We can't let it overwhelm us!"**

The others pressed on, their weapons blazing with light as they struck at the creature from all sides. Every time their blades connected, the darkness hissed and recoiled, but the creature was relentless, its form shifting and reforming as it attacked.

Mae knew they couldn't keep this up forever. The creature was too powerful, too deeply rooted in the darkness. But then her gaze shifted to the altar—to the artifact still pulsing with dark energy.

"The artifact!" she shouted. **"It's feeding off the artifact! We have to destroy it!"**

Kade nodded, understanding immediately. **"Cover me!"** he shouted as he broke away from the fight, making a dash toward the altar.

Mae and the others fought with renewed determination, doing everything they could to keep the creature at bay as Kade raced toward the artifact. The creature, sensing his intent, let out a furious roar and turned its full attention on him.

"No, you don't!" Mae yelled, charging at the creature with everything she had. She slashed at its tendrils, drawing its focus back to her as Kade reached the altar.

Kade's hands trembled as he raised his sword, the blade glowing with the light of his gift. **"For Elysar,"** he whispered, and with a mighty swing, he brought the sword down on the artifact.

The moment the blade connected, the artifact shattered with a blinding flash of light. The force of the explosion sent shockwaves through the cathedral, and the creature let out a soul-piercing scream as its form began to unravel, the darkness dissipating into nothingness.

Mae shielded her eyes from the light, her heart pounding in her chest. When the brightness faded, the creature was gone, its presence erased from the world.

The silence that followed was overwhelming.

Mae lowered her sword, her body trembling with exhaustion. Kade stood by the shattered remains of the artifact, his chest rising and falling as he struggled to catch his breath.

The fighters gathered around, their faces a mixture of relief and disbelief. It was over. They had won.

But the cost had been high.

Mae looked at the spot where their fallen comrade had been taken, a pang of sorrow tightening her chest. She had promised not to lose anyone else, but the darkness had claimed another life.

Kade approached her, his expression weary but grateful. **"We did it,"** he said softly. **"Elysar is free."**

Mae nodded, though the victory felt bittersweet. **"For now,"** she said quietly. **"The darkness is always waiting. But we'll keep fighting. Together."**

And with that, they left the ruins of the cathedral behind, their footsteps carrying them toward an uncertain future—but one lit by the hope of the light they now carried within.

The group stepped out of the ruined cathedral, the cool night air washing over them like a breath of new life. The once suffocating weight of darkness that had clung to the city was gone, replaced by a strange, almost eerie calm. The distant fires that had blazed across the city were now dying embers, flickering weakly against the skyline.

Mae's legs felt heavy, every step an effort, but she pressed on. The others followed in silence, their faces etched with exhaustion and grief. Kade walked beside her, his face set in grim determination. Behind them, the cathedral stood like a dark sentinel, a reminder of the battle they had fought—and the lives they had lost.

They reached a small square just outside the cathedral's grounds, where a crumbled statue of an old king lay in ruin. It seemed as good a place as any to stop. Mae lowered herself to the ground, leaning back against a broken pillar. The fighters spread out, some sitting, others standing in silence, all lost in their own thoughts.

Kade broke the silence first, his voice low. **"We did it, but it doesn't feel like a victory."**

Mae didn't respond at first. Her eyes were on the distant horizon, where the first hint of dawn was beginning to touch the sky with pale light. She felt the weight of everything they had been through pressing down on her. The battles, the loss, the constant fight against the darkness—it never seemed to end.

"It's never going to feel like a victory," she said finally, her voice quiet but steady. **"Not when there's so much left to fight for. The darkness will always come back, in one form or another. We just have to keep pushing it back."**

Kade nodded, though there was a heaviness in his gaze. **"I thought... after this, maybe things would get better. That the darkness would be gone for good."**

Mae shook her head. **"It doesn't work like that. The darkness is part of the world. We can't destroy it completely, but we can stop it from consuming everything. And we can protect what matters."**

Kade sat down beside her, his eyes fixed on the ground. **"You've been fighting this for a long time, haven't you? Not just here, but... everywhere."**

Mae's chest tightened at his words. She thought of the Watchers, of all the worlds she had seen fall, all the people she had lost along the way. **"Yeah,"** she admitted softly. **"A long time. Too long, maybe."**

There was a long pause before Kade spoke again, his voice barely more than a whisper. **"Do you think it'll ever end? The fighting, the darkness?"**

Mae's eyes drifted back to the horizon, where the sky was now tinged with the faintest hint of pink. **"I don't know,"** she said honestly. **"But I do know that as long as we're here, as long as there's light left to fight with, we can keep it at bay. We can make sure the darkness doesn't win."**

Kade was silent for a long moment, then he nodded, his resolve hardening. **"Then that's what we'll do. We'll keep fighting. For those we lost. For Elysar. For whatever comes next."**

Mae felt a small spark of hope flicker inside her. It wasn't much, but it was enough.

As the first rays of sunlight broke through the clouds, casting the city in a soft, golden glow, Mae stood up, her strength slowly returning. She looked at the fighters around her—exhausted, battered, but still standing. Still alive.

"There's more out there," she said, her voice carrying across the square. **"More worlds like this one. More people who need our help. We stopped the darkness here, but it's not over. We can't rest just yet."**

The fighters looked at her, their eyes filled with determination. They had fought alongside her, faced the worst the darkness had to offer, and they had survived. Now, they understood. The fight wasn't just for Elysar—it was for every place threatened by the same shadow.

"Where do we go next?" one of the fighters asked, stepping forward. His armor was dented, his face streaked with dirt and blood, but his eyes burned with the fire of someone who had found a purpose.

Mae smiled faintly. **"We go wherever we're needed,"** she said. **"There are more battles to fight. More people to protect. But we don't have to do it alone. We have each other now. And we have the light."**

The group rose to their feet, their spirits lifting as the sunlight bathed them in warmth. Mae felt the familiar pull of the Watchers, a distant whisper in her mind, guiding her toward the next place, the next fight.

"We'll rest when we can," she said, glancing at Kade, who was now standing beside her. **"But we're not done yet."**

Kade nodded, a faint smile tugging at the corners of his mouth. **"No, we're not."**

Together, they turned toward the horizon, toward whatever lay beyond the ruins of Elysar. The road ahead would be long, the battles unending, but for the first time in what felt like an eternity, Mae didn't feel alone.

With the rising sun at their backs and the weight of the past behind them, they moved forward, ready to face whatever darkness dared to stand in their way.

And this time, they would do it together.

Vivi Returns

Vivi had always known that the darkness was never truly gone. No matter how many times she pushed it away, it always lingered—watching, waiting, whispering. As she made her way back to the cemetery, the air was thick with the weight of the past, and her thoughts were heavy with memories she'd tried to leave behind.

It had been years since she left the cemetery—her sanctuary—and wandered into the world beyond. The battles she had fought, the lives she had touched, all felt like faded echoes in the cold silence of the night. The world was still dark, but not the kind of darkness she had grown accustomed to. This was a more subtle, creeping shadow that clung to everything, even to her.

Vivi stepped through the iron gates of the cemetery, her boots crunching softly on the gravel path. The roses in her garden had withered in her absence, their once-vibrant petals now black and brittle, curling inward like the dead things they had become. She knelt down and touched one, the delicate stem crumbling beneath her fingers.

"I'm sorry," she whispered, though she wasn't sure if the words were for the roses, for the cemetery, or for herself.

The cemetery was eerily quiet, the tombstones standing like sentinels in the fog that swirled around the edges of the graveyard. The faint scent of decay mixed with the damp earth, but it was a familiar smell—one she had always found oddly comforting.

Vivi stood and made her way to the center of the cemetery, where her rose garden had once been a vibrant oasis amidst the graves. Now it was nothing but a desolate patch of earth, overgrown with thorns and weeds. She had thought that leaving the garden behind would help her move on, that the battles in the world beyond would fill the void inside her. But the truth was, the garden had always been more than just a place of beauty—it had been a part of her.

As she approached the stone bench that sat at the heart of the garden, she noticed something strange. In the center of the desolate patch, where no light had touched in months, a single rose stood tall, its petals the deepest shade of red she had ever seen. It was untouched by the decay that had consumed the others, glowing faintly in the moonlight.

Vivi's heart quickened as she knelt beside the rose. There was something otherworldly about it, something ancient and powerful. She reached out, her fingers hovering just above the delicate petals. A strange energy pulsed from the rose, and for a brief moment, she felt the presence of something—someone—watching her.

"You returned," a voice whispered from the shadows.

Vivi stood quickly, her hand instinctively going to the small knife she kept hidden in her coat. She knew that voice. She had heard it before, in her dreams, in the darkest moments of the battles she had fought.

"Who's there?" she demanded, her eyes scanning the shadows.

From the fog, a figure emerged—tall, cloaked in black, their face hidden beneath a hood. Their presence was unsettling, like a cold wind that chilled her to the bone, but there was something familiar about them, something that tugged at the edges of her memory.

"You've come back to the place where it all began," the figure said, their voice soft but dripping with menace. **"But you've never truly left, have you? You've carried the darkness with you all along."**

Vivi's grip tightened on the knife, but she didn't move. **"I don't know who you are, but you've made a mistake coming here."**

The figure chuckled, a sound that sent shivers down her spine. **"Oh, I think you do know. You've felt it, haven't you? The pull of this place, the way the shadows cling to your soul. You and I are the same, Vivi. We are both born of the dark."**

Vivi's chest tightened, her pulse quickening as the words sank in. She wanted to deny it, to push away the truth that had been gnawing at her for so long, but the figure's presence felt too familiar. Too real.

"You're wrong," she said, her voice steady despite the fear gnawing at her insides. **"I've fought the darkness. I've kept it at bay."**

The figure stepped closer, their form shifting like smoke in the moonlight. **"You can't fight what you are, Vivi. You can't run from the truth forever. This garden, these graves—they've always been a part of you. And now that you've returned, the darkness will reclaim what it lost."**

Vivi felt the weight of the figure's words pressing down on her, suffocating her with their truth. She had always felt different, always known that something dark lurked within her, something she couldn't fully understand. But she had never let it control her. She had fought it, and she would continue to fight it—no matter what.

"I'm not afraid of you," she said, her voice firm as she met the figure's gaze. **"Whatever you are, whatever you think you know about me, you're wrong. This garden, this place—it's mine. I decide what it becomes."**

The figure paused, their head tilting slightly as if considering her words. Then, slowly, they lowered their hood, revealing a face that made Vivi's blood run cold.

It was her own.

The figure smiled, a twisted, dark reflection of Vivi herself. **"You can't escape what's inside you,"** the doppelgänger said, her voice echoing like a cruel whisper. **"You can't deny what you were meant to be."**

Vivi took a step back, her heart pounding in her chest. This wasn't real. It couldn't be real.

But the figure moved closer, mirroring her every step, every breath. **"Embrace it, Vivi. Embrace the darkness. It's the only way to survive."**

For a long moment, Vivi stood frozen, the world around her seeming to blur as the weight of the figure's words crushed down on her. The cemetery, the roses, the graves—all of it seemed to fade, leaving only the suffocating presence of the darkness.

But then, from deep within her, a spark of defiance flared to life. The same defiance that had carried her through every battle, every loss, every moment of doubt.

Vivi raised her knife, her hand steady. **"I may have darkness in me,"** she said, her voice strong and clear. **"But it doesn't own me. I control it."**

With a swift motion, she slashed the knife through the air, and the figure dissolved into mist, vanishing into the night.

The garden was silent once more, the only sound the faint rustle of the wind through the trees. Vivi stood alone in the moonlight, her breath coming in short, sharp bursts as the adrenaline slowly faded.

She looked down at the single red rose still standing in the center of the garden. It was untouched, its petals glowing softly in the pale light.

Vivi knelt beside it once more, her fingers gently brushing the petals. The darkness inside her was still there, but for the first time, she felt like she could control it. It wasn't something to fear —it was something to harness, to use.

And she would use it to protect this place, her sanctuary.

The cemetery was hers. And so was the darkness.

Vivi whispered her secrets to the rose, and the rose whispered back.